A TOUC

"Kindly let me pass. I think I've humiliated myself sufficiently for today."

Jon chuckled. "Nonsense, Duchess. On the contrary, I'm the one nonplussed." He grinned. "You make me feel like a callow schoolboy, I'm afraid."

Not proof against his infectious smile and grateful he wasn't treating her like a strumpet, Andy unbent enough to scoff, "I can't imagine you ever being a callow schoolboy. But that is really neither here nor there, my lord. If you'll excuse me?" she said. striving for some dignity and performing a small curtsy as though nothing untoward had occurred, needing to distance herself mentally and physically from his intoxicating presence.

"So formal, Duchess? It was far more exciting to hear you whisper my name. You must be sure to continue calling me by name—at least when we're in private."

"I think it best if we try to avoid any further private moments, don't you?" She glanced at Jon and regretted her question when she saw his rakish grin.

"My valet might agree with you, but I'm not sure I do." He ran his fingers lightly over her arm. "I'm a bounder and a cad to have taken advantage of you," he stated, his devilish features masked with the honest chagrin of the not-so-innocent. "Forgive me, Duchess?"

Since she had been as responsible for the episode as Jonathon, Andy knew there wasn't anything to forgive. However, it wouldn't do to let him know that. Instead, a slight smile tugging at her lips, she admonished him, "Insufferable rake," and turned to leave.

"Jon?" he asked, his voice soulful.

"We shall see," she replied over her shoulder.

A TOUCH OF CLASS

Lydia Trusz

Zebra Books
Kensington Publishing Corp.

http://www.zebrabooks.com

ZEBRA BOOKS are published by

Kensington Publishing Corp.
850 Third Avenue
New York, NY 10022

Zebra and the Z logo Reg. U.S. Pat. & TM Off.

First Printing: May, 1997
10 9 8 7 6 5 4 3 2 1

Printed in the United States of America

"To Babushka, Anna, Eva and Sarah—true Amazons each and everyone of you. I couldn't have made it without your help."

Chapter One

Skittish horses fought the coachman for supremacy. The driver won and gingerly led his cattle out of the courtyard's mire. Andy leaned forward to wave at the friendly innkeeper. He waved back. For a moment, he shuffled his feet in the mud. Then, swiping the rain dripping from his bulbous nose, he rushed back to the warmth of the inn.

What had he meant when he'd said their arrival was unexpected? Andy wondered. She shrugged and brushed back wet strands of hair clinging to her forehead. The carriage rocked. Andy cracked her head against the hard mahogany side and bit back a moan.

Forgetting the innkeeper's peculiar comment, she peered out the swaying carriage's window once more. The scent of damp wool already filled the closed space and she longed for fresh air. Her neck jerked when they hit a rut. With a hand steadied against the padded red leather squabs, she groaned and cursed the downpour. "Bloody English weather! I am so weary of all this traveling."

"Please, Andy," Edgar Fitzgerald rasped. "At least we're

back home in England. Furthermore, I shouldn't have to remind you such language is unsuitable for a female of your station. Besides, people here will understand your *bloody* imprecations.'' He softened his rebuke with a smile.

''I suppose you're right, Papa, and truly, as interesting as the Continent was to visit following the defeat of Napoleon, it is good to be back on British soil. But to land in this brumble-broth, after the god-awful Channel crossing we had, is disheartening. No wonder you've caught cold. We should have accepted the Count de Silensia's request to explore his genealogy instead of the Marquess's. Besides, it's so much warmer in Milan! . . . If only it weren't so full of mad Italians.''

Edgar chuckled at her grimace. ''Yes, your height certainly drew an admirer or two.''

Instead of slouching at the reminder of her height as she would have a few years ago, Andy grinned. ''Truth to tell, Father, admirers I could handle. The bruises on my backside from the pinching, though, were something else. Worse was being treated like a helpless, ignorant female, lacking in sufficient wit to participate in even the simplest political or intellectual discussion.'' Disgusted, she shook her head.

''My dear child,'' Edgar teased, ''I've caught you making a most grievous error for the first time in ages. You forget there's absolutely nothing simple about Italian politics! However, I still can't understand how I let you talk me into going to some country manor in Kent instead of to London.'' His smile slipped.

''Papa, please . . . '' Andy fussed with the fine woolen lap robe. They'd had this discussion before.

''No, Andy. You missed your come-out because of your mother's illness. Traveling to the Continent after she died may have helped both of us deal with our loss but we've tarried too long. It's been four years now and it's high time you take your rightful place in society. How can you find a proper suitor with all our gadding about? Perhaps we should reconsider the Marquess's commission until after the Season?''

Andy ignored the cajoling tone of his hoarse voice and pushed aside the blanket. The knee she'd cracked upon entering the carriage was sore. She rubbed it through her damp gown.

"Nothing's changed, Father. London would be wonderful to visit, but not for the entire Season. Besides, can you imagine me flitting about the Marriage Mart in search of a mate from amongst the fops and dandies stumbling drunkenly out of their clubs? How would I fit with the latest crop of debutantes preparing to trip through their first waltzes at Almack's?"

Unpleasant memories of her aborted season flickered through her mind. She shook her head, denying them. The crashing thunder echoed the tumultuous thoughts. She massaged the scar on her palm, a nervous habit she'd had for years. Her forehead puckering, Andy sighed. "Is it so very unrealistic of me to hope for a relationship such as you and Mama had?"

Edgar leaned his head back after coughing harshly. Wiping a handkerchief across his lips, his almost inaudible sigh echoed Andy's. "Remember, my dear, ours was a love match. I suppose that's why I'm not trying to rush you to the altar—although some might consider you on the shelf at such a ripe old age." Fidgeting to hold on to his blanket, he reached across and tweaked her straggly hair.

Andy grinned. "You're right. Twenty-three does make me rather ancient." Her chuckle became a groan as the cold permeated the bouncing carriage. Shivering, she brought the lap robe to her chin and grumbled, "These ancient bones *really* despise traveling."

Edgar's blanket slipped when he patted Andy's knee. "Just think how much worse it would be if the carriage weren't well sprung. Seems the old Marquess didn't believe in pinching pennies when it came to his comfort."

Taking in the elegant fittings of the carriage, Andy nodded in agreement. "Am I correct in assuming Sir Malcolm, the former Marquess, was not a universally likable man? With you handling all the correspondence while I packed for our return to England, I'm not really prepared for this venture."

Her father coughed harshly before replying. The cough was getting worse. Andy bit her lip, noting his flushed Patrician features.

White knuckles clenching the handkerchief, Edgar struggled to clear his throat. "I'm afraid you might be right. Sounds like there's some dirty linen to be found there. Of course, every family has some, but normally it's relegated to the distant past. The new Marquess, however, appears to be cut from a different cloth from his uncle. He's commissioned the genealogy to placate his aunt, Sofia, the Marchioness."

"So the Marchioness feels her departed husband besmirched a fine old family name and now she wants us to rewrite history," Andy added caustically.

Edgar frowned. "While I certainly hope that isn't the case— even though it wouldn't be the first time something like that has happened—I'm surprised at you being so judgmental."

"I'm sorry, Papa. The travel must be making me more crotchety than usual."

Edgar muffled another cough.

Andy tried to stifle her concern. He'd only accuse her of cosseting him if she said anything. Allowing him time to recover, she asked in a more conciliatory tone, "Wasn't the Marchioness related to her husband?"

"Second cousin—no love match, that one." Edgar's clipped words were interspersed with shallow breaths.

Andy wondered how much farther it was to the Marquess's. Her father needed warmth and a proper place to sleep. Each bout of coughing left him looking weaker and weaker. He no longer sat tall, carrying his lean height with pride as he was wont to do. Instead, he'd been replaced with this gaunt-faced individual, whose lank graying hair gathered at the edge of his collar.

She feigned a yawn, nearly poking out an eye when the

carriage jolted yet again. "Why don't we get some rest, Papa? We can talk more when we start going through the papers tomorrow."

"Not trying to mollycoddle me, are you, child?"

"Of course not, Papa." Andy met his suspicious gaze without blinking.

He snorted. "I don't believe you, but I'm too tired to argue."

Silently, she watched him fidget, trying to get comfortable in the corner of the bouncing vehicle. Giving up with a ragged sigh, he tucked the blanket more securely around himself and finally closed his eyes.

Left to her own devices, Andy pulled the curtain back to peer out at the countryside. In spite of her praises of Milan, she'd missed England. The rain had stopped, but the pastoral scene she sought was obscured by a fine mist and advancing twilight. It would be just their luck to get caught in a good old-fashioned English fog . . . the kind of thick fog where one could bump into the Devil, without the Devil ever realizing it.

After what seemed an interminable amount of time, the swaying carriage finally came to a halt in front of a Palladian manor. With darkness settling in between layers of mist, the only hint of its grandeur came from the carriage lamps and the warm light spilling out from the mansion's windows.

Stiff and exhausted as she was, Andy's knees nearly buckled when she descended from the carriage. Before she and her still-groggy father could walk up the front steps, the door was opened by one of the most imposing butlers Andy had ever seen—a veritable Goliath. The shadowy candlelight from the hallway only served to accentuate his stature.

Upon closer inspection, he looked as though he'd gone several rounds in the boxing ring—without success. The squashed-in, weary face was all the more astounding for its pair of unusually benevolent eyes. He bowed and waved them into the foyer. Andy's jaw snapped shut. She hoped the butler hadn't caught her gaping.

"Welcome, Sir Edgar," he said in a solemn baritone, award-
ing Andy a lesser inclination of his balding head. "Ma'am."
An odd hint of a question colored his voice. He passed their
cloaks to a nearby footman and introduced himself. "My name
is Simms." The lofty tone implied kinship to Saint Peter, pro-
tecting the portals of heaven. Instead of leading them to a sitting
room or to their chambers, however, Simms continued to stand
guard in the foyer, with the front door still open.

Andy's desire to chuckle faded. She shot a puzzled look at
her father. He shrugged and they sat on nearby velvet-covered
chairs.

Edgar leaned his head against the yellow figured silk of the
wall. His eye lids drifted shut. With nothing else to do, Andy
clasped her hands, surreptitiously twiddling her thumbs. Footmen, loaded with their luggage, scurried across the black and
white marble floor, masking the sound of her tapping foot.

Her father's intermittent coughing troubled her. Gazing at
the central staircase, Andy wondered what Simms would do if
she and her father made a dash up its subtly defined carpet to
find their rooms. She discarded the idle thought quickly. Simms
wouldn't hesitate to tackle them, even if it meant knocking one
of the precious Oriental vases off the Italian marble pedestals
lined along the hallway. Cracking one of the Gainsborough
paintings over his head for attention probably wouldn't do any
good, either. His skull looked too solid.

Simms peered out into the dark.

Andy heard the carriage clatter away. Simms finally glanced
at them, his features perplexed. She straightened.

"I beg your pardon, sir, but are you not missing one of your
party?"

"You've obviously been misinformed, Simms. I believe my
letter clearly stated there would be only the two of us."

Andy could tell her father was losing patience by his tone.
Simms, however, wasn't appeased. He opened his mouth as if
to protest, but before he could say anything else, a young lady

of about twenty years rushed from one of the arched hallways, and into the foyer.

Brushing short, curly brown hair shyly away from her face, she extended her hand. "Sir Edgar? I'm Lady Helen Parker." She glanced at Andy, who was now standing alongside Edgar. Her voice faltered. "Ma'am . . . ? I trust the journey was not overly difficult."

"Traveling conditions were less than ideal for early March, but we made it," Andy replied. Her father's coughing interrupted her. Andy took in his hunched shoulders and bit her lip. Her father had suffered an inflammation of the lungs in Italy two years ago. Was the same about to happen again? She shot their hostess an apologetic smile. "Perhaps Sir Edgar could have some tea with brandy? I'm sorry to be so forward, but he hasn't been well."

Simms was more put out by her effrontery than Lady Helen. His bushy eyebrows snapped together. After sending her a glare, he turned back to his mistress and justified his lapse in etiquette. "Forgive me, milady. I was awaiting Sir Edgar's son to leave the carriage, but it seems he did not make the trip. It appears this"—Simms hesitated ever so slightly—"young lady did instead."

Edgar growled. "Pardon me, but I've never had a son, and at my age, I doubt I ever will. Furthermore, at the rate you're moving to settle us for the night, I may never even live to see a grandson. Wherever did you get such a harebrained idea?"

Andy clapped a hand over her mouth, swallowing a groan. *The unexpected arrival.* The innkeeper's peculiar comment now made sense. She took her father by the elbow and fixed him with a pointed stare. "We have some explaining to do. Lady Helen?"

"Oh, of c-course." Recalled, their hostess allowed an offended Simms to lead the way. The younger woman halted at the entrance of the drawing room. Her hand on the door frame, she peered hesitantly over her shoulder. "You are Sir Edgar Fitzgerald, aren't you?"

Edgar's face mottled. *And* he'd *been surprised at* her *crotchety mood?* Andy shook her head and patted her father's arm, shooing Lady Helen forward. "Of course he is." The response apparently satisfied her and she sent the butler for refreshments.

"I shall be back promptly, Lady Helen."

Andy caught his not-so-subtle tone of warning and bit back a chuckle. When Lady Helen sank into a Sheriton winged-back chair, Andy chose the sofa across from her. The younger woman plucked at the skirt of her rose muslin gown and her silk-shod foot nudged at the Aubusson carpet's pile. An uncomfortable silence descended.

Andy cleared her throat. Glancing at the pale jade walls accented with a cream-colored wainscotting, she smiled. "This is a lovely room."

"Thank you." Helen's soft voice was uncertain.

Andy caught her father's irritated glare and responded with an impish grin.

"Well, my dear. Let's have it. What's the joke?"

Just then, Simms entered, pushing a cart laden with tea, brandy, and a plateful of dainty sandwiches. Andy wondered if he hadn't been listening on the other side of the door. Probably. Everyone, including the butler, now looked at her expectantly. It was obvious Simms wouldn't leave until convinced his mistress wasn't in danger from a pair of escaped bedlamites.

Andy accepted a cup of tea. She took a sip and settled more comfortably against the sofa's low back. Edgar's frown deepened. Andy's smile widened. Elbow on the curved armrest, cup properly balanced, she asked him, "Do you recall how strangely first the innkeeper, and then the coachman, looked at us when we arrived?"

"Yes. What of it? We looked like a pair of drowned rats. . . . Well?" Edgar punctuated his question with a sneeze. Turning aside, he blew his nose, then accepted a brandy from Simms.

Andy drew in a deep breath, surveying the inhabitants of the room. At last, she focused on their hostess. "Really, I am *not* here under any false pretense, Lady Helen. Normally, I take care of the correspondence for Sir Edgar. But caught up as I was with the chores related to moving back to England, he handled the matter with your cousin. I'm sure he referred to me in the letter, only not by my proper name."

Edgar smote his forehead, groaning in acknowledgment. "Devil take it! You're right. I referred to you as my child and assistant, 'Andy.'"

"Andy?" Lady Helen whispered.

Andy nodded. "Andrea Samantha Fitzgerald. Sir Edgar is my father."

Helen flushed. "Oh, dear . . . "

Simms murmured a quiet "Aha!" then, mollified, inclined his head toward Sir Edgar in a civil nod. "Mrs. Simms is preparing her special toddy for you, sir. I'll see to it that a more suitable room is prepared for Miss Fitzgerald as well." Simms ignored Andy's protest and favored everyone with a beatific smile before regally bowing his way out of the room.

"I'm sorry my mother was unable to greet you, but she wasn't feeling particularly well this evening, either. I'll speak to Mama about the, uh, error in identity so that she won't be too . . . surprised." Helen faltered. Her flush deepened and her gaze fluttered downward, fixing on her twisting hands.

"Cousin Jonathon should be back from London by the end of the week, so there really isn't any point in writing to him. When he and Mr. White, Jon's secretary . . . when they arrive, I'll speak with Mr. White. He'll know how to best explain the misunderstanding to my cousin."

Andy waited patiently for Helen to conclude and glanced at her father. No longer paying attention, he sipped brandy by the fireplace, obviously trying to chase the cold from his system. She turned back to Lady Helen. Their hostess, her speech over, bolted from her chair to rearrange a perfectly fine bouquet of yellow spring roses and nearly knocked the delicate porcelain vase off the side table when her skittering gaze met Andy's.

Good humor waning, Andy dug her nails into the scar on her left hand. The scar reminded her of too many things. Sighing, she massaged a temple. "Do you expect a problem with my being female, Lady Helen?" Andy asked bluntly.

"Please call me Helen. It feels more comfortable." She returned to her seat and took a long sip of tea. Andy waited.

Helen's nostrils pinched. She fanned crimson-stained cheeks with one of the linen napkins. "Well, the long and short of it is . . . while Jonathon is, in fact, looking for a wife—he does have the title to consider, you know—he doesn't think very highly of females in general. I feel I should warn you. He might not appear very welcoming . . . Jon's always been very kind to my mother and myself, though."

Seeing her discomfort, Andy answered gently. "Since I'm only here to help my father, not to apply for the position of his wife, there shouldn't be any difficulty."

Unconvinced, Helen gulped. "Unless your presence is misconstrued." She rubbed at her forehead and pinned Andy with an intent, defensive look. "You see, Jon's not only a war hero and popular Corinthian, but he's also very handsome and rather wealthy. Unfortunately, the women in his life haven't exactly exerted a positive influence on him. I'm sure you'll find out about all of this as you work on the genealogy, so there isn't any point in my dressing it up. What with Jon's stepmama, then so many society matrons, uh . . . seeking his favors . . . " Helen paused to recover from another blush.

During Helen's speech, Andy alternated between sipping the refreshing China tea and studying her fingernails. Short as she now kept them, they were still chipped from traveling. When Helen stumbled over her words again, Andy arched an eyebrow, hoping her pasted smile wouldn't slip and reveal her image of Helen's adored cousin. "No doubt debutantes and ambitious mamas have tried to entrap him into marriage as well?"

"Oh yes! More than once. That's why, knowing Jon as I do, I'm afraid he might misinterpret the error in identity."

Andy shrugged. "I suppose he has some justification for his attitude, but you're probably making much ado over nothing. It's unlikely his lordship will see much of me. After all, I'll be working with my father most of the time."

And thank heavens for that. I don't need another Lothario adding to the bruises on my backside, Andy thought once she'd had a hot bath. Drying herself off, she made a moue of distaste at the mirror. The Marquess was probably nothing more than another vain coxcomb.

She sat and hugged her mother's silver-backed brush before beginning her nightly routine of brushing her chestnut hair one hundred times. After about fifty strokes, she bent her head forward. Her hair billowed down, nearly reaching the floor. She continued counting. *Sixty-one, sixty-two, sixty-* . . .

Her hand froze.

The brush slipped from numb fingers and hit the carpet with a dull thud. Andy stared at the curtained window.

The drapes, heavy as they were, couldn't block out the sound, and her ears rang from the most mournful baying she'd ever heard.

No, not the most mournful. Demillo, the springer spaniel she'd had when she was nine, had wept the same way when his constant companion, Venus, a ginger tabby, was crushed beneath the wheels of a carriage.

Andy rushed forward, stumbling over the hem of her dressing gown. She yanked back the window coverings, but couldn't see anything.

The clouds moved. A pale half-moon shone upon the crest of a hill, outlining the body of an animal. Its head up, the specter gave one more poignant howl, then disappeared.

Dazed, Andy returned to the dressing table, stooping only

to pick up the fallen hairbrush. She couldn't finish her nightly routine. Even with the passage of so many years, the memories were still strong. Dashing away surreptitious tears, she went to the four-poster, recalling how Demillo licked the bleeding, motionless Venus. She remembered how her own whimpers echoed the dog's.

A faint recollection of powder-soft perfume teased her nostrils, just as it had when her beloved mother's consoling embrace enfolded her all those years ago.

Clutching the bedcovers to her breast with one hand, Andy leaned over and blew out the lone candle. If only she could extinguish the bittersweet memories as easily.

A wet and irritable nonpareil cantered up the long drive with his companion. "Bloody English weather," he muttered.

Dominic White, his equally pained comrade, responded with a groan. "Wasn't my idea to leave the comfort of your London townhouse with a storm coming on."

"I couldn't take it anymore, Dom! The last episode turned my stomach. If Lady Cynthia hadn't been there and overheard the plans of Marion and her mother, I'd be well on my way to getting leg-shackled." Jonathon Charles Albert Sterling, the Marquess of Baldwin, swore.

Dominic snorted. "Oh, come now, Jon. Thought you considered the Lady Marion a bit of a beauty. Furthermore, as a much decorated veteran of Waterloo, you should be impressed with her mother's strategy—arranging the closed carriage, missing maid and all. Actually, it was rather amusing. Wonder how that old dragon felt when she saw Lady Cynthia entering the carriage together with the two of you. Dashed bright of her to beg a ride. Must say, Jon, you have the devil's own luck."

Jon chuckled. "I wish you *could* have seen Marion's petulance as she rearranged her cloak to cover the bodice her mother had ripped. What a waste of a good dress! Inviting Cynthia for a house party was the least I could do in return for her warning.''

Jon directed his horse around a fallen branch. ''She's rather a taking piece—might even do as the next marchioness,'' he mused.

Dominic didn't answer. Jon could almost hear his friend *cum* secretary grinding his teeth. His lips tightened. They'd had this discussion before. So what if his careless tone suggested he was merely choosing a new cravat. Was there any difference? Both a cravat and a female could form a noose around a man's neck. Hadn't his own father choked to death because of a woman? Jon gazed at the manor they were rapidly approaching. His cousin and his aunt were the only two women he knew who were exceptions to that rule.

A light flickered out in one of the upstairs guest rooms. The Fitzgeralds must have arrived.

Dominic broke the awkward silence. ''St. James will be coming as well, won't he?''

'' 'Fraid so, Dom, although I still can't figure out how he wangled the invitation. I must have been deep in my cups that evening. Sorry.''

''No need to apologize. You know what they say about relatives. Just be grateful that he's more my cousin than yours,'' Dominic offered wryly.

They clattered into the stable yard, handed the reins to a pair of sleepy grooms, and dashed to the dark manor. Entering through the side door, they startled Simms just as he was making his final rounds.

Jon stripped off his damp jacket and affectionately cuffed the butler on the shoulder before bounding toward the stairs. ''It's a pleasure to see your homely face again, Simms.''

''And yours, too, I'm sure, m'lord,'' the butler declared. Regaining his equanimity, he nodded at Dominic. ''A good evening to you as well, Mr. Dominic. I'll have some hot water for baths brought up for each of you shortly.'' Not with a twitch of a scarred eyelid did he indicate they weren't expected for another week. "And, m'lord, about the Fitzgeralds . . . "

"If they're here already, I'll meet them in the morning. Right now, all I want is a bath, a bite, and my bed." Halfway up the stairs already, Jonathon paused and turned, catching an odd expression in Simms's eyes. He looked almost . . . worried. Impossible. He hadn't seen a crack in Simms's stately façade since he and Dom had pulled the man, bleeding and beaten, from a pugilist's ring many years before. No . . . he *must* have imagined it. Jon grinned and shook his head, continuing on his way. Dominic, now only a few steps behind, was obviously in just as much a hurry to dry off as he was.

Jon jerked to a sudden halt. His hand gripped the oak railing for support and Dom slammed into his back.

"What now, Jon?"

Slowly, reluctantly, Jon turned and stared beyond his disgruntled companion. Head cocked to the side, he listened intently.

There it was again. A faint, eerie howling.

"Did you hear that, Dom?"

"Hear what?"

Jon listened for it again. Nothing. "Sorry. I must be more tired than I thought." He shrugged and shot a rueful grin at his puzzled friend. Turning back, he continued on his way, a faint uneasiness slowing his steps.

Chapter Two

Weak morning sunlight filtered through partially open drapes. Andy sat up and the last remnants of depressing dreams of whimpering animals faded. With a groggy smile, she accepted a tray from a fresh-faced maid who'd introduced herself as Lily.

The aroma of fresh coffee, chocolate, and pastry was enticing. Andy sniffed appreciatively and bit into a still-warm, flaky croissant. Eschewing the chocolate, she washed the pastry down with cream-thickened coffee. "Mmmm, heavenly!" she murmured.

"Will you be needing any help getting dressed?" Lily busied herself with Andy's luggage, nodding gratefully when Andy shook her head. "Things are a bit topsy-turvy today, what with you folk coming in the evening and the Marquess and Mr. White coming late at night when they weren't expected."

Andy brushed away the delicate flakes still clinging to her lips and stifled a groan at the news. At the same time, she remembered the baying dog—if a dog it was. "Lily . . . "

"Yes, miss?"

"Did you hear a dog howling last night?"

"Howling? No, miss." Her fingers curled around a silk petticoat and stilled. She shot Andy a queer look as if she'd just thought of something. "What sort of howling?"

"Oh, you know . . . the sad type of wail."

"Ain't no dogs 'round here as howls like that."

Andy shrugged, thinking perhaps it couldn't be heard from the servants' quarters. She took a last sip of her coffee and shook off the memories the dog had raised. "Have you heard if my father is feeling better this morning?"

" 'Fraid he's still abed. Simms stopped to see him earlier, but his lordship—your father, that is—asked you start without him. He's hoping to be up and about by luncheon." With a final curtsy and one last, curious look at Andy, the diligent maid bustled off to her other tasks.

Frowning, Andy put aside the tray. Normally, her father rose early. Any change from his routine did not bode well.

She got out of bed, hopping lightly when her feet hit the still chilly carpet. Quickly, she whisked through her morning ablutions behind the Chinese lacquered screen. There was a lot of work to be done, especially if she had to do her father's portion.

After donning one of the freshly pressed dresses, Andy added a gaily colored, knotted shawl about her shoulders and twisted her hair into a knot. She stuck her tongue out at her image in the mirror and laughed, recalling the horror of the maids on the Continent at her negligent attitude toward dressing.

She grabbed her notebook from the Queen Anne desk and stepped into the hall. Pausing, she gazed at her father's door and shrugged, deciding to let him rest a bit longer. Slowly, she made her way down the stairs. The air, redolent with beeswax, emphasized the trappings of a well-kept home. She reminded herself, however, that they were here to find out what was beneath the veneer. Caressing the smooth oak balustrade, Andy wondered who had built this home and about what the walls had seen. Humming a dreamy tune as she waltzed down the stairs, she began spinning tales of the distant past. Rounding the bend, she hesitated.

At the bottom of the staircase, Simms was speaking with a gentleman. The Marquess? Her forehead wrinkled. He certainly didn't match her idea of a dashing Corinthian. With sunny, open features and straw-colored hair, he resembled a comfortable country gentleman more than anything else. Reluctantly, Andy continued her way down.

The butler looked up, fretting. "Good morning, miss. I was just informing Mr. White of the previous evening's turn of events." Simms turned to introduce the Marquess's secretary.

Andy smiled when she realized this was the man whose mere name could bring a flush to Lady Helen's cheeks. "It's a pleasure to meet you, Mr. White." Once they'd observed the formalities, she alluded to the problem raised by Helen. "Allow me to assure you that my presence shouldn't overly disturb the household."

"Neither Simms nor Lady Helen had a chance to speak to Lord Baldwin before he left for rounds with the steward, but I'll be sure to clarify the confusion as soon as he comes in," Dominic White promised. "He ought get a chuckle out of it. I can just imagine Simms standing guard over you last night. He does tend to be overprotective of the ladies of the house," he added with a charming grin.

Andy covered a quiet laugh. She hadn't expected such a forthright response. Simms, however, wasn't amused and stalked off in the opposite direction. Turning to her companion to share the humor, she caught a fleeting glimpse of melancholy in the secretary's gentle eyes and her words stuck in her throat. Quickly recovering, she asked, "Would you be so kind as to show me to the library now? Since my father is still feeling the effects of the journey, I'll need to begin the research without him."

"Certainly, Miss Fitzgerald. Allow me." Dominic extended

his arm and ushered a now silent Andy into a richly appointed library.

One of its two desks was extremely large and littered with papers and she glanced at Dominic in question.

"It's Lord Baldwin's. He prefers to work in here. You'll be sharing the library with him."

Andy hid her surprise. That the Marquess took his responsibilities seriously didn't fit her preconceived notions of the man. Dominic distracted her by pointing out the family Bible and various diaries, and she forgot the incongruity. When he left, she began the painstaking work of preparing an initial list of descendants, starting from the current Marquess and working her way back into the past.

Engrossed as she was, the hour for the midday meal came far too soon. She only hoped she wouldn't be late if she took a few moments to freshen up and glanced ruefully at her ink-stained fingers. How could her father expect her to fit in with the London group of ladies? *They* preferred dabbling in water-colors.

Jonathon shrugged off his greatcoat with a curse. Behind schedule, he'd have to settle for a tray in the library instead of joining the family. "Confounded women! A more manipulative lot I've yet to meet. Flash a title in front of them—with or without an attendant packet of gold—and before you know it, they're falling all over you. That Lady Metcalfe and her mealy-mouthed daughter held me up for nearly an hour by the village, trying to wangle an invitation to dinner."

Simms wrung his hands. His mouth opened, only to promptly close.

Taking note of his butler's uncharacteristic agitation, Jon paused in his tirade against half of the human population. "What is it, Simms? You've heard this diatribe before. You know how I detest the false pretense most women adopt."

"Yes, of course, my lord." Simms cleared his throat. "If you could spare a moment, I believe Mr. White would like to see you before luncheon ... about an unexpected guest."

The butler's unusual formality and glum appearance didn't halt Jon's rush to change. "If that's all that concerns you, you know it shouldn't. We've plenty of rooms, so one more person certainly won't be a problem."

Simms followed him to the stairs, huffing to keep up. Jon grinned. Simms was definitely not his normal, unflappable self.

"But, sir, it's about the Fitzgeralds ... " he stuttered, still trailing behind.

"Later, Simms." Jonathon dashed around the curve, tugging off his cravat at the same time. Suddenly, he skidded to a halt.

Directly in front of him, a tall vision's gaze reflected his own amazement. And what a vision! Dark, chestnut tendrils framed bold, square features.

The startled woman let go of her skirt to steady herself and simultaneously tripped over her hem.

"Not another one," Jon muttered as he wrapped his arms around the woman to break her fall. She struggled free and lost her balance, landing ignominiously on her backside. Resigned, he bent to help her.

Simms groaned.

Jon looked back at the butler from his awkward position over the woman. The farcical situation got the better of him and he fought back a grin. "The new assistant housekeeper your wife has been begging for?"

Simms shook his head in unhappy denial.

"I didn't think so." Jon turned back to the woman, now struggling with her long skirts. He passed an experienced eye over her revealed petticoats. Their seductive silk was too fine for anyone of the serving class. "The unexpected guest."

So much for having a few quiet days alone with the family. Jon gave a heartfelt sigh and continued his examination. Her dashing gray morning dress, slashed with panels of teal green, did nothing to hide her ample charms. Delicate Brussels lace on the collar brought attention to her graceful neck. And her features, stormy as they were . . .

Jon sighed again. With little other choice, he extended his arm in a gesture reminiscent of the most debonair gallant at a ball. His wicked sense of humor reasserted itself. He purposefully spoiled the effect by taking the offensive and stared boldly into her eyes.

"That really is the oldest trick in the book, m'dear," he drawled. "I would have thought a woman of your obvious, ahem. . ."—he paused blatantly—"your obvious attributes would be more creative in bringing a man to his knees."

His gaze caressed the neat turn of her exposed ankle. The delightful baggage brushed aside his assistance, muttering imprecations against him and his antecedents under her breath in Italian. Jon smirked. Thanks to a good tutor and an extended Grand Tour, he'd known Italian since his salad days.

Her rich curses brought out his full laughter. A woman who actually challenged him? How refreshing! No English miss, this one, he thought, staring pointedly at her heaving breasts. His dear dragon of an aunt must have lost some of her reservations about the upcoming house party and hired an opera singer for entertainment. "I'm sure your voice will more than compensate for your mediocre method of capturing the attention of a man, *cara mia,*" he crooned in Italian.

Andy's blush deepened at this last barb, even as her stomach churned in reaction to the intimate, hot gaze of his ice-blue eyes. She swallowed hard and swatted at the hands caressing her legs under the guise of tugging her skirt into place. Glaring at the somewhat mud-bespattered, but ruggedly handsome man, she hissed in English. "Disagreeable coxcomb!"

The vibration of his chuckling extended to the fingertips touching her skin and echoed in the sinking pit of her belly. *Please don't let this be the Marquess.* He looked to be about thirty, the right age. His hand brushed against the curve of her elbow. She jerked, slapping his outstretched palm before observing a mortified Simms peering anxiously at them. Her muttering faded. Memories of the "Awkward Amazon" resurfaced, tormenting her once more.

"M'lord, milady. Oh dear, oh dear," the pugnacious butler stuttered, reaching out a shaking hand. "Are you hurt, miss?"

Andy shook her head and stifled a desire to run and hide. Her fingernails dug into the old scar, the same as they had during her aborted Season. Seeing the huge butler incongruously fluttering about her like a fragile Sphinx moth—a harbinger of ill luck according to superstition—she managed a weak smile.

"Except for my bruised pride, I'm fine, Simms. Truly, I am." She accepted the butler's help, thinking she'd probably added to the bruises on her backside. However, she wasn't about to bring attention to any intimate part of her body with *that* unprincipled rake around.

On the other hand, observing him surreptitiously through lowered lashes, Andy admitted the man before her—if he were the Marquess—wasn't the dandy she'd expected. No buckram padding on his calves, if the tight-fitting knee-high riding boots were anything to go by. Even standing a step below her as he was, she still had to look up at him. Broad shoulders and narrow hips enhanced his tall physique. Thick ebony hair, too long for the current style, brushed against his collar.

Andy's gaze narrowed, noting the arrogant angle of his nose. Lips far too sensuous hinted at his virility. She shook her head, disgusted. Whoever he was, he was obviously the type of man who fascinated women without effort, she thought. He interrupted her musings with a roguish grin.

"If you've finished your inventory, perhaps Simms would be so kind as to perform the introductions."

"You came up short," Andy shot back, instantly regretting her words. However, they were no more than what his insolence deserved. Simms's gasp of shock mingled with the man's rich laughter. Nostrils thinned, she reminded herself she was no longer a blushing debutante. The man moved to join her on the step. Andy's spine pressed into the railing and she looked up at his twinkling eyes.

"Still short?" he asked with a grin. Without awaiting a reply, he bowed over her hand with a flourish. "Allow me . . . Jonathon Charles Albert Sterling, Marquess of Baldwin, et cetera, otherwise known simply as Jon." His voice lowered. Now plaintive, like a puppy teased with a tasty morsel, he said with a trace of regret, "And with your obvious command of the King's English, I can only presume you are not an opera singer."

Simms huffed. "A man of your years and experience with Quality ought to know better than that, m'lord!"

"Pray forgive my impertinence," the Marquess offered with another bow.

The butler's indignity on her behalf did more to appease Andy than the Marquess's glib apology. Resisting the impulse to push the Marquess onto his precious derriere, she graced the flustered butler with a warm look, without reminding him that he'd also questioned her identity.

Chest puffed out, Simms bowed again. "Allow me to introduce Miss Andrea Fitzgerald, better known as 'Andy,' daughter to Sir Edgar Fitzgerald and come to help him with the study of your family tree—bent twigs and all," he added, scowling at the Marquess.

Andy pasted on an insincere smile, wishing the Marquess weren't standing quite so near. "Not at *all* as talented or exciting as an opera singer. How disappointing for you, I'm sure." Nudging past him, she excused herself with a curt nod. "I do believe luncheon is being served." Thanking Simms politely for coming to her rescue, she flounced down the stairs more quickly than she had in the morning. She wasn't quick enough, however, to miss the Marquess's quietly uttered reposte.

"Actually, I believe you might be even more exciting than an opera singer . . . and far more to my taste."

Andy's cheeks were still flaming when she entered the dining room. Simms followed closely behind to announce the Marquess would be having a tray in the library. She darted an anxious glance at the others to see if anyone heard her unguarded sigh of relief. Apparently not.

Flushed, her father was fiddling with his cutlery. Dominic cast her a guilty look, as though apologizing for not warning the Marquess about her presence. Helen was staring at her plate, as if expecting her fish to swim off. At the other end of the table, a handsome, tight-lipped woman of Junoesque proportions—presumably the Marchioness—exuded the dark aura of someone who'd been deceived. Once Andy was seated, the woman pierced her with a fierce glare and fired the first salvo, confirming Andy's supposition as to her identity.

"My daughter explained the error in identity. And while I am aware of your father's impeccable reputation in the field of genealogy, what qualifications do you have to be assisting him?"

Edgar grumbled. Andy hushed him with a speaking glance. She straightened her already stiff back, refusing to give in to the old feelings of inadequacy. Managing a slight smile, she spoke evenly. "I have the same qualifications you were willing to accept a son of his might have, Lady Baldwin. I've been helping with his research for the last four years."

Out of the corner of her eyes, she caught Helen's sympathetic glance and felt better. Andy lowered her gaze to concentrate on taking a bit of the poached salmon filet. She only hoped she wouldn't disgrace herself by dropping the delicate morsel onto her lap.

Edgar cleared his throat. His irate voice was hoarse when he spoke. "None of the families who have commissioned my services have ever complained of Andy's skills."

Andy's gaze rolled heavenward. Why couldn't he let go of the matter? Her usually urbane father, whom hostesses counted on to thaw the most frigid duchess, was only adding to the tension. Why did he have to take the questions as a personal affront? She began regretting her insistence upon accepting this assignment, and barely managed to forestall her father from making matters even worse. "I'm sure Lady Baldwin just requires some evidence of your assurances. You must admit, Papa, that your respect for my abilities *is* out of the ordinary way of things."

The comment, while mollifying her father, did little to satisfy the Marchioness. She snorted and arched a disbelieving brow before turning the conversation to an upcoming house party.

Andy took a sip of the fruity white wine and studied Lady Sofia, as they had been reluctantly invited to call her. Nearing fifty, her attitude toward Helen, Dominic, and the servants was distantly kind without being condescending. Unfortunately, Lady Sofia was anything but kind toward herself and her father.

While making an occasional reference to material for their research during the uncomfortable meal, the Marchioness's civility was tainted with barely concealed displeasure. Sofia scowled at Edgar when his hacking cough interrupted her yet again. At the end of the spell, the Marchioness stood. Tossing her napkin beside her unfinished meal, she called for the nearby Simms. "Kindly assist Sir Edgar to his room and summon the physician immediately." Without another word, Lady Sofia turned on her heel and stormed from the room.

Incensed, Edgar shook off Simms's help and glared at Andy, as though she were responsible for his banishment. "A little cough and it's treated like a cholera epidemic. I will rest now, but only because the journey must have fatigued me more than I thought." He marred his exit with another bout of coughing.

It was as if the two senior members of the party had just completed some animalistic ritual of staking out territorial rights, with neither coming out a clear victor. Taken aback at the behavior of both her father and the Marchioness, Andy could only stare at the table's two remaining occupants. They stared back, equally speechless.

Lady Helen bit her lip. Her gaze slid from Andy's. Voice faint, she apologized. "I'm so terribly sorry, Miss Fitzgerald. I don't understand what came over Mama. Normally, she can be counted on to keep her head about her in the most dire of circumstances." Dominic patted her shoulder awkwardly. She looked at him with a grateful, hesitant smile.

"Please, Helen. We promised to dispense with formality last night. Moreover, I'm the one who owes you an apology. It's obvious that my father is truly ill. Your mother was absolutely correct to send for a doctor. As a matter of fact, I am glad she did so."

Helen didn't appear much mollified by her attempt at easing the atmosphere. Andy tried changing the subject. "Perhaps you could show me the portrait gallery now? It helps if one can envision the people one is writing about. Any anecdotes you know, might also add some insight to their lives." Besides, Andy thought, this would also give her an excuse for avoiding the library . . . and the maddening Marquess. She wasn't ready to meet him again just yet.

Lady Helen embraced the distraction, her relief obvious. She shook off her dejection with a game smile. "I'd be more than happy to share the little I know, although Mama is really the person who should take you. She's much more knowledgeable about the history."

Dominic stood. "In that case, I'll be off." He hesitated, patting Helen's shoulder once more before leaving with a final nod. Helen gazed after him, her fingers busily tearing the bread on her plate into tiny pieces.

Andy was sure something was afoot. Was the Marchioness aware of the emotional bond between the two? Did she oppose it? Andy recalled herself sternly. It wasn't her concern. Still, she couldn't help but comment. "What a pleasant gentleman Mr. White is." It was true. With his light hair, warm brown eyes, and ready smile for all, he resembled a ray of sunshine under which Helen fairly blossomed.

"He is everything that is kind." A rosy hue crept up the soft plains of Helen's face.

"Have you known him long?"

"Oh, Dom—that is, Mr. White—and I grew up together." She hesitated, glancing at Andy. "It's a rather sad story."

Andy held up a hand. "There's no need to share it if you find it troubling, Lady Helen. I didn't mean to pry."

"Dom is a distant relation, so I'm sure you'll hear about it sooner or later. It isn't that uncommon a story. No doubt you've heard similar tales." Helen sighed as they left the dining room. Her words clipped, she related the events.

Dom's mother, Emily White, was betrothed to a wealthy, older crony of her father's when she met and fell in love with Richard St. James, a young Baron. Her father refused to sanction the match, so they ran away to the Continent. Nearly a year later, a pregnant Emily returned alone.

Their ship had capsized. Richard drowned, but Emily survived by clinging to her small valise. When rescued, she claimed to be Richard's widow. However, because she couldn't produce the marriage lines, no one believed her, least of all her father or the Baron's family. They thought her unhinged over the tragedy and cast her off.

"Unfortunately, you're right, Helen. The story isn't that uncommon." Andy made a moue of distaste, again grateful her own father wasn't forcing her into a loveless marriage, and tucked her arm through her agitated companion's. The swishing of their skirts along the upstairs hallway added a soothing chorus to the age-old tune of the fate of star-crossed lovers. Andy patted Helen's white-knuckled hand.

Thus encouraged, Helen added more details. "Having nowhere else to turn, she came to my mother, a cousin with whom she had been best friends at school. Emily succumbed to a fever within days of arriving here, never speaking of the marriage again. She died three weeks later, after giving birth to Dom. My mother, still childless at the time, couldn't bear to part with him.'' Helen's fingers dug more deeply into Andy's arm.

A sudden idea popped into Andy's mind. Ever the sleuth, her gaze narrowed. ''Forgive me, but do you have any idea if Emily kept a diary? If one exists, it might contain some clues to confirm her claim. Although Father and I are here to work on your genealogy, I'm sure I could find time to see if anything can be discovered on Mr. White's behalf.''

Helen gnawed on her bottom lip without replying.

Mentally berating herself for raising recent ghosts, Andy tempered her brash proposal. ''Please don't consider me presumptuous for offering. I would understand if you refuse. Unpleasant memories would have to be resurrected.''

Helen shook her head. ''That's not it. It would be wonderful to discover proof of the marriage. It's just that I've never heard mention of any diary. I'll speak to Mama about it. But please,'' she added hurriedly, ''don't mention any of this to Dom. He's rather sensitive about his mother.''

After Andy's assuring nod, Helen picked up the threads of her tale. ''Four years later, I was born. When twelve-year-old Jon arrived not long afterward, Father accused Mama of running a home for foundlings. However, there wasn't any real choice but to take Jon in. Jon was his heir.'' Brightening, Helen laughed softly. ''Father was furious. Jon was a hellion, if you'll pardon my saying so. But he *was* understandably unhappy at the time, you know.''

A sadness due, no doubt, to the fact that he'd just been orphaned. Andy promptly scolded herself. She ought to know better than to make assumptions. Still, she hoped Helen wasn't about to treat her to a litany of the Marquess's escapades.

Andy recalled his devilish grin as he'd stroked her leg, and shivered. She couldn't help being intrigued, in spite of herself. What was it about the Marquess—and his his rakish air—that piqued her interest? And legions of other women as well, she reminded herself dryly.

Their arrival at the gallery frustrated her whetted curiosity. Helen paused at the portrait of the first Marquess. He'd earned his title from Charles the Second, shortly before the Battle of Worcester in 1651, and the rise of Cromwell.

The Marquess's deep blue eyes mesmerized Andy, drawing her closer. If not for the period clothes, she would've thought the current Marquess and he were brothers. They certainly shared the same laughing, teasing looks. Her gaze slid to the tall, fierce wolfhound pressing against his thigh. Andy moved closer still. Her hand hovered over the image of the hound, as if to stroke the rough fur captured so vividly by the artist. Abruptly, she stepped away. "What happened to him?" Andy wasn't honestly sure if she was asking about the Marquess or the dog.

Helen couldn't quite meet her eyes. "He died."

Andy examined the ornate plaster work on the ceiling, trying to quell a sudden impulse to chuckle. If she and her father had to drag out each necessary detail like this, it was bound to become a lengthy process. Fortunately, Helen spoke up before Andy was forced to prod her.

"A gang of Roundheads killed him. According to accounts, it was rather grizzly. Burne, his dog, was fatally wounded trying to protect him. Apparently, it took Burne hours to die and he howled for the full time. Cromwell's forces laughed and wouldn't allow anyone to put him out of his misery."

Andy's internal smile faded at the chilling words. Now she understood Helen's reluctance to speak.

"Near the end, unable to bear Burne's ghostly cry as he shielded the Marquess's body with his own, they made a game of who could kill the dog hand-to-hand. Burne fought them off. They finally speared him. Since then, no Marquess has ever kept a dog in the house."

Andy shuddered. She looked between the Marquess and his dog again, wondering about the incredible bond between man and beast.

"According to legend, Burne still prowls the estate . . . "

"Yes?" Andy prompted, repressing another shiver.

" . . . howling in prophesy of danger." Helen wrapped her arms around herself and looked away. "The last time was about eighty years ago, when a disgruntled tenant wounded the third Marquess's wife."

Accustomed though she was to legends and ghost stories, Andy's throat went dry. Her voice low, she asked, "That reminds me of last night . . . that *was* one of the dogs loose from your kennels, wasn't it?"

"I beg your pardon?" Helen looked at Andy, perplexed.

"Didn't you hear the animal last night? I saw it atop a knoll. It looked and sounded like a very large dog."

"I didn't hear anything. We have no dogs like that. Are you sure?"

Andy knew she couldn't have imagined that mournful weeping. She nodded.

Helen's eyes widened. Her gaze slid back to the portrait. "Oh, my," she whispered.

Andy's gaze followed. "Preposterous!" Only the answer to Helen's unspoken question sounded hesitant, sliding as it did over an odd lump in her throat.

Chapter Three

"Confound it, man! Must you discharge your duty with such vehemence?"

Her father's weakly muttered exclamation, followed by a string of curses interspersed with a hacking cough, greeted Andy's ears when she opened the door to his room. It was all she could do to bite back her worry as she took in the tableau.

Under the guidance of a stern-faced Lady Sofia, a servant was pounding Edgar's back with cupped hands to loosen the phlegm in his lungs. Steaming bowls of hot water surrounded the bed, and the pungent odor of tincture of Friar's Balsam assailed Andy's nostrils.

Gripped by a sense of foreboding, she quietly slid the door shut and stepped forward. As she did so, her sudden fear eased. Even if it had been Burne she'd heard, he only warned of danger to the Marquess's family.

"Ah, Miss Fitzgerald." Lady Sofia glanced up from the bedside. Dismissing the servant, she folded her hands in her lap and frowned at Edgar. "Your father is in a poor way. Of course, it doesn't help that he is behaving like a stubborn old fool about the regimen necessary to restore his health—not that I would expect a man to act any differently,'' she added with a disparaging sniff.

"Andy . . .'' Her father turned slowly onto his back. "Kindly inform this behemoth that I'll be just fine in a few days.'' His voice cracked during the insult.

Andy cast an apologetic glance at the Marchioness and sat beside her father. His hand was hot to her touch, his countenance flushed and accentuated by eyes glazed over with fever. Taking the proffered cloth from the Marchioness, she gently wiped away the gathering sweat from his forehead with a frown. "The physician's been here?''

Glaring at Lady Sofia, Edgar spoke first. "Bah! That quack was worse than an old woman.''

The Marchioness glared back as if he were nothing more than a recalcitrant schoolboy. "Be grateful Dr. McDonald doesn't hold with bleeding patients and the like. You might as well accept the fact that you have inflammation of the lungs.''

Her father's face mottled and he looked prepared to do battle.

"Papa!'' Andy shot him a warning look to prevent any rejoinder. The diagnosis confirmed her earlier suspicions. She only hoped the convalescence would be easier than it had been in Italy. With an austere tone, she prompted, "Lady Sofia is all that is kind for ensuring you have the best possible care. You know you're not well. You really do owe her an apology.''

"All right, so it may be a day or two before I'm up and about.'' Edgar acknowledged his daughter's rebuke with a grumble in Lady Sofia's direction. Turning back to Andy, he continued, his breath rattling and shallow. "You go ahead and start the research. Don't forget to check old copies of *The Gentleman's Magazine* for any printed information on marriages and deaths . . . might prove a good source of biographical information.''

Propping himself up on an elbow, he coughed harshly and waved his hand in frustration. "Oh, you know the methodology as well as I do. Hopefully you won't have too many suggestions regarding a revisionist history. And if you do, ignore them.''

Instead of reminding him that he'd rebuked her for making exactly the same assumption during their journey, Andy darted an anxious glance at the older woman.

Edgar didn't notice. He stared pointedly at the Marchioness before collapsing back on the pile of pillows. Through with his blustering, he patted Andy's hand. "I'll survive. Don't worry on that score.''

"Of course, Papa.'' Andy brushed back damp strands of hair from his face and maintained a soft tone while reviewing the procedure. Reassured, he listened as she went on to relate some of Helen's anecdotes—without mentioning the legend of Burne. After a few minutes, her steady, quiet tone lulled Edgar into a restless sleep.

Andy faced the Marchioness. "Perhaps I could do some of the research here, so as to help care for my father?''

"Nonsense,'' Sofia responded haughtily, as if her abilities had been impugned. "While I had no idea we'd be operating an infirmary when you were invited, I'm certainly capable of overseeing your father's recuperation. Of course, it means the Marquess and Mr. White will have to be more involved in assisting you with your research, but I'm sure they will manage to find the time.'' She paused and stared down her nose at Andy. "I do hope your father is correct in assuring us you are capable of starting the work.''

"Certainly, Lady Sofia. I'd best be off then.'' Andy offered a hesitant smile, swallowing her dissatisfaction at working with the Marquess. She doubted he'd be much help, but it wouldn't do to further exacerbate the Marchioness. After a quick peck to her sleeping father's cheek, she departed as quietly as she'd come.

Andy entered the library with trepidation, but a quick glance around confirmed the Marques was absent. She breathed a sigh of relief, pleased at being able to start her work without his disturbing presence.

She worked steadily until a tingling at the back of her neck interfered with her concentration. Rotating her head from side to side to release the building tension, she told herself she was spending too much time buried in the past. Its ghosts must be starting to haunt her. Even so, the neatly piled papers on her desk attested to the amount of work she'd accomplished in the last couple of hours, despite intruding thoughts of the Marquess.

Andy glanced at his lordship's vacant desk and rubbed her neck. Thinking to pace off her vaguely irritable mood, Andy stood and pushed away her chair. The chair rocked, hit an obstacle, and fell back against her.

"Gads, woman!"

Andy's ears burned at the choked oath. She darted a startled glance over her shoulder. *That* was the obstacle she'd hit with her chair? Her eyes fluttered closed at the sight. Memories of her clumsy Season mocked her. The old scar still burned.

The Marquess . . . a now very pale Marquess . . . had come up behind her with a stealth probably honed during the Napoleonic campaigns . . . a Marquess now doubled over and gasping for air. One hand clutched at emptiness for support. The other hand covered an unmentionable part of his anatomy.

Blushing furiously, Andy shoved aside her chair to help him regain his balance. She tucked her hands under his arms, and when he braced himself against her shoulders, she prattled nervously, "You must think me a clumsy goosecap, my lord. Let me assure you that I'm not usually so graceless." *At least, I haven't been for years.*

Gasping, Jonathon couldn't reply. Opening and closing his eyes, he fought to stop the room's spinning. Throbbing pain, unlike anything he'd ever known, ripped through his body and he feared he'd shame himself by casting up his accounts. Bile lodged at the back of his throat. He gulped several times before finally succeeding in pushing it down.

He had been leaning against one of the massive oak book-
cases lining the walls, observing Andy as she flipped through
the journals on her desk, inexplicably drawn to the woman who
had rejected his teasing advances. There was something erotic
about the way she arched her back and massaged her neck with
a slim white hand. Mentally caressing the sensitive path from
her ears downward, imagining his tongue trailing after her hand,
he'd stepped forward without paying attention—directly into
her moving chair.

He stretched painfully and grasped Andy's shoulders. Balance regained, he shot her a faint smile, revived somewhat by
her refreshing violet scent. "There are those who might accuse
you of attempting to do permanent damage to my most esteemed
self. However, I'm sure your clumsiness was unintentional."

When the blood rushed to her cheeks, his smile widened.
"In fact, the fault was probably all mine," he rasped into her
ear. He moved closer. His overconfidence had cost him dearly.

Another wave of pain and nausea washed over him. His
knees buckled and his fingers dug into her. Haloed black spots
swam before his eyes and he was forced to swallow hard again.
It took a while before he could summon up a sangfroid he was
far from feeling. "I could probably use a brandy."

Instead of sitting down and letting Andy bring him the drink,
he limped to the liquor cabinet in the corner with her assistance.
She poured out the brandy with a shaking hand and some drops
spilled. Something about that imperfection warmed Jon more
than he suspected the brandy would.

Keeping one arm around her shoulder, he accepted the glass
she thrust at him. For a slow moment, he brushed his fingers
over her soft, trembling ones then took a gulp of the burning
liquor.

His vision wavered again.

Slowly, the pain eased to an uncomfortable pulsating, echoing the drumbeat in his skull. He took another sip and put down
the glass. Eyes closed, he mentally flexed the various parts of

his body. Pleased to feel no irreversible harm, he thanked God and began to savor his armful. Without letting go of Andy, he opened his eyes gradually, only to find temptation staring back at him. Rising to the challenge, he exchange a fleeting smile with another grimace of pain.

Andy stopped licking her brandy-spattered fingers and chewed at the corner of her lips. "My lord?" Her gaze skittering away from his, she brought a hesitant hand to his chest. "Are you sure you're all right? Perhaps I should fetch some help?"

Careful not to overdramatize, he answered weakly. "No, I'm fine." Seeing she was unconvinced, he admitted, "Well, perhaps I need another moment. You don't mind if I lean on you a bit longer?"

When she shook her head, he lay his cheek against her shoulder. His breath teased her loose, glossy tendrils of hair. Tipping her chin up with his forefinger, he inched his face forward, focusing on her ripe mouth. "I had come to see if I could assist with your research, but you were so engrossed, it seemed a shame to disturb you. Do say you'll forgive me," he murmured.

"Don't be ridiculous, Lord Baldwin," Andy uttered, still not daring to look at him. He continued clutching her shoulders. When he didn't respond, she peeked up at him.

Jon was waiting for just that. His lips, so near hers now, curved in satisfaction. He gazed steadily into her hazel eyes, looking for signs of deceit or cunning. None. He drew her closer. His mouth hovered above hers, as though seeking permission to taste her sweetness.

She gazed back at him, eyes widening. He smiled softly. Without another word, he brushed his lips against hers. Once. Twice. Ever so lightly, a third time. Andy's eyes fluttered shut. Nibbling gently, he teased her firm lower lip. His tongue flicked out to trace the outline of her mouth. Her lips parted. He nibbled once more.

His hands tangled in her hair, he drew her face nearer. Was

it his imagination or did she really welcome his kiss? When her tongue accidentally brushed his before quickly darting away, Jon nearly came undone. He dragged her closer. The air he breathed vibrated. His hands, now running along the column of her spine, burned from her heat and she moaned against his neck.

Andy's soft whimpers brought Jon back to awareness with a sudden jolt. *Bloody hell!* He was acting like a rogue with a gentlewoman. He gave her earlobe a last, frustrated tug with his teeth, then grazed the pulsating vein at the base of her throat. Unable to resist, he kissed her yet again, his tongue intentionally brushing against hers.

Finally, he leaned his forehead against hers, listening to her harsh breathing, feeling the pounding of her heart. Or was it his? Did it matter? The point was, he'd nearly lost his control. That in itself was unusual. What was it about this tall, square-faced Amazon that drew him?

Reluctantly, he stepped back. Best stop now, or risk a servant discovering them—grappling with desire *and* each other on the carpet. He couldn't permit that, no matter how much his ardor and anatomy—obviously undamaged—argued against letting her go.

Hypnotized by her glazed look and parted mouth, Jonathon's resolve floundered. He dragged her back into his arms and nuzzled her neck, stroking it to calm her hammering pulse. Taking a deep breath, as much to calm himself as to breathe in her elusive perfume one last time, he grasped her head and quickly kissed her lips before withdrawing and clasping his hands behind his back.

"I really don't think this was what my aunt had in mind when she suggested I see if you required any help." A self-deprecating laugh accentuated his chagrin. He walked toward the French doors leading out to the gardens and enviously observed the serenity of the gardeners. He and Andy, on the other hand, both needed a moment to compose themselves.

He also needed a change in topic to bring his still throbbing arousal under control. Otherwise, Andy might succeed in doing permanent damage to him without having to lift a finger. Jon sucked in a deep breath and clenched his jaw. Forcing a nonchalance he was far from feeling, he began. "No one has ever inventoried the family's journals. Although most of the chronicles appear to be in here, there's a possibility others exist in the old muniments room behind the estate office."

Mortified, Andy wondered what the deuce had come over her. Barely able to comprehend the Marquess's speech, she put a hand to her breast, trying to still the racing of her heart, and glanced down at the green and white patterned carpet. Fallen hairpins stared back at her accusingly. Her hands flew to her disheveled hair. The enormity of her actions struck her and her mortification intensified. Appalled by her utter loss of control, she wished she could disappear. It didn't happen. Instead, she bent and, with fumbling fingers, picked up the pins.

Andy tried to concentrate on the Marquess's steady voice, speaking as though nothing untoward had occurred. Although grateful for his discretion, Andy was nevertheless piqued by his casual attitude. Glaring at him in frustration, she stuck the pins in her hair and wondered if he ached the same way she did. Perhaps he hadn't been affected by the encounter at all. That possibility was too much to be borne and she fought a sudden urge to take one of the pins from her mouth and jab it into his back.

Reining in her vexation, she tugged at her bodice, blushing at the rustling sound of material, before replying in a cooler tone than she thought possible. "The chronicles here seem to contain the major diaries. It will probably take a few weeks to review all of them. I'll be free to search out other data after that." Her voice quivered on the last few words. She gulped back her embarrassment. "How well do you know your family's history?"

"Actually, fairly well," the Marquess answered. "My aunt

made sure of that. She's always felt remembering one's roots helps keep a sense of perspective. She claims, and probably rightly so if one considers the number of profligate members of the aristocracy, that to forget one's past is to lose touch with the soil and a person's obligations to others. To her, the past is linked with the present, forming part of the chain to the future. A link by itself lacks strength or purpose."

A point in the lady's favor, Andy mused. Unfortunately, that he had obeyed his aunt in learning the history was also a point in favor of the Marquess—and she was definitely out of charity with him at the moment.

Now as tidy as she could make herself without a mirror, Andy went to the shelves, pretending a need to double-check some references made in the journals she'd been reading. She had to occupy herself somehow until the unsettling man left. "Do you have a favorite amongst your ancestors?"

"Oh, I have some definite favorites—and they were all black sheep," he replied with a wicked grin and came toward her.

"Somehow, that doesn't surprise me," Andy shot back, mentally trying to brace herself against his potent magnetism. Standing on the tips of her toes, she stretched up to reach a book on the history of the region during the early part of the eighteenth century. She nearly lost her balance when he touched the small of her back.

"Allow me, my sweet," he breathed into her ear.

She shuddered at the contact, glad when he went to place the book on her desk. She buried the fleeting thought that had he chosen to embrace her again, she probably would have been tempted to return his touch.

The door opened.

Andy gave a guilty start. She hadn't heard a knock.

Simms entered to announce tea would be served shortly.

Fumbling with her papers to hide her embarrassment, Andy was supremely grateful he hadn't arrived any earlier. And if the observant Simms noted anything peculiar about her shaking hands, for once he hid his curiosity beneath the visage of a well-trained servant.

The Marquess led her out, indulging in only one comment to remind Andy of her folly.

"I wish you'd call me 'Jon,' and . . . you really are much more interesting than an opera singer, you know," he whispered roguishly.

The delicate blush staining Andy's cheeks was her only reply to his effrontery.

Not thinking clearly, Andy escaped directly to her room on the pretext of needing to get some notes. She hadn't stopped to think one wouldn't take notes into tea. No wonder the Marquess's chuckle had followed her up the stairs. Now, still feeling horribly gauche, Andy hesitated at the drawing room door.

She glanced at the footman and silently blessed all well-trained servants. He didn't bat an eye at her indecision, allowing her to stand and listen to someone inside playing the piano. Finally gathering up her courage, she nodded and the footman opened the door.

The Marquess was the only one there. Comfortably seated on the low bench at the pianoforte, he ran his strong fingers smoothly over the ivory keyboard.

The same strong fingers which had played her like an instrument not long ago.

Andy bumped into a side table. Its vase rattled and her grasp flew to prevent it from tipping. An unclipped thorn from one of the yellow roses bit into her hand. After managing to right the flowers without further catastrophe, she sucked on her wound.

Jonathon turned at the disruption. He left the pianoforte and came toward her. Grasping her hand, he inspected it carefully at the same time as stroking her wrist. "Not seriously hurt, I pray." The gleam in his eyes belied the innocence of his tone. He brought his lips to Andy's hand.

Somehow resurrecting her hard-won assurance, Andy yanked her hand back and strode toward the sofa. "I believe I shall survive to see the light of another day."

"You cannot imagine how that pleases me." The Marquess grinned and followed her.

Andy immediately regretted choosing the sofa when he joined her. He draped his arm casually behind her shoulders and cast an appreciative glance at her snug bodice. She couldn't ignore his gaze as it caressed upward, lingering suggestively at her mouth, before finally meeting her eyes.

"As a matter of fact, it pleases me very much," he declared with another shameless grin.

Andy stared into his eyes. Wherever had she gotten the idea they were an icy blue? Right now they were melting her, starting at some inner core she hadn't even realized existed. She jerked when his hand brushed against the back of her neck.

Dominic entered, preventing Andy from making any acerbic comment on his forwardness. Her fingers curled over the old scar on her hand as she struggled to focus on Dominic's concerned comments about her father.

"You're most fortunate to have Lady Sofia watching over him. She'll make sure his health improves, won't she, Jon?"

The Marquess nodded in agreement, his eyes rolling. "The woman is an absolute Tartar in the sickroom. She'll alternate cajoling and appealing to your father's manly instincts, to arguing with him and insisting he has no choice but to recuperate with all possible speed. Her sparring techniques are tougher and dirtier than Gentleman Jackson's were at the height of his career. Or yours, for that matter, Simms," he added, including the butler who had just entered.

"Of course, m'lord," the butler agreed graciously. "The ladies ask that you start tea without them," he intoned in his stentorian voice as he pushed the cart forward.

"He would've been wonderful on the boards, wouldn't you say?" Jon murmured into Andy's ear.

Simms, whose hearing was evidently as powerful as his voice, puffed up his broad chest at the compliment.

The Marquess's comment so closely echoed her own thoughts of the day before that an unwilling laugh escaped Andy's lips. At least her equilibrium was restored.

Preparing for bed, Andy reviewed the day's events. Dinner had gone off surprisingly smoothly. Although her manner was still stiff, Lady Sofia unbent enough to ask pertinent questions about the research and to offer some sharp insights into the family's history. She also promised Andy that her father would receive the best possible care. The Marchioness's brusque manner reassured Andy. Dominic and the Marquess were probably correct. Lady Sofia would likely cow her stubborn father into recuperating, whether he wished it or not—at least Andy fervently hoped so.

She frowned as she brushed her hair. The only blight to her day other than her father's illness was her encounters with the Marquess. He'd kept her on tenterhooks during the evening meal as well, carrying on a subtle flirtation seemingly unnoticed by the others.

If only he hadn't disarmed her with his unfeigned solicitousness in regard to her father. The Marquess had more facets to his character than the fabulous crystals hanging from the Austrian chandeliers gracing the hallways of his home. She brushed her fingers against her lips, recollecting his kisses.

Glancing up, she caught the glazed look of her eyes in the mirror. Vexed with herself, Andy tossed her brush on the dressing table. She strode to the window and yanked aside the curtain, telling herself angrily that she was no chit just out of the schoolroom to be dazzled by a pretty face and broad shoulders.

"Was that you last night, Burne?"

A soft knocking interrupted Andy's chaotic thoughts of ghost dogs running alongside the Marquess. Startled out of her reverie, she rushed to answer the door, castigating herself for mooning over a modern-day Lothario while her father could have taken a turn for the worse.

"Lady Helen, what is it? Nothing's happened to my father, has it?"

"Oh, no. I'm terribly sorry if I frightened you. It's not that at all." Helen hesitated. "It's about our earlier conversation in the portrait gallery. Mama was late in retiring this evening, so it was a while before I could speak to her about any journals Emily might have left behind. . . . Forgive me for troubling you at this hour, but I saw your light from under the door. Would you prefer we speak in the morning?"

"Nonsense, Helen. Please, come in." Cutting off her protestations, Andy ushered her in and closed the door. She donned a wrap to cover her blue silk night rail and led the younger woman to the seats near the fireplace. "Was your mother able to shed any light on the matter?"

Despondent, Helen shook her head. The shadows of the room deepened the gloom evident on her features. "Nothing definite. Apparently Dominic's mother salvaged a small portmanteau from the shipwreck which might have contained some records. Mama remembers that Emily brought it here, but she isn't sure what happened to it—she was quite distraught when Emily died."

She brightened. "Since Mother rarely discards anything, however, there is a chance it may be in the attics, or in one of the other storage rooms. On the other hand . . . if Papa got to it first, we may never see it again," she concluded glumly. "Nevertheless, I'll start looking in the attics tomorrow."

Andy's brow rose at the unconscious aspersion against the old Marquess. It reminded her of the Marchioness's negative remark about men earlier in the day. She shook her head to clear her thoughts and offered Helen a gentle smile. "A capital idea. One word of caution, though. You mustn't get your hopes up. Even if you are able to locate some record left by Emily, it might only confirm that her relationship with the Baron was what people have believed all these years.''

Helen's soft gaze hardened. Leaning over, she gripped Andy's hand. ''I know, but it won't change my regard for Dominic.''

''He means that much to you?'' Helen flushed and lowered her gaze. There wasn't any need to say anything. It was obvious. Andy patted her hand. ''I didn't mean to pry. Forgive me.''

Helen stayed Andy's apology with a shake of her head. Her chin tilted at a stubborn angle. ''I've cared for Dom longer than I can remember. It's just this foolishness about his parentage that keeps us apart. He insists I could do better for myself and worries the stigma of his birth would attach itself to me. As if I care. So what if he is . . . illegitimate?'' Helen flushed once more, stumbling over the word, and swallowed hard.

''Mama knows of my feelings. She doesn't discourage them, but she is speaking of going to London for the small Season. Even though her heart doesn't really seem to be in it, the possibility worries me. Once our year of mourning is over, I'll run out of excuses. I don't want a Season or anything else which might separate me from Dom.''

Andy could only think kindly of Lady Sofia as a result of Helen's artless disclosures. Many another society matron would be appalled if a daughter were hanging out for a bastard as husband. Brusquely, Andy stood and led Helen to the door. ''Your mother obviously cares very much for your happiness. However, tomorrow's another day, and from all appearances, the attics you'll need to search through are quite large. You'll need to get plenty of rest for the task ahead.''

Helen squeezed Andy's hand before leaving. ''Thank you.''

Andy's thoughts were troubled as she went to sleep. But they weren't of Helen's revelations, or of her father's illness, or of ghostly animals. No. Instead, a vision of ice melting in a pool filled her imagination. Glacial blue eyes burning with desire. Strong hands caressing the keys of a piano.

Somehow, somewhere between consciousness and slumber, the black and white of the keys blended into each other and changed into long, chestnut hair, captured by powerful fingers. Bold hands pulled on the hair, pulled her closer.

But closer to what?

Andy moaned. She didn't know.

Chapter Four

Disgruntled after a restless sleep, Andy paid even less attention to her ablutions than normal. An odd feeling of guilt nudged her as portions of last night's dreams, wrapped in soft gauze, flitted through her mind. Sternly, she reminded herself she was here to work on a genealogy and nothing more.

Before getting down to work, though, Andy stopped in to see her father. Lady Sofia was already there, personally dabbing his forehead with a wet cloth. Groaning, Edgar tossed and turned in an attempt to escape her ministrations. Andy curtsied briefly at the Marchioness and sat, taking her father's hand. "How is he?"

There were no servants and they could speak freely. The Marchioness shrugged. "The fever has yet to break. The miserable man spent an uncomfortable night. We've bathed him in cool water every few hours and forced him to drink at least some of the concoction the doctor left. It was quite a battle, I can assure you. I suppose I must give him his due, though. He's certainly stronger than I thought. If only he could be convinced to fight the fever instead of me. Sooner or later, however, I shall prevail,'' Lady Sofia ended confidently.

The two women studied each other silently. Andy noted the older woman's rolled-up sleeves and the apron covering her fawn-colored silk gown. The water stains on her gown's shoulder, just above the apron's edge, looked like dark autumn leaves. Andy's sense of guilt returned twofold. "Lady Sofia . . ."

"If it's about your father, there's no need to say anything." She brushed the topic aside, as if Sir Edgar's recovery were a foregone conclusion, in spite of his resistance. "Did my daughter speak with you yet?"

At Andy's affirmative nod, she sighed. "I would spare her the pain of Society's rejection if I could, you know. But sometimes it's wiser to follow the heart than the strictures of the aristocracy. I've warned her the search might be futile, or worse. I trust you've done the same?"

"Yes, I have," Andy acknowledged.

"Thank you. Best leave me to my work now. You get on with yours," Lady Sofia admonished. She shooed Andy out of the sickroom, her mask firmly back in place. "We must see to it that your father's confidence in your abilities isn't misplaced."

The change to an intimidating tone was too late to conceal the vulnerability Andy had glimpsed, and as she left the room, she felt herself softening yet again toward this grand dame. Here was a woman, she imagined, who had followed the rules of her class and paid the price.

Edgar's fever raged another four days. The household settled into a routine to accommodate his illness. Andy visited him before descending to work in the morning and before retiring at night. The Marchioness also permitted Andy to nurse him for a few hours before teatime in order that she, herself, might rest. Sofia refused to permit her to do more than that, declaring Andy lacked experience in dealing with cantankerous, sick men.

Unfortunately, it was true—not just that Andy didn't have

much expertise in the sick room, but also that her father was an irascible patient. She wondered if they could ever repay the debt owed to Lady Sofia for the care and attention she lavished on a virtual stranger without major complaint. The Marquess and Dominic were correct in their evaluation—the Marchioness was an excellent nurse. Even her father confirmed this opinion.

While delirious most of the time, he reacted violently once when Andy tried to help him take a drink. "Where's Sofie?" he choked, sputtering when the water dribbled down his chin. "That behemoth may be a fussbudget and tyrant, but at least she can help a man take a drink without making him drown." He glared at Andy for a moment, then delirium reclaimed him.

At dinner, Andy apologized once more for her father's illness casting a pall over the household.

The Marchioness dabbed delicately at her mouth with a crested napkin and took a fortifying sip of the red wine before replying. "Stuff and nonsense. As if we would allow a slight inflammation of someone's lungs to inconvenience us." She waved toward the others at the table. "Lord Baldwin and Mr. White carry on handling estate matters. My daughter is rummaging through the attics contentedly, and I am feeling useful," she concluded, brushing off Andy's concern.

Andy allowed the comment regarding the seriousness of Edgar's illness to slip by. Lady Sofia did indeed seem more purposeful and less overbearing. Nevertheless, she argued, "But what about the house party? Surely we're interfering with your need to prepare for it. I must insist on doing more of my share in nursing Father. My research can be done just as well from the sickroom."

A glimpse of the Marchioness whom they had met upon their arrival reappeared. Lady Sofia bristled, as though shocked at Andy's temerity. "Balderdash! The house party will only consist of a few people. No one really expects much from a house party in the country anyway. It's more of a repairing lease from the rounds one must make in London. . . . I suppose you've forgotten that with all the time you spent gadding about foreign parts.''

Lady Sofia's nose rose a notch before she unbent. ''Besides which, Jonathon reports you're coming along quite well with your work. It would be best if you continue concentrating on that. Unless, of course, you still doubt my abilities to nurse your father back to health?''

''Of course not, Lady Sofia,'' she hastened to appease the Marchioness. Andy flushed slightly, but whether it was in response to the implied rebuke, or owing to the Marquess's grin as he raised his glass in a silent, mocking toast to her, she wasn't at all sure.

In the days which followed, Andy continued with the research, missing her father terribly. Every time she found a particularly amusing passage, she looked up to share it with him—only he wasn't there. Instead, she would find the Marquess's enigmatic gaze fixed on her, and she'd hurriedly lower her head.

The one thing she hadn't been able to find, though, was more information on the legend of Burne. Even convinced as she was that she must have imagined the howling, she was still curious and had spoken with the Marquess about it. He'd shrugged off the stories, but promised to find what he could.

Once Edgar's fever finally broke, constant nursing was still necessary to care for his lungs. Therefore, the routine settled into during his crisis remained the same. His back and chest were beaten regularly to keep the lungs clear. A kettle continued boiling in the fireplace to fill the room with purifying steam. The only major difference was that whoever tended Edgar now had to bear with a *conscious* churlish patient.

Andy entered her father's room one afternoon in time to hear Lady Sofia's crow of triumph. ''Checkmate, you old coot! There's no way for you to weasel your way out of this trap.''

''It wouldn't have happened if I weren't so weak and tired,''

Andy tucked her hands into her pockets, gloating over the few times she'd bested him during their sometimes tart exchanges. Was that how the Marchioness felt winning at chess?

If only she could ignore that wicked tilt to his dark eyebrows whenever *he* bested her ... Only it wasn't possible, not with the two of them working together in the same room.

Too flustered to do as she had been bid, Andy turned and made her way toward the portrait gallery. Lily, the maid, passed her with a cheerful greeting.

"Not having a rest, miss?"

Andy shook her head. "No, I think I'll spend some more time in the gallery." She continued on her way, pausing only once to glance into a large ornate mirror and wished she hadn't.

Turning away from the sight of her square jaw and bold features, her gaze dropped to her large feet. Although she was disgusted with their size, they were at least proportionate to her long legs—as if that were any consolation.

Thoughts scattered, she stepped to the lead-cut window, observing the sheep on a far hillside. Even in their meandering, they had a purpose. What was hers? She hugged herself, her hands sliding around her waist. At least that was slim. A pity her hips were so full. If only she weren't so tall. From her experience in London, she knew men enjoyed looking down on a woman and she was far from petite. On the Continent, it had been a different story. Her brow knit and she lifted a hand to the drapes, crumpling the fine damask in a fist.

Catching her ephemeral reflection in the glass, she chanced a downward glance. Perhaps her breasts weren't so bad. Immediately, her cheeks grew warm—such thoughts simply weren't proper! Quickly, she stepped away from the window, determined to make her way to the gallery.

Only, escaping her reflection couldn't dispel other images. Andy's steps slowed; her lids grew heavy as she recalled how the Marquess had caressed her during that one episode in the library. Languorous heat invaded her body. She had fit so well against him. . . . Enough!

Jaw squared, she stomped into the portrait gallery, determined to banish all thoughts of that rogue—a task made more difficult by the fact that it was the portrait of the first Marquess with Burne which drew her attention. Time passed without her even being aware of it when suddenly something brushed the hair from the nape of her neck . . . or, rather, someone.

"Hello, Princess," the Marquess crooned softly into her ear.

Andy jerked back and darted a quick glance about, hoping no one had seen his familiarity. Unable to totally quell a tiny thrill from his touch, she rounded on him, telling herself that sometimes, the best defense was offense. Hands on her hips, she demanded, "Have you no sense of decency?"

The Marquess appeared totally unmoved by her icy tone and clasped his hands loosely in front of his stomach in a manner which was so angelic it reminded Andy of a little boy caught rummaging through Cook's fresh pastries. His expression didn't move her a whit, and crossing her arms akimbo, she arched her brow.

Laughing, he put up his hands, as if to ward off an attack. "I'm here on the orders of my aunt, Princess. I met her in the hallway just now. When I asked Lily to pass my aunt's message to you, she offered that you were on your way here, so I decided I might as well deliver the message in person."

Flustered by his warm tone, Andy said the first words which came to her mind. "Stop calling me 'Princess'!"

His voice lowered, "Would you prefer that I call you 'Duchess'? There's something so innately regal about your attitude, that to call you 'Miss Fitzgerald,' or even 'Andy,' doesn't really do you justice." Gradually closing the space between them, he tapped his finger against the cleft in his chin—the one she'd noticed the many times when she'd looked up from her work in the library.

Belatedly, Andy recalled that sometimes the best defense

was retreat, with its inherent opportunity to regroup and fortify one's forces. She wrapped her arms around herself, trying to quell the shivers Jonathon's seductive tone sent down her spine.

He came closer still. She backed away. Definitely time to retreat.

When Andy's shoulder pressed into the edge of the gilt frame of his ancestor and she had no place left to flee without looking foolish, he finally murmured, almost to himself, "Yes, I do believe I'll call you Duchess."

Clutching the edges of her shawl together with one hand, Andy put out the other to stop his advance. Unconcerned, he walked straight into her palm and her knees weakened.

"You said your aunt sent you?" she reminded him, unable to prevent the throaty whisper in her voice, trying to sidle away without appearing totally ridiculous.

Jonathon halted her retreat by reaching out and tipping up her chin, brushing her trembling lower lip, then sweeping back the hair from her cheek. For a moment, he did nothing more than stare at the soft curl twisted around his finger. It captivated him more than he had expected.

Her guileless eyes widened. "Your aunt . . . ?"

Even with the hesitant reminder, Jon had a problem recalling his original intent. "My aunt? Mmm . . . yes," he finally murmured. "Since it's such a pleasant day, she's decided to have tea in the conservatory and asked I pass on the message."

Andy made a small sound as his hand traversed its way to her earlobe. Jon wasn't entirely convinced it was protest. "I suppose I should play the gentleman, apologize for disturbing you, and leave, but . . ." His voice tapered off.

Andy shook her head. "Jonathon. No," she whispered as he drew her toward himself.

His hands slid to her spine and he stared at her again, wanting nothing more than to kiss her.

Andy's knees buckled. The back of her head knocked the first Marquess's portrait off-center, succeeding in bringing her to her senses. She opened her eyes and flushed. "What are you doing, my lord?"

He grinned and, loosely resting his hands on the wall on either sides of her shoulders, glanced beyond her. "*He* is one of my favorite ancestors. Apparently had quite the way with company."

"Women, you mean," Andy muttered, refusing to look back at him, trying to ignore the heat from his body as well as the pleasure his touch had given her. When he didn't immediately respond, she peeked up at him through her lowered lashes.

His grin had faded. "I do believe I've mentioned this before, but considering the circumstances, perhaps you could use my name. Please . . ."

Hypnotized by his parted lips, she acquiesced before she knew what she was about. "Jon. Please. . . . This is madness . . ." Her voice trailed off even as her hands slipped between their bodies, meaning to push him away. Instead, they rested against his hips.

"I've died and gone to hell," Jon moaned brokenly, tracing the outline of her jaw. "I'm being made to suffer for all my sins. If I haven't died, then the ache I feel will surely kill me." His voice was a harsh, frustrated whisper and he lowered his head to her mouth.

Andy tightened her grip on his hips—just as his body jerked into hers. Her fingers clenched in reaction. Tightly.

The sound of cloth tearing thundered in her ears. Andy drew back, scorched. A handful of buttons had lost their moorings on his pantaloons. Some were now in her palm; others were on the floor. Twisting to the side, Andy clenched her eyes shut. She'd made a fool of herself. Again.

Clinging to her shoulders, refusing to let her go, Jonathon choked back a pained laugh as his frame shuddered. Timidly, Andy's eyes peeked open.

His self-deprecating grin slowly disappeared. His lips descended for another kiss, this one gentle, exploring. When he finally drew back, he stared at her intently and Andy struggled to draw breath. Her hands clenched at her sides and something bit into them.

The buttons. She opened her hand to glare at them, as though they were somehow to blame for her shocking lapse of decorum. A wash of heat swept over her cheeks. She didn't dare look up at him and, instead, shoved the buttons into his outstretched hand before he could touch her again, then quickly spun on her heel.

Jon grasped her elbow, holding her from fleeing. She made the mistake of glancing back at him and wished she hadn't. His breeches hung open, half the buttons missing. However had she come to such a pass, she asked herself, wishing she could simply vanish.

"What have you done to my legendary finesse?"

She tried to brush off his lighthearted question and evaded his gaze by speaking toward the wall. "Please don't. Kindly let me pass. I think I've humiliated myself sufficiently for today."

Jon chuckled. "Nonsense, Duchess. On the contrary, I'm the one nonplussed. My valet is either going to have my head, demand a raise, or leave my employ," he added dryly, letting her go and stooping to gather up the remaining buttons from the floor. He glanced up and grinned. "You make me feel like a callow schoolboy, I'm afraid."

Not proof against his infectious smile and grateful he wasn't treating her like a strumpet, Andy unbent enough to scoff, "I can't imagine you ever being a callow schoolboy. But that is really neither here nor there, my lord. If you'll excuse me?" she said, striving for some dignity and performing a small curtsy as though nothing untoward had occurred, needing to distance herself mentally and physically from his intoxicating presence.

"So formal, Duchess? It was far more exciting to hear you

whisper my name. You must be sure to continue calling me by name—at least when we're in private.''

"I think it best if we try to avoid any further private moments, don't you?'' She glanced at Jon and regretted her question when she saw his rakish grin.

"My valet might agree with you, but I'm not sure I do.'' He ran his fingers lightly over her arm. ''I'm a bounder and a cad to have taken advantage of you,'' he stated, his devilish features masked with the honest chagrin of the not-so-innocent. ''Forgive me, Duchess?''

Since she had been as responsible for the episode as Jonathon, Andy knew there wasn't anything to forgive. However, it wouldn't do to let him know that. Instead, a slight smile tugging at her lips, she admonished him, ''Insufferable rake,'' and turned to leave.

"Jon?'' he asked, his voice soulful.

"We shall see,'' she replied over her shoulder, maintaining a stately pace during her exit, not rushing until she rounded the corner. Then she picked up her skirts and ran the rest of the way to her room, grateful to reach it safely without encountering any servants.

Closing the door softly, she rested her forehead against its frame, hoping he, too, would make it to his room undetected— and that his valet wouldn't make too much of a fuss over his disheveled state. On the other hand, the poor valet was probably accustomed to his master's philandering ways by now. Drat the Marquess anyway!

Her back pressing against the door, Andy finally began to tremble. Hesitantly, she brushed her fingers against her lips. Whatever in the world had come over her? She'd been kissed before, but never had she been so affected by those kisses. Slowly, her gaze narrowed. More proof that the man was indeed a successful libertine, just as she'd suspected when Helen first described him. Surely that was the only reason she'd lost her wits.

Chapter Five

In spite of her resolution to be cool toward the Marquess, Andy entered the conservatory with trepidation. What if he were the only one here? She glanced around nervously. She just wasn't ready to test her determination to maintain a polite distance from him when they were alone.

Fortunately, the room appeared to be deserted. So, why was she disappointed all of a sudden? Frustrated with her fluctuating emotions, she began wandering through the collection of unusual plants.

Only the room *wasn't* empty. Helen and Dominic were already there, hidden behind potted palms. Startled by Andy's entrance, an embarrassed Helen jumped away from her escort's side. Dominic filled the awkward breech and greeted Andy.

"You couldn't sleep, either?"

Forcing herself not to recall just why she'd had problems resting, Andy avoided a direct answer. "I decided to enjoy the flowers for a while. With the blustery weather of the last few days, it's been difficult to get outside. It was a lovely idea on your mother's part to have tea in here," she added, smiling at Helen.

"Oh, yes. Exactly. We just came to look at Mama's orchids. Their exotic appearance makes one forget our unforgiving climate." Her blush and the longing with which she gazed at Dominic belied her claim.

The arrival of Lady Sofia saved all of them from further discomfort. The Marchioness nodded at Andy. "I see you received my message. I trust Jonathon didn't disturb you," she said just as the Marquess strolled in behind her.

Now, it was Andy's turn to blush.

Jonathon came up beside her and took her elbow. "Of course she received the message, didn't you, Miss Fitzgerald?"

Not trusting that innocent look of his, Andy bit back an urge to hiss at him to be quiet.

"Did I disturb you, Duchess?" he asked as he led her to the sofa. Seating her, he whispered, "You certainly disturbed me."

"Duchess?" Lady Sofia's brow rose a notch.

Andy's shoulders hunched. She'd been right not to trust him. At least the Marchioness hadn't overheard Jon's whispered comment, or her eyebrows would have risen even higher.

"Yes, Aunt. Miss Fitzgerald's regal bearing is reminiscent of royalty. Wouldn't you agree?"

Andy grit her teeth at his effortless response. The Marchioness greeted his remark with an unladylike snort. Jon merely smiled and made a show of rearranging Andy's skirt in order to sit beside her, totally ignoring her attempts to bat away his hands.

The man must have led too many cavalry charges. He simply didn't know when to stop. But then, did she? Recalling the scene in the gallery, she swallowed and another wave of heat crawled up her neck. Feeling guilty, she darted a glance at the Marchioness. Busy as Sofia was with the tea tray brought in by Simms, Sofia hadn't noticed either Jon's familiarity or her blush. *Thank goodness!* Andy thought.

"Did you rest well?" Jonathon finally asked his aunt.

"Actually, I was preparing the menus for the house party. Apparently Cynthia's cousin, Barbara, will be coming as well." Sofia poured Andy's tea and graced her with a benevolent glance. "We're planning to introduce the guests to the local gentry at a dinner party towards the end of next week. Perhaps your father might even be well enough to attend by then. I believe Sir Edgar would enjoy meeting Mr. Green, the vicar, who dabbles somewhat in genealogies. He might even have something to add to your research."

Helen and her mother began discussing whom else they should invite to the dinner. Dom indicated his attention by offering the occasional suggestion.

Andy sidled to the far end of the sofa and did her best to follow the conversation. At least this time, the Marchioness made an effort to include her in the conversation—unlike during the luncheon when they'd first arrived. Unfortunately, the Marquess's proximity interfered with her concentration.

Jon shot Andy a wicked grin. "And did *you* rest well, Miss Fitzgerald?"

Andy's cup rattled on its saucer. The Marchioness looked up sharply. Jonathon maintained his angelic expression. Andy inspected the fronds of a nearby asparagus fern. Once Sofia returned to her conversation, Andy turned and glared at him. She should have known better than to expect him to behave as a gentlemen. Drat him for reminding her of her folly—as though she might forget.

Not put off by her silence, he continued in an undertone. "Personally, I was rather distracted. Can't say I rested well at all. My valet stomping around the dressing room in a huff didn't help, either," he added, shuddering.

Dominic overheard and laughed. "Now what did you do to damage his sense of consequence, Jon? Scuff the polish off your boots, or get some mud on your cloak?"

"Not this time. Something far more grievous in Marsh's

opinion. I managed to lose some buttons from my apparel. In too much of a hurry . . . desire to be free of the constraint and all that.''

Andy's grip on the ear of the fragile porcelain cup tightened. She considered the idea of dumping her tea in his lap. Maybe that would wipe the droll expression off Jonathon's face. However, she supposed she should be grateful that he didn't mention he hadn't been alone when the accident occurred or that the missing buttons had come off his breeches. Nevertheless, she was definitely out of charity with him.

Finishing off her tea as if it were fortifying brandy, Andy stood and shot Jon a look suggesting she was tempted to crash the cup over his head. His smothered grin of awareness only set her teeth on edge. She took a deep, steadying breath and carefully replaced the cup and saucer on the tray, refusing Sofia's offer for more. Drawing Helen off to the side, she asked, ''How is your search coming along?''

''Oh Andy, I'm so discouraged. I've gone through every conceivable nook and cranny in the attics and haven't found a single thing which might have belonged to Dominic's mother. The only place left to look is the muniments room.''

Andy remembered Jonathon mentioning the room. She also recalled the circumstance in the library and hurriedly glanced at one of the vivid orchids at her side to hide her blush.

Helen didn't notice. ''Perhaps I should just admit defeat. If we've been able to look beyond Dom's so-called questionable lineage all this time, then Society can learn to do the same. If it can't, then it can go hang for all I care,'' she ended with a stoic shrug.

Andy forced herself to focus on Helen's concerns and clasped her hand. ''Whatever happens, I think you're extremely fortunate to have found someone who means so much to you. You're also lucky your family considers your happiness more important than Society's approbation.''

Helen's tone and features assumed a bitterness quite contrary to her nature. "True, but then Mama learned the hard way, didn't she, that marrying where one was expected to and earning Society's approval wouldn't necessarily bring happiness." She glanced back at Andy. "You know, I'm not really sure how Mama survived Papa's alternating moods as well as she did. At least the three of us—Dom, Jon, and myself—had each other to deflect his rages. It's horrible to admit," Helen added with a guilty sigh, "but none of us wept when he broke his neck riding."

They lapsed into silence. Like Helen, she was an only child, Andy thought. The similarity in their situation ended there. Besides being loved by parents who had also loved each other, Andy belonged to a happy extended family.

Thinking of her three uncles, and several cousins, brought a soft smile to her lips. Despite the strictures Society normally placed on the upper Ten Thousand, her family was unusually close, with a strong work ethic—thanks to her great-grandfather, the Earl of Durham. How very different from the Marquess's family which, on the other hand, had more than its share of resentful profligates of late.

Andy recalled herself before the silence became uncomfortable. "According to the journals, your father's attitude bears a strong resemblance to his grandfather, Horace. Did you ever know him?"

"No, thank heavens." Helen shuddered. "He was responsible for raising my father."

"No doubt he influenced your father's attitude. Both positive and negative patterns in personality are often carried from one generation to the next unless there's a conscious effort to break the mold. It takes a very open-minded individual to recognize the occurrence of a destructive pattern. Such an individual must also have tremendous strength in character to alter life-long habits. That's why a family history can be so very valuable."

"I suppose you're correct. I hadn't ever really thought about it that way,'' Helen responded, successfully diverted from her morose thoughts.

"Most people don't,'' Andy nodded. "When Father sets out the genealogical map, he tries to subtly point out why people had certain foibles—good or bad—hoping those who commission him will learn from their ancestors. Genealogies are useful for medical purposes as well, since certain ailments recur throughout a family line. People often forget that.''

"So a family's history should be more than a collection of dates and anecdotes?''

"Absolutely! I remember one of the genealogies we did in Milan, not long before coming here. The family was in the habit of denigrating its females in a most atrocious way. It was a practice handed down through generations, accepted not only by Society, but by the majority of the family's women. A few notable exceptions strove to make their spouses appear ridiculous, flaunting their cisebos *and* their intelligence.'' Reminiscing, Andy paused and grinned.

"Papa made the women look like heroines. It was all he could do. You see, sometimes people commission my father simply because it's the current mode and they never bother reading his work. So, Papa wasn't really sure what would happen in this case. Well, the matriarch who'd allowed herself to be downtrodden took the time to read the tale. Then, she made the other ladies in the family read it and the men ended up with a minor revolt on their hands. It was quite the talk of Milan for some time although no one connected it to Father's work.''

"So, trite as it might seem, the pen really is mightier than the sword,'' Helen said.

"Old adages almost always contain kernels of truth.''

With a mischievous smile, Helen asked, "What kind of trouble will Sir Edgar create with our history, I wonder. Lord help us all if it prompts Mama to assert herself.''

Andy chuckled, pleased she'd been able to distract Helen. "I don't think we need have any fear on that score."

"There's still some time before dinner. I think I'll have a look at the muniments room now. If Dominic goes back to the estate room, I'll just tell him that I'm helping you look for material—if that's all right?"

"That will be just fine."

Andy managed to avoid the Marquess for the balance of the tea. When it was over, she escaped in the company of Helen. Parting in the hallway, she waved Helen good luck and went to visit her father.

Andy bent over the stack of papers on the bed and planted a kiss on her father's forehead. An incredible feeling of relief washed over her as she studied him. While his face had thinned during the illness, at least it no longer looked pasty. Even his hair looked healthier, springing as it did in waves across his forehead.

"It's so good to see you sitting up and working again."

"Yes, I was rather under the weather, wasn't I?" Edgar admitted with a wry grin, putting his work aside after making one more notation. He leaned back against the stack of pillows. "The doctor's negative prognosis didn't influence Sofie, though. Incredibly obstinate woman, Sofie is. Wouldn't let me slip away. I'm very grateful for her care. The woman should have been in the battlefields. Could've saved a lot of British soldiers."

"There's no doubt about that, Father. The Marquess and Dominic both sang praises of her sickroom abilities . . . but 'Sofie'?" Andy arched an eyebrow. "I really can't imagine anyone being allowed to call the Marchioness 'Sofie.'"

"Ahem." Edgar cleared his throat. A slight flush rose to his cheeks. "Privileges of the sick room and all that, you know.

It's rather difficult to maintain the formalities with someone who changes your sheets.''

"Oh come now, Father. Don't gammon me. The Marchioness didn't change your sheets.''

"Well, she supervised the changing of them, so it's almost the same,'' Edgar replied huffily and changed the subject by motioning to the papers scattered about on the bed. "The work on the genealogy is coming along nicely. The family has fine, strong roots although some of the off-shoots in recent memory have been a disappointment. A rather unhappy family of late, wouldn't you agree, my dear?''

"It is rather sad, isn't it, Papa?''

"Yes,'' Edgar agreed. "Seems to have started with the fourth Marquess, Horace. Nothing worse than a bitter second son coming into the title late in life.''

"Primogeniture at its very worst.''

"Absolutely.'' Edgar nodded.

They settled into their routine, established from years of working with each other, and reviewed the research. It was a practice which often resulted in new information coming to light.

Horace, an ignored second son, had ignored his own second son, Samuel. By the time Horace's eldest was killed in a duel over some remark about the cut of his coat, Samuel was unmanageable. He ran off to Gretna Green with an actress, a union which produced Malcolm. Samuel drowned and Horace, now a Marquess, was forced to take on the responsibility of raising a seven-year old Malcolm.

"According to the journals of the Marchioness's mother—Horace's second cousin—Malcolm appeared particularly cruel.''

Edgar shook his head. "Unfortunately, she couldn't influence her husband when Horace sought a match between the two families.''

Andy shot her father a curious look. "Has Lady Sofia said much about her marriage?"

"She certainly hasn't complained about it. Sofie's not like that, you know. Even so, evidence of his cruelty has crept in to some of the stories she's related. They aren't germane to the genealogy so there's no need to go into those."

Edgar's protective attitude surprised Andy, but before she could comment, he continued.

"Since she was unable to change Malcolm, she contented herself by raising the three children. It kept her from seeing too much of her husband. Malcolm disliked children and did his best to avoid them, granting Sofie some peace as a result. She was particularly pleased with having a hand in raising Jonathon since he was also starting to go wild. She realized he needed a firm, loving hand in order to make the most of his life. He reminded her very much of the first Marquess. Would you agree?"

Swallowing a smile for the way her father had so deftly turned the subject away from the Marchioness, Andy nodded. "On the surface at least, I would agree with Lady Sofia. When you see the portrait gallery, you'll know what we mean. Apparently, the first Marquess was very much the dashing blade, as well as a responsible landowner. Lord Baldwin does have a similar reputation," she added honestly.

"It shouldn't be too much longer before I can visit the gallery. Thank God! Being bedridden is enough to drive a saint to insanity," Edgar muttered. "Sofie's promised to release me by the end of the week. In the meantime, I'm very grateful for all of your research on this commission. You've done a fine job, Andy, and I'm proud of you."

Andy gave her father a warm hug. "I'm just glad to be of some help and so very, very relieved you're feeling better."

Edgar held her tightly for a moment, awkwardly patting her on the back. Clearing his throat, he brushed off her comments. "Now you should have a bit of time to yourself and relax . . .

enjoy the upcoming house party.'' Before Andy could argue, he added, ''How are you finding the members of the household?''

Andy grinned. ''I am eternally grateful for the attention the Marchioness is lavishing upon you. Because of that, I feel the sharp edge of her tongue only during meals.''

Edgar didn't smile. In fact, her father's stormy features informed her she had chosen the wrong moment to be flippant.

''Really, my dear?'' Edgar's nostrils thinned and he sat forward. ''I'm afraid I must disagree with your evaluation of her character. Although she has a sharp wit, I would never infer she's a shrew because of it.''

That was the third time he'd taken umbrage with her and come to the defense of the Marchioness. Chastened, Andy hastily apologized. ''I was just teasing, Papa. Actually, I must agree with you about her sense of humor, although she tries to hide it most of the time.''

Apparently satisfied, Edgar relaxed and settled back against the pillows. ''Sofia can be very reserved. Her experiences in life have made that necessary. It takes a great deal of patience to cut through that façade.''

''No doubt. It probably helps, too, if one is gifted with such legendary charm as you,'' Andy replied with a cheeky grin and was rewarded with another flush rising to her father's cheeks.

''Enough of this nonsense. Charm has nothing to do with it,'' he denied vehemently. ''Now tell me, how are the others in the household?''

''Lady Helen is truly all that is sweet. As gentle and somewhat naive as she initially appears, you can feel an undercurrent of strength running through her character. She's also surprisingly mischievous and it's fun to see that impish light enter her eyes—usually when Dominic is around. He, too, is excellent company,'' Andy added, trying to think of a way to escape her father's room before he could question her more about the Marquess.

''Mmm, yes,'' Edgar interrupted thoughtfully, taking her

bait. "Sofie's mentioned that. A suitable couple, but not necessarily a suitable match. Any luck in locating Emily's diary?"

Andy's brow rose a notch. She hadn't realized Lady Sofia had discussed the matter with him. "Nothing yet." She wondered if they had talked about other intimate matters. Her surprise and curiosity must have shown.

"Have to talk about something while we're playing chess," Edgar grumbled before shaking his head. "Sofie can't imagine what could've happened to Emily's things. She's not very optimistic about the chances of Helen finding anything, but doesn't have the heart to disabuse her daughter from having some hope.

"Truth is, Sofie doesn't much care one way or the other if anything is found. Dominic is very much a son to her. She sees how happy Helen is with him. The only problem is, the couple could be ostracized due to the question of his legitimacy. If that happens, Sofie fears it won't bode well for the relationship. She's thinking of taking Helen to London for a Season, which should prove Helen's feelings one way or the other."

Edgar, ever the genealogist, paused and frowned. "I'm a little surprised, however, that she hasn't mentioned the repercussions and ensuing scandal if Dominic's legitimacy is proven."

"Lord, that certainly would wake the sleeping dogs, wouldn't it?" Andy agreed.

"Unfortunately, yes. It would revive the old gossip of how both families cast off first Emily, and then the responsibility of raising Dominic as the heir."

Andy flinched. "The scandal would be unavoidable—especially since, by proving his legitimacy, Dominic could claim the baronetcy."

"Yes. Phillip St. James would be considered a usurper and would lose his position—a fact which should please a number of people since the current Baron appears to be an irresponsible, if harmless, bounder. But such speculations are neither here nor there until some evidence of a marriage is uncovered." Edgar sat forward and folded his hands on his lap. "Now tell me, how are you getting along with the Marquess? Has he practiced any of his vaunted charms on you? Hasn't tried to lead you down the garden path the way the Italians used to try?'' he asked, chuckling at the memories.

This was the topic Andy had been dreading. ''Really, Papa,'' she replied, pretending to be shocked and trying to conceal her blush by dropping her gaze to the books surrounding her father. She busied herself by rearranging the piles.

He covered her hands. ''Do I detect some interest in that direction on your part? Has someone finally kindled your fancy?''

''Nonsense, Father. Our relationship is strictly formal,'' she answered, this time unable to hide the heat flooding her face at the bald-faced falsehood. Eyes downcast, unable to lie to her father, Andy corrected herself. ''Well, almost strictly formal. He can be a very charming, attractive man. I wouldn't be human if I didn't notice.''

Edgar tipped up her chin and looked directly into her eyes. ''I just want you to be happy, my dear. You do know that, don't you?'' he asked softly. At her nod, he continued in a lighter vein. ''Just sit back and enjoy this visit, then. Who knows, you may not need a Season in London after all.''

''Putting the cart before the horse, aren't we?'' Andy shook her head before grinning slyly. Unable to resist a little dig in retaliation for his teasing, she asked, ''Unless, of course, you're referring to yourself?''

Edgar's mock horror couldn't quite cloak his discomfort. He paused and gazed at the Constable painting on the far wall. ''There hasn't been anyone since your mother died. And while Sofie is a fine figure of a woman, she isn't one to dally with.'' He shrugged. ''At my age, I'm past all that. Besides, no one could ever replace your mother.''

Andy tucked a loosened strand of hair behind her ear and dropped her hands to her lap, staring at them until the edges of her fingers blurred as her eyes misted. She gulped past the lump in her throat. "Of course, it isn't possible to replace her. Mama *was* incredibly special, wasn't she?"

They sat quietly for a moment, each lost in their own memories.

Andy finally broke the silence. "Still, I'm positive Mama would want you to be happy, too. After all, you're not exactly doddering off to take the waters in Bath to maintain your health. Who knows, you might be fortunate enough to find someone equally special, just in a different way. And ... Lady Sofia certainly is different," she added with a grin.

"Bah, off with you now. I have work to do." Edgar dismissed her with a wave of his hand.

After giving her father a final hug, Andy paused at the door and glanced over her shoulder. Instead of poring over his work, Edgar was still gazing pensively at some distant point. There was a melancholy slope to his shoulders.

Was he remembering her mother, thinking of how lonely it was without her? Was Lady Sofia a serious contender for her father's affections? Exactly what had been going on in this sickroom? Did the Marchioness return her father's interest?

So many questions. Andy intended to find the answers at the first opportunity and closed the door quietly, not wanting to disturb her father's meditation.

Fudge! Andy halted midstride. She had forgotten to ask what her father had learned about Burne. He'd finally heard of the legend, apparently through Lady Sofia. It would just have to wait for another time. Head bent in thought, Andy walked down the hall.

A hand shot out and, with one swift motion, pulled her into the privacy of the alcove.

"Hello, Duchess." The Marquess's voice was a seductive whisper as he pressed her against the wall.

Startled, Andy shot back, "You oaf!" She aimed a blow to his shoulder to gain some space between their bodies. It landed with a satisfying thud. "Pray, what the devil are you about, frightening me like that?"

He bit back a chuckle and pursed his lips. "Such shameful language." His hands against the wall on either side of her head, he crooned into the curve of her neck. "I'm so sorry for startling you, Duchess." The apology rang false.

Andy twisted her head away, simultaneously slapping at the hands now traveling down her shoulders. "Stop that, Jon!"

"Whatever you say, Duchess," he answered agreeably, "as soon as you tell me why you've been avoiding me. Your machinations are severely damaging to my manly pride, you know." He pulled her closer.

Andy couldn't stop herself from leaning into Jonathon's hard frame. Her hard-fought resolutions which had aided her in dodging his attention the last several days suddenly disappeared. How tempting it would be to slip her hands to his shoulders and "enjoy" herself as her father had suggested. Only, this wasn't what her father had in mind. She looked up at the darkly handsome aristocrat. *Sheer folly!* The Marquess was a practiced rake.

Finally finding her voice, Andy denied his claim. "I haven't been avoiding you," she declared rather weakly, somehow finding the strength to escape his loose embrace. Stepping back, she hugged herself protectively.

"Really?" Jon asked, his expression disbelieving. "What would you call it then? Every time I come into the same room, you find an excuse to either leave or move to where another person or piece of furniture can separate us. Just what is that?"

"Self-preservation?" Andy asked wryly, embarrassed that he'd noticed her tactics. Sidestepping past him to go back into the hallway, she changed the subject quickly. "Was there something in particular you wished to speak to me about?"

He followed her, closing the distance between them. "Yes, actually. The guests are expected to arrive tomorrow. Since your work with your father is basically completed, I shouldn't need to remind you that you're expected to join in the activities.''

He raised his hand as she opened her mouth to object. "Nothing too strenuous, just the normal country fare of picnics and riding. All activities will be properly chaperoned, of course,'' he added when she hesitated. "Besides . . . my aunt insists upon it.''

There was no polite way to decline, Andy thought, frustrated. "Thank you. However, it really will depend on my father and his work.''

"Retreating again, Duchess?'' he asked with a knowing smile.

Andy gave him a chilly glare, spared the search for a suitable reply at the sound of footsteps coming up the stairwell. A pensive-looking Helen came in to view.

"Hullo there, Helen,'' Jon greeted.

Startled, Helen looked up. "Oh, Jon. Yes . . . hello,'' she mumbled, including Andy in her distracted greeting.

Jon reached out for her arm before she could walk away. "Why the long face, puss?'' His voice was gentle.

Arrogant and infuriating though he might be at times, Andy couldn't help but silently salute his sensitivity. Helen's mood was unusually gloomy.

"Doldrums, I guess,'' Helen responded with a halfhearted smile and absently patted his comforting hand.

"I was just going out to enjoy some fresh air. Won't you join me?'' Andy asked, praying Jon wouldn't offer to come along. There was no doubt the man affected her balance.

Helen shook her head. "I don't think so. I'm afraid I won't be very good company. You go on ahead with Jon.''

"Oh no!'' Andy interrupted. "Lord Baldwin was just on his way to, mmm . . . on his way to . . .'' Unable to think quickly of a destination for the Marquess, she looked beseechingly in his direction.

"The estate room, I believe," he replied, gallantly coming to her aid.

Andy's smile of appreciation soured when he grinned and added, "Or was it the library, Duchess? Perhaps to confer with the gamekeeper?"

His innocent expression set Andy's teeth on edge. She glanced away, only to notice a delicately patterned bowl filled with potpourri on a hallway table. How would it look overturned on Jonathon? "Yes, actually I believe you mentioned something about checking with the gamekeeper—regarding any deadly traps which may be about in the woods. Safety of the guests to consider, I think you said," she shot back, her glare suggesting she wouldn't regret it if he were stuck in one of them. Turning back to Helen, she suggested, "Why don't you get a shawl and meet me in the rose garden?"

Helen gnawed her lip before agreeing, totally missing the byplay between her two companions. "I suppose we could clip a few of the spring blossoms for the house. I'll be down soon then, if you're sure?" She walked away, her shoulders still slumped.

"Adieu then, Duchess." Jon bent over Andy's hand and placed a warm kiss on the inside of her wrist. Straightening, still holding her hand, he leered. "As you said, I must check for traps which might ensnare unsuspecting guests."

"Just be sure not to set any," Andy warned, yanking her hand away.

Jon winked, but allowed her the last word. With one final grin over his shoulder, he tucked his hands in his pockets and strolled off whistling a jaunty tune.

Chapter Six

Andy donned the sturdy gardening gloves Helen offered her and flexed her fingers. They were a tight fit, obviously made for a more delicate woman's hand. Ignoring the minor discomfort, she picked up a basket and clippers, glad to be outdoors.

She and Helen wandered about the walled garden, bending over bushes rounded with early spring blossoms. However, each time Andy tried to chat, even of the most inconsequential matter, she was met with a halfhearted response. Finally, Andy dropped her basket full of roses and Queen Anne's lace, and sat on the park bench.

The afternoon had grown warm. Andy stripped off her gloves and removed her hat. With the back of her hand, she swiped off beads of perspiration from her forehead. Eyes closed, she raised her face to the warm rays of the sun. "I'm so glad you suggested cutting some flowers. The scent here is divine and it's turned out to be a lovely afternoon. Quite different from the evening we arrived."

Helen quit her pacing and sat beside Andy, arranging and rearranging the folds of her skirt. "Yes, it is rather lovely.

Mama will appreciate the flowers, too, I'm sure. She very much enjoys the sense of freshness they bring. Some of them will probably end up in your father's chambers to push away any hints of it having been a sickroom." She then took one of the roses from the basket and began plucking at the unfortunate blossom, unheeding of the torn petals scattering about her feet. Another flower soon suffered a similar fate.

Andy placed a gentle hand over Helen's. "If you're not careful, there won't be any flowers left for either your mama or my father," she said softly, breaking the lengthening silence.

Helen jumped to her feet and resumed her pacing in the quiet enclave. With a pensive glance at Andy, she broke her stride. Hands clasped tightly together in front of herself, she apologized. "I'm sorry. I'm really not very good company today."

"Please don't be concerned about it. We all have days like that. I'm just glad for your company. The fresh air has done us both good." She allowed Helen to continue her pacing. As both the pacing and silence continued, Andy hazarded a guess that Helen needed to unburden her woes. "I won't ask what's troubling you, but is there anything I can help you with?"

As if presented with the opening she'd been hoping for, Helen dropped to Andy's side. Her forehead puckered and she again twisted the folds of her skirt. "It's just that I'm so discouraged at being unable to find Emily's portmanteau. Having Dominic in the next room hasn't helped any. He's constantly coming to visit, to see if I need any assistance and interrupting my search."

She gulped and sent Andy a helpless look. "I was rather rude to him a few times. Now, he's quite put out and has stopped coming by. If I don't find anything by the time our guests arrive tomorrow afternoon, the search will have to be postponed."

Andy sighed. It was her fault. "I feel responsible for your current mood. You lived without any thought of Dominic's antecedents until I came along and blithely suggested there might be some documentation. I'm sorry. I never meant for this to come between the two of you.''

"No, don't blame yourself.''

"Why don't you let it be for now? If the material has been there this long, it will survive for another week until the house party is over.''

Helen's hands balled into fists. "Oh, why did Jon have to invite the guests?'' she wailed. "I don't know Barbara and only have a passing acquaintance with Lady Cynthia. As for Phillip St. James, Dom's half-cousin, I don't like him at all. Mama doesn't either, and even though he's a neighbor, his rare visits haven't been encouraged. The few times he's been here, he's been horribly condescending to Dominic. After each visit, I've noticed a bitterness in Dom which is difficult to dispel.''

Helen sucked in a breath, trying to calm herself. "Besides which, I just don't trust Phillip. During those visits, we'd sometimes find him poking around places a guest wouldn't normally be found. Now that I know there's a possibility of a marriage between Emily and Richard, I suspect Phillip may have been searching for the same evidence we are in order to destroy it.''

"It would certainly be to his advantage to do so. If the marriage is proven, that would mean Dominic, not Phillip, should be the Baron.''

Helen thrust out her chin. "I'm fully aware of that, as well as of the repercussions if conclusive evidence is found about a marriage. The scandal . . . it simply doesn't bear to think upon,'' she shuddered. "Dom would gain Phillip's title and a substantial estate—although that isn't the reason for my search.'' Helen paused and shot Andy a puzzled look. "But why would Phillip still be looking for something after all these years?''

"First of all, unless there's any hard evidence such as disturbed documents, it would be unfair to suspect Sir Phillip of having some nefarious purpose. Did anyone notice anything out of place during any of his visits?''

"If anything was out of place, no one seemed to connect it with him," Helen admitted.

"Furthermore, since everyone has accepted Dom's apparent lineage for so long, there wouldn't be any reason for Phillip to search your home." Andy gazed thoughtfully at a small butterfly hovering over the bushes. "Unless, of course, he had access to the journal. Is it possible that your mother or father gave Emily's effects to either her family or the Baron's?"

Helen shook her head. "No. I asked Mama about that. The only contact between the families was through messenger. They didn't even attend Emily's funeral." Her lips twisted at a hurt which had occurred before her birth.

"Then I suggest we both keep a close watch for any untoward movements by the Baron during his visit." Andy picked up her gloves. "If your mother doesn't have any activities planned after dinner this evening, why don't we spend some time searching the muniments room together?"

Helen declined with a sigh. "I appreciate the offer, Andy, but I just can't. Not tonight. I promised to go for a walk with Dom. If I back out now, he'll either think I'm upset with him or he might suspect something is going on. The search will just have to wait."

Seeing her regret, Andy made one final offer. "I'm in the habit of waking early and breakfasting with Papa. Since my research role is diminished, I'm sure he'd let me have a few hours to myself tomorrow without any questions. If you like, we could meet directly after breakfast. It would give us at least a few hours to search before the guests arrive."

Helen's features lightened. "Are you sure you wouldn't mind?"

"It will give me something to do. Besides, I'm curious to see if the room is as dank and dusty as you've described. I can't imagine any room in your mother's home being like that," Andy assured her with a smile.

"Well, it isn't quite as bad as I've described it," Helen

Reassured by the thought, she decided to be more careful around him in the future. Really, all she had to do was avoid being alone with him, on guard against his lures. She could do it.

After all, forewarned was forearmed.

Andy, still startled by the encounter she had just witnessed, turned apologetically to Lady Sofia in the hallway. "I seem to be spending an inordinate amount of time trying to excuse his behavior, but really . . . Father normally isn't so ill-mannered. I am terribly sorry."

"You shouldn't pay him any mind. It's the slow process of recuperation," Sofia replied without rancor, patting Andy's arm. "Your father was quite ill. There were moments when even I was concerned about his chances."

The passing reference to the nights when her father was so ill confirmed Andy's suspicions that Edgar had been carefully watched over by Sofia after everyone else had retired. She looked at the Marchioness. No words could express her gratitude.

Sofia continued before Andy could say anything else. "His petulant behavior is due to forced inactivity and the normal weakness following a ravaging illness. I'm experienced enough in the ways of the world to realize your father isn't a mean man by nature. In fact, I have even observed an innate chivalry in his behavior—something I almost stopped believing in." With a wry shrug, she changed the subject. "You've put in a full day. Now go and nap before tea. You're beginning to look a bit peaked. Some rest will do you a world of good. It might even give you a better advantage in your dealings with my nephew," she added knowingly before sailing down the hallway toward her own room.

Mortified, Andy stood still for a moment, wondering at Sofia's complacent smile. Was it because the Marchioness was pleased to beat Edgar at chess, or was it because she was pleased to catch Andy unawares? Andy hadn't realized others might notice the thrust and parry of the verbal sword play she and the Marquess conducted whenever they chanced to meet. At least, she'd hoped no one had. How naive!

If only she could avoid the Marquess . . .

If only she didn't enjoy his sharp wit . . .

Edgar complained. He turned on his side to greet Andy, accidentally knocking over the chess pieces.

Lady Sofia merely arched her brow and smiled at Andy. "And to what do you suppose he would attribute his thorough trouncing of me in yesterday's game? Could that have been a result of your ill health as well, Edgar?" she asked innocently.

He grumbled. "Oh, stop plaguing me, Sofie. Truth to tell, you are a fairly decent hand at chess," Edgar admitted grudgingly before grinning. "But you've yet to beat me at backgammon." He finally looked back at his daughter. "How's the research coming along, Andy?"

Andy, who had been turning her head from one protagonist to the other, paused a moment, expecting a tart rejoinder from Lady Sofia. To her surprise, none was forthcoming. Instead, the older couple worked together, calmly gathering up the spilled parts.

Andy swallowed her surprise and answered her father. "Quite well actually, Papa. The genealogical table is basically complete and I'm about halfway through verifying the journals. While quite dry at times, there were some excellent records kept. The research really needs your light touch."

Edgar rubbed his hands together. "I can hardly wait to get started. Unfortunately, my *warden* has other ideas at the moment." His good humor vanished abruptly and he glared at the Marchioness when she stood.

"You're absolutely correct, Sir Edgar," Lady Sofia answered with equanimity. "I'm so pleased you recognize my superior abilities in the sickroom. Be sure to remember that. I simply will not brook any foolishness which might bring on a relapse. Behave now and take your nap like the good fellow I've been assured you are—although I've yet to see evidence of any charm. Perhaps I'll allow you to start working towards the end of the week—from your bed, mind you." With that final warning, she took Andy by the arm and swept both of them out of the room.

admitted with a grin before wrinkling her nose. "But it is fairly dark due to the lack of windows. That's probably what makes it seem so depressing."

"I will come prepared. Shall we say at eight o'clock then?" At Helen's nod, Andy picked up her basket of flowers and stood, linking her arm through her much-cheered companion's. "Now we had best get in to prepare for dinner. I'm positively famished after missing tea, aren't you?"

The soft scent of roses greeted Andy as she entered her father's room early the next morning. Edgar was already sitting at a table set with breakfast things near the window, reading some of his notes and sipping coffee. A delicate bouquet of red and yellow blossoms with sprigs of white was at his elbow. Andy smiled. Helen was right. Some of the flowers they cut had found their way there.

She came up from behind Edgar and bent to kiss his forehead. "Good morning, Papa. Such lovely flowers," she added innocently.

"The art of setting a good table isn't just in having fine food," a much-healthier-looking Edgar replied absently. His gaze still focused on the work before him, he made a notation on the side of a page before putting the papers away and pouring Andy some coffee.

"Have you discovered anything on Burne yet? I've only been able to find a few passing references," Andy said, helping herself to lightly scrambled eggs.

"You mean, the first Marquess's legendary wolfhound?" Edgar shook his head and automatically passed her the strawberry jam she liked so much. "Nothing of any consequence. Do you think there's any truth to the tales?"

Andy smeared a thin layer of the conserve on a fresh croissant. "I don't know. But I'm very curious. Let me know if you discover anything."

Edgar peered at her as she took a bite of the pastry. "Come to think on it, Sofie mentioned a maid said something to Simms about you hearing a dog howling. It seems the maid was rather nervous since the only dogs here are the ones in the kennels by the stables. What was that all about?"

Andy suddenly lost her appetite. She'd done her best to forget that episode, linking her desire to learn more to the tale Helen had told in the portrait gallery. She sat back and dabbed her lips with a snowy napkin, shrugging off the question. "I daresay it was just my imagination."

Her father accepted her answer and buried his head in his notes, preoccupied once more. Loath to leave him just yet, Andy pushed back her chair and wandered toward a chess game set up in the corner of the room. She was positive this set was different from the one her father and the Marchioness had used before. She picked up the ivory queen and admired it, stroking the intricate workmanship. "What an exquisite chess set," she murmured, more to herself than to her father.

Edgar's head snapped up. "Don't touch it!"

Andy was so startled by the unaccustomed sharpness in his tone that she fumbled the piece, nearly dropping it. If this had occurred during her long-ago Season, she probably would have. Thank goodness she'd gained some confidence since then. "Sorry, Father," she apologized, gently returning the queen to its place. "Is it a very valuable set then?"

"Actually it is, but that's not the reason I asked you to put it down," Edgar mumbled, unable to meet her gaze. He cleared his throat. "I'm the one who should apologize, Andy. Sofie and I are in the middle of a game. It was her queen you picked up. She warned me yesterday that if any of the pieces are moved, she'll suspect me of cheating. Can you believe that?" he asked, his affronted voice rising.

Andy didn't bother trying to hide her grin. "Appalling, Papa. Would you like me to have a word with her? I should be very well pleased to vouch for your character, if you think it might help,'' she offered, smothering a chuckle.

His eyebrows drew together in a mock frown. ''We'll have none of your impertinence, young lady.'' Pushing back his chair, he came up beside her and, with a sheepish grin, asked, ''You did put the queen back in its original place, though, didn't you?''

Andy's eyes rolled. ''Of course I did, Papa.'' Her gaze returned to the game. Tapping her chin, she studied the layout for a moment. ''Lady Sofia has the white?'' Edgar nodded in confirmation. ''Might I offer you some advice, Papa? Unless you think it might be construed as cheating, of course.''

''I know you're an excellent chess player, my dear. After all, I taught you myself. However, I got myself into this mess,'' he said with a rueful look at his men neatly lined up behind Sofia's side of the board, ''and I'll just have to get myself out. Let me tell you how. You see the placement of my knight to Sofie's rook,'' he began, pointing to the pieces.

''Edgar!'' Lady Sofia's frigid voice boomed from the doorway.

Both father and daughter started guiltily.

''Are you trying to get help with weaseling your way out of the deep hole you've dug? I must say, I had thought better of you.'' She turned frosty features to Andy. ''Good morning, Andrea.''

Jonathan, escorting the Marchioness, glanced at Andy's chastened features and chuckled. ''Isn't it amazing how my aunt can do that without raising her voice? All it takes is a lift of her brow and an imperceptible chill in her voice.''

Sofia tapped his wrist in admonishment and shook her head, resigned. ''You, of all people, should know.''

''Good morning, Lady Sofia, Lord Baldwin,'' Andy said before rushing to defend her father and herself. ''We just finished doing some work over breakfast. Father was showing me how good a chess partner he's found. He wouldn't even consider accepting advice from me.''

''No point in doing it up brown,'' Jon snorted, meeting Andy's glare with a grin. ''She doesn't gammon easily.''

Sofia ignored his comment. She glanced at the work on the table and frowned. ''You haven't been overtaxing your father, have you?''

Andy clasped her hands behind her back and quickly shook her head. ''Absolutely not, my lady. He was already working when I joined him for breakfast.''

''Edgar!'' Sofia rounded on him. ''What have I told you about overdoing it? You know you must take it slowly if you wish to regain your strength. Otherwise, there's the risk of a relapse.'' Her voice softened; the stern lines along her mouth eased. ''The work can wait. How many times must I tell you there's no need to hurry with it?''

Jon watched Edgar shoot a dark look at Andy for interfering. When he turned back to the Marchioness, his expression was as abashed as his daughter's a moment ago. Highly diverted, Jon swallowed another chuckle and went to stand at Andy's side. They didn't understand his aunt's gruff exterior was just that, an exterior.

Edgar spoke up. ''Now, Sofie, I swear I'm taking it as easy as any man can.''

''*That* is not saying much,'' the Marchioness shot back.

''Really, Sofie,'' Edgar affirmed, taking Lady Sofia by the arm and patting her hand. ''I woke up early this morning and thought to do just a bit to occupy the time until you came.''

Andy's jaw slackened at the familiarity. Transfixed by their words and actions, her gaze darted between the two of them.

Jonathon noted it, too. If his aunt's softened expression was anything to go by, Edgar's efforts to cajole Sofia out of her bad humor were working. So, Edgar did know about his aunt's façade.

He tugged at Andy's elbow and winked. She returned his

look with a surprised one of her own before looking back at the tableau. Jon ran his fingers absently over the worn twill of Andy's sleeve, enjoying the feel of her arm. He, too, watched Edgar gallantly seat the Marchioness to resume the chess game. His aunt's upturned features nearly glowed.

The Marchioness glanced over her shoulder and spoke to Andy. "I believe my daughter is awaiting you in the muniments room."

"In other words, we're dismissed?" Jon teased, answering before Andy.

Edgar chuckled. "Quite the autocrat, aren't you, Sofie? It's almost a shame that Malcolm couldn't inherit a dukedom."

The Marchioness stiffened at the mention of her dead husband.

Edgar held up a hand, crying pax. "Almost, I said—although one shouldn't speak ill of the dead, of course. Still, you would have made a truly wonderful Duchess."

Sofia unbent and brushed off Edgar's compliment with a wave of her hand.

Jon was reminded of the way he liked to refer to Andy and swallowed another grin. He gazed down at her, noting the way her hair captured the morning light in a blazing halo and felt something within himself ignite.

Andy smiled at the older couple. "I get the message, Papa, and so I shall retire gracefully." He was too preoccupied with the Marchioness to notice her departure and Andy's smile widened only to slip when she glanced back at the Marquess. His overly warm gaze seemed to devour her and she stumbled as he escorted her from the room.

Jon broke their silence in the hallway. "I hope my aunt didn't offend you. She really isn't the Tartar she appears. It's just that she's concerned about your father's health."

Andy glanced up at him and shook her head. "I understand and appreciate that. No, I was just thinking about how peculiar it was for a biographer to declare one shouldn't speak ill of the dead.''

"My aunt tends to have that effect on people.''

Andy pulled her gaze away from the wicked way his full lips slanted, wondering if the Marquess knew the effect *he* had on people, more specifically, women. Probably, she thought, disgruntled. His quiet voice dragged her gaze back to his arresting features.

"Thank you for agreeing to help my cousin with her search.'' He covered her hand with his.

Andy made a noncommittal noise, unsure of just what Helen had mentioned. Her skin tingled when the rough pads of his fingers stroked her hand.

"Both Helen and my aunt spoke to me about the possibility of Emily's diary.''

Forcing herself to concentrate on the topic, Andy stared straight ahead and responded in a tone as hushed as his. "I'm glad. She's very troubled by it.''

He shrugged in resignation. Understanding, she placed a hand on the arm holding hers. "Emily's family and the Baron St. James are neighbors of yours?''

Jon nodded. "Actually, Emily's family moved away not long after her death. They couldn't bear the whispers. I'm not sure what happened to them.''

"Was there any enmity between the families?''

He hesitated. "I don't know. There was very little contact until St. James—the current Baron—was old enough to attend the same clubs as myself. I always thought it was because they were embarrassed by our assuming responsibility for Dom. Why do you ask?''

Andy cleared her throat. "Helen mentioned that her father might have destroyed Emily's effects. I was trying to understand why.''

"With my uncle, there didn't have to be a reason. Believe me.''

"I see." Andy looked up at Jonathon's hardened features and recalled how the Marchioness, too, had stiffened at the mention of Malcolm. She waited for him to say more, but he had nothing else to add. Thus, they walked down the stairs in silence until they reached the library.

There, Jonathon paused and took her hands into his. "Let me know if there's anything I can do to help. Both Helen and Dom mean a lot to me."

Andy nodded, touched by his concern. Without any warning, his expression changed and his eyes crinkled at the corners. Before Andy could escape, he pulled her into his embrace and gave her a hard, fast kiss.

He stepped back quickly and rested an index finger against her lips, hushing her outrage. "Observe," he invited with a wave. "There isn't anyone else about. Adieu, Duchess. Good luck." He winked and slipped into the library.

Audacious libertine, Andy thought, making her way to the estate room, only her outrage was less heated than it should have been. Brushing her fingers against her lips, she couldn't help a rueful smile. The smile faded only when she entered the estate room.

A morose Dominic looked up from the papers he had been shuffling at the desk and responded to her cheerful greeting without much enthusiasm. "Oh, good morning, Andy. If you're looking for Lady Helen, you'll find her through there," he said, thumbing at a door in the corner.

"*Lady* Helen? Feeling formal today are we, Mr. White?"

"One shouldn't forget one's station in life, should one?" he muttered, a slight flush visible above his collar. He continued in a cool tone, "I believe you're expected." So saying, his shoulders slumped and he turned back to his documents. Clearly, their conversation was over.

Andy doubted he had any idea as to what he was reading. He didn't respond to her brief thanks. Lost as he was in his dark mood, he probably hadn't even heard her. She shot another glance at the brooding gentleman. Something had obviously occurred between Helen and him. With a shrug, she entered the muniments room.

"Oh my!" Andy exhaled slowly, unprepared for the sight which greeted her. This room was nearly as large as the one she had just passed through. However, whereas the estate room exuded a sense of orderliness, this one was the exact opposite. Books were laid flat upon each other in a haphazard fashion— some on shelves, others on boxes which were themselves stacked one upon the other. Pieces of odd furniture were mixed in between trunks of indeterminate ages. There was even an old assortment of clothing.

"Oh my!" Andy repeated and sucked in her breath, turning slowly to look around at the bewildering assortment of odds and ends. This time, her exclamation was heard by the room's other occupant.

Sitting cross-legged on the floor, in the middle of a pile of boxes near the room's only window, Helen responded. "Looks pretty grim, doesn't it?"

"I'm certainly glad I wore one of my older dresses," Andy agreed. "It appears this room was too much even for the efficient Mrs. Simms to tackle," she said in awe. With no place else to sit near Helen, she brushed the dust off a trunk. "What a daunting task you've set for yourself. No wonder you were depressed yesterday. I wish I could've helped you sooner."

Shrugging, Helen waved off Andy's regret. "Do not concern yourself so. The search could end up being fruitless anyway." She brushed the hair from her face with the back of her hand and stretched. "Mama says the jumble here is because only the men of the family used this area for storage. Since it's just behind the estate room, they claimed any attempts to rearrange things would distract them from their work. As a result, we're dealing with what can only be described as several generations of trash."

"Well, perhaps not all of it," she amended, handing Andy

a delicately engraved pre-Georgian silver snuff box. "Isn't it lovely?"

Andy examined the piece, impressed by the exacting workmanship. She knew a number of collectors who would be pleased to own it. Saying so, she passed the article back to Helen and gazed about to survey the mass of material. Her brow rose. "Have you been able to make any sense out of the order here? Or perhaps a better question would be, is there any order?"

Helen pointed to the space opposite from them. "I don't know if you can call it order, but the oldest items appear to be the ones against the far wall over there. Since I might have missed the material, it doesn't matter where you start. I'll continue on in this spot. If you need extra light, the spare candles are over there," she said, waving toward one of the trunks near the door. Helen grinned, adding, "Don't allow any snuffboxes to distract you."

Smiling absently at the admonishment, Andy rested her elbow on the arm hugging her midriff and pressed her knuckles against her chin. If this was an exclusively male domain, and Helen's father hadn't destroyed Emily's portmanteau, he *could* have stored it here. Would he have put it with the more recent material accumulated? Too obvious? Hands on hips, Andy turned and interrupted Helen.

"Helen, where would you say the oldest and dirtiest collection of what you referred to as trash might be?"

"Over there." Helen motioned with a thumb over her shoulder in the direction of the darkest corner. Straightening, she looked at Andy, her gaze curious. "I looked there briefly, but really didn't see anything."

"I think I'll try there again. That is, if you have no objections?" When Helen shrugged as if to say she hadn't any, Andy took a brace of candlesticks and settled down to work.

Ugh! Andy thought after an hour of hot, backbreaking work moving trunks, piles of furniture, and assorted books. Someone

should speak to Jonathon about getting this room organized.
A knock on the door interrupted her musing.

Helen darted a worried look at Andy but, being closer, got
up to answer. It was Simms, with a footman bearing a tray of
refreshments.

Chapter Seven

"Good morning, Lady Helen." Simms bowed and turned his benign gaze toward Andy. "Miss Fitzgerald. It's good to see Lady Helen having company this morning." He bent and dusted a trunk for the tea tray. "The gentlemen ordered tea for you."

"How very thoughtful of them." Relieved at the break, Andy swiped her grimy hands against her skirt and came forward. Her raw throat reminded her of just how desperately she needed a restorative.

Helen thanked Simms and warned him they might not make it for luncheon. After the footman placed a pair of chairs by the trunk, both men bowed and departed.

Helen glanced at the door to the estate room. "It was probably Jon who sent for our tea. Dom seems particularly busy today. He was even too preoccupied to finish our walk last night."

"Oh, dear. Feeling ignored, is he?"

Helen nodded.

Andy sat down with a tired plop, mopping the sweat off her brow with the back of an arm. The overly warm room lacked any air circulation and her kerseymere dress clung to her breasts. She tugged at it, trying to make it more comfortable—an impossible task—and she soon gave up trying. "Perhaps you should just explain what you're trying to do."

"I will soon enough, but not yet." Helen looked up from pouring the tea and laughed. "Oh, Lud! Look at you."

"Do I look that bad?" Andy asked with a rueful smile, tucking another loose strand of hair behind an ear.

"Like Tom, the pot boy, on a bad day," Helen chuckled, glancing again at Andy.

Accepting the cup of tea and a warm scone, Andy retorted, "It's no wonder, then, that you didn't want to do much in that corner." She took a bracing sip of tea and sighed. "You really should speak to your cousin about having something done to this room."

"I intend to," Helen confirmed. "Have you had any luck?"

"Except for a couple of interesting letters which Father will find useful, I'm afraid not. There are a few locked trunks, though, which I'm curious about. Would you happen to know if any keys exist for them?"

"If they do, it would take forever to find them. However, there is a pry bar in here somewhere. You have my permission to break into anything you wish . . ." Helen stood to survey the room. "Now, where had I seen it?"

"Are you sure no one in your family will mind the damage? Some workmanship on those trunks is exquisite."

Helen dismissed Andy's concern with a snort. "How can anyone mind a bit of damage to something they didn't even know existed?" Helen bent and scrambled under a pile of furniture not too far away. She came back almost as grimy as Andy, proudly flourishing the pry bar. "Here you are. Let's have a look at the trunks now."

"All right," Andy agreed. "But you can do the honors of prying them open. I insist," she added, smiling.

"You're right. Inflicting damage on something inanimate might even make me feel better." Helen strode toward Andy's corner, brandishing her weapon as though willing to fend off a horde of intruders. The marshal gleam in her eyes brightened. "Where are they?"

"Good heavens, Helen! Such vehemence!" Andy stepped back, her arms crossed in front of her face, pretending to ward off an attack.

Helen answered with a giggle, her voice tinged with relief. "It feels good to laugh at something. I've really been frustrated these last few weeks."

"I understand." Andy patted her gently on the back and led her to the trunks.

The first one required little work to open. Its rusted lock quickly gave way to Helen's determined jabs. Tossing down the pry bar, Helen lifted the lid and started passing an odd assortment of articles to Andy, who efficiently separated out a few more journals her father might use. Helen wasted no time getting to the bottom. Dejected at finding nothing else there, Helen sat back on her heels.

"Well, we have discovered more material for the genealogy and there's still one more trunk for you to vent your fury upon," Andy prompted brusquely.

The second trunk proved to be more difficult to break into. Of a newer vintage, its sturdy lock stubbornly refused to budge. Trying to find a way to gain more leverage, Helen ordered Andy to sit on the trunk so it wouldn't move. Then, revealing a most unladylike amount of stockinged leg, she braced a foot against the trunk. She leaned forward and grunted, putting all her strength into trying to break open the lock.

"Would you like me to try?" Andy offered when Helen's efforts proved unsuccessful.

Helen straightened, pressing her hand against the small of her back. "Let me try a little longer. The lock's beginning to give. I've got a strange feeling about this one."

"Better not get your hopes up," Andy cautioned. In spite of her dampening words, she, too, felt a rising anticipation.

Helen ignored the warning and attacked the trunk once more. After a few more attempts, the wood ripped and the lock loosened. Andy crossed her fingers superstitiously. Helen redoubled her efforts without stopping to look up, toppling onto the trunk when the lock unexpectedly gave way.

"Are you all right?" Andy asked, helping Helen right herself.

Helen reassured her with a gamin grin. "Other than a few blisters starting to appear on my hands, I'm fine. I just wasn't ready for the lock to come off and lost my balance." Brushing her hands on her now filthy skirt, Helen knelt in front of the case. She rested a hand against the trunk's lid and shot Andy a hesitant look. Andy stepped back.

Steadying herself with a deep breath, Helen nodded and tried to speak calmly. "Nothing ventured, nothing gained," she said. She opened the trunk and began tossing out articles over her shoulder. After a few more minutes of rummaging, Helen sat back clutching several letters. She looked at them, her expression puzzled.

"These are my father's. Some of them indicate they're copies of correspondence he had with Lord St. James, dated around the time of Emily's arrival. That means they could only have been addressed to Phillip's father." She passed them to Andy as if they were contaminated. "I'd rather you read them."

Overcome with a sense of foreboding, Andy carefully accepted the brittle papers, glancing at the backward-slanting script on the letters. For some inexplicable reason, she recalled the legend of Burne. Her skin crawled at the memory of the eerie howling she'd tried to deny she'd heard.

Malcolm's copies of three letters written to the new Lord St. James. The Baron's two responses. Dates noted on the corners of the envelopes. A total of five letters. The vellum crackled when Andy pulled the letters out of the envelopes.

The first letter dealt with Malcolm's displeasure at housing a pregnant Emily and his demand the Baron accept responsibility since Emily had supposedly married his predecessor. The second contained a frigid refusal from the Baron, declaring Emily had nothing which substantiated her claim. Andy passed the letters to Helen. The copy of the next letter from the Marquess was so malicious that Andy paused reading midway.

Helen, who had scanned the other two letters, looked anxiously at Andy. "What is it?"

Andy gnawed her bottom lip. "This isn't a pleasant one, I'm afraid, and just might confirm your worst fears. Written just after Dominic was born, it declares there *was* a journal. You might even find it here if you dig a little deeper. Unfortunately," she added as Helen began tossing items out of the trunk in search of the diary, "it appears your father tore out some pages and sent them to the Baron, teasing him with the possibility he might, in fact, be a usurper since Emily bore a son."

Helen's search came to an abrupt halt. She sat back with a stunned look. "That means Phillip *was* searching for the diary every time he was here. And now he'll have the opportunity to do so again during this visit. We have to find it first!" She frowned, redoubling her efforts. "It just has to be in here."

With a quick glance at her companion, Andy continued to read, describing the contents as she did so. "Amazing how the Baron changes his tune after receiving the excerpts from Emily's journal. He insists on taking Dom in, even if Dom is not legitimate, claiming it's his Christian duty since Dom was the deceased Baron's by-blow—my apologies for the language, but the words are his."

Swallowing back a few unchristian thoughts about the two men, Andy continued her perusal of the Baron's response. "He makes veiled threats about commencing legal action to gain custody of Dom if your father doesn't release him to his care." Picking up the copy of the last letter from the Marquess, she gave an unladylike snort. "Your father didn't take kindly to the threats and made a few of his own. I don't suppose we'll ever know what made them discontinue their posturing."

Helen interrupted. "I found it!" She hugged a faded blue diary reverently to her chest. "I found it," she repeated more softly. The gentle candlelight reflected the sudden brightness pooling in the corners of her eyes. She stood and gave Andy a fierce hug, then passed her the journal. "Please read this. Find out what you can."

"Wouldn't you rather read it first?" Andy asked, unwilling to take the somewhat tattered diary Helen had searched so hard for.

Helen shook her head. "No. With your experience, you're more qualified to unravel any mysteries it might contain. I wouldn't know what to look for. I'm just glad we could find it before Phillip's arrival." Brushing at a tear which streaked through the grime on her face, she hiccuped and hugged Andy again.

Accepting the diary reluctantly, Andy returned the hug with a sigh. "You may be right. However, I'll need to find a safe place to store it." She slipped the diary into her pocket and picked up the other material for her father's research. "It's getting late. We'd best go up and change. If Dominic hasn't left the office yet, you might even be able to entice him out for a walk before the guests arrive."

Helen rewarded Andy's smile with a wavering grin. Taking a napkin from the tray, she dipped it in the carafe of water and ran the moistened cloth lightly over her face and hands. Andy considered doing the same but shrugged, deciding she might as well go straight to her room and do a proper job of it.

Dominic was still at his desk when the women walked through to the estate room. Not put off by his stiff greeting, Helen winked at Andy and sat down on the corner of his desk, chatting gaily. "You wouldn't believe some of the material we found! Andy has everything she needs now and I won't need to search for anything more." Following each phrase, Helen moved closer and closer to Dominic's side.

Andy swallowed a chuckle, leaving Helen practicing the age-old feminine wile of fluttering her eyelashes at Dom. As she rounded the bend in the hallway near the main staircase, she wondered why she'd never been able to master the art of batting her eyelashes without looking ridiculous. Was it a question of practice? By all appearances, it could work wonders—not that she meant to entice anyone, she told herself, trying to banish Jon's dark visage from her mind.

Tucking a hand into her pocket, her fingers brushed against the diary. A sudden chill swept through her and she froze midstep.

The howling. She raised her head to look around.

There it was again. A dog bayed. Andy withdrew her hand from the pocket and tried to still its trembling by pressing it to her breast. She waited.

Stillness.

She looked around the hallway. No one. Was she dreaming? When there was no more sound, Andy drew a shaky breath. She clutched her skirt and slowly proceeded forward. She must have imagined it.

A honeyed tone coming from the front entrance distracted her. *The guests!*

Andy pressed her back against a recess in the wall, praying the party would soon pass from the foyer and allow her to make her escape unnoticed. She looked down at her grubby hands and regretted not cleaning herself when she'd had the chance.

"You simply *cannot* imagine the horrible journey we had, Jonathon. Isn't that right, Mama?" an aggrieved stranger asked.

Andy chanced a peek around the corner before drawing back

sharply. An elegantly clad blonde allowed the Marquess to remove her wrap and rested her arm possessively on his after he passed her cloak to Simms.

Lady Cynthia Duvall, no doubt. Andy swallowed a silent groan. The older woman must be her mother, Tabitha. The dandy, Phillip St. James, the Baron. But who was the third woman, standing quietly behind Tabitha? Oh yes, the Marchioness had mentioned the cousin, Barbara. Andy peeked again.

Leaning heavily on the arm of the medium-height, sandy-haired Baron, who patted her hand solicitously, the older woman spoke. "The agonies we suffered! Had it not been for the tender care of my daughter and the thoughtfulness of Sir Phillip here, I'm sure I would have expired *en route*. Of course, Barbara's company was invaluable, too." This last was added almost as an afterthought.

The blonde took up where her mother left off. "The roads were atrocious and the treatment at the hostelries along the way wasn't much better. If it weren't for the presence of Sir Phillip, I doubt we would have received any service at all."

Andy edged forward. She noted the woman didn't let go of Jon's arm even though her glance focused on the Baron, who preened visibly from her praise. Andy's nose wrinkled. She and her father had made a much longer trip, in far worse weather, without any theatrics. Cynthia, however, made it seem as if they had crossed the Pyranees on mules.

The Marquess's soothing noises set her teeth on edge. What was it about fluttering eyelashes that turned men into malleable marzipan? Whatever it was, Andy vowed to practice at the first opportunity. First of all, though, she had to escape from this predicament. She turned and crept farther along the wall, looking for an avenue of escape when the Baron spoke up. She halted with a backward glance, wondering what the fop had to add.

"It's incomprehensible how anyone can bury themselves out

in the country. Really, Jon. It's *so* uncivilized," he declared, his tone languid.

The party moved, but didn't go up the stairs. Andy saw Jonathon shoot a dark look at the Baron. Her eyes rolled. *Men!* Why hadn't he taken umbrage at the similar comments made by the two females, instead of standing over them solicitously?

Quickly, Andy reminded herself this wasn't the time to ponder on the inconsistencies of the male species. If she could see them clearly from where she stood, they only had to turn to discover her. Wishing to avoid this at all costs, she decided to make a dash back to the estate room. Only, when she dropped her hands to her side, the papers she'd been holding at her breast rustled against her skirt.

Unfortunately, Jonathon wasn't paying as much attention to his guests as she'd thought. He pivoted on his heel at the sound. Spotting Andy, he greeted her with a smile. "I was beginning to wonder if you'd gone into hiding."

"Why ever would I wish to do that, my lord?" Submitting to the demands of propriety, Andy stepped forward and curtsied briefly before the guests. "If you'll excuse me?"

The blond goddess frowned. She quirked a thinly plucked eyebrow and gave Jon's arm a subtle tug. "It's so difficult to get unobtrusive help nowadays, isn't it, Jonathon?"

Andy faltered at the rudeness. Her shoulders straightened and she jutted out her chin, raising her own brow in return. She hugged the armful of material just the slightest bit closer to her chest, as if to ward off further barbs. Her fingers dug into the old scar on her hand. She nodded once more in their general direction and turned. Jon's voice stopped her.

"The Duchess is definitely not hired help. Allow me to introduce you." Jon offered a satiric grin in response to Andy's glare.

"Duchess? Oh my," Lady Tabitha gushed, putting out her hand.

A furious blush at her *faux pas* stained Cynthia's features.

The Baron leaned forward, his interest obvious. Barbara merely stood quietly behind them all.

Jonathon pulled Andy into the circle. "Well, she's not actually a duchess," he qualified, grinning at her smudged features and squeezing her hand, "but she has the makings of one."

"Pardon me," a recovered Cynthia interrupted. Lips thinned, she crossed her arms. "If she isn't the hired help and she isn't a duchess, then just who might she be?"

Andy sucked in a quiet breath. Based on past experience with this type during her short London season, she doubted anyone who made sport of Cynthia got off lightly. Andy also realized she'd end up taking the blame for the Marquess's jest. Her chin rose another notch and she cast a steady gaze around the company, waiting for Jon to continue.

Tabitha withdrew her hand, as if afraid to shake hands with a housekeeper, or worse, someone's lightskirt. Sir Phillip came closer, apparently titillated by Jonathon's qualifications. Only Barbara hung back with a placid smile, her hands folded neatly in front of herself.

After a long pause to draw out the moment of suspense, Jon finally drawled, "This is Miss Andrea Samantha Fitzgerald."

Observing the flaring nostrils of the reigning toast of the ton, Andy wasn't sure who would stomp on the Marquess's foot first—she or the lovely Lady Cynthia. Just as she opened her mouth to explain her presence, Jon interrupted her to introduce the others. Andy clamped her jaw shut with a decided snap.

"Miss Fitzgerald is here to assist her father in compiling our family's history. You are all familiar with Sir Edgar Fitzgerald, I'm sure." In response to Cynthia's puzzled look, he explained, "He's the only writer ever asked by both our own Prince Regent as well as by Napoleon to work on their genealogies."

Andy suppressed a shudder, recollecting her father's tirade in response to both of those requests. It happened a few years prior to her come-out, but she could still remember him asserting that Prinny was little more than an overgrown pompous ass and Napoleon a frightening, if brilliant, megalomaniac. Needless to say, he never did any work for either man.

Recognition dawned on the faces of the guests. Unsure as to how to greet someone who was definitely not a duchess, but not exactly the hired help because of her connection to the renowned genealogist, the ladies made noncommittal noises.

With a glare warning the Marquess of reprisal at the first opportunity, Andy tore her hand from his and made another perfunctory curtsy, noting how Sir Phillip stiffened.

He peered myopically at Andy. "A bluestocking, eh?" As if realizing he'd muttered the insulting words aloud, the Baron rushed on in an attempt to mitigate the comment. He took the hand she had just recaptured from the Marquess and bowed over it. "A pleasure, I'm sure. One as lovely as you shouldn't be troubling her pretty head or hands with such work," he declared pompously before noticing her grimy state. He quickly dropped her hand and pulled out a handkerchief. Wiping his palm with meticulous care, he turned back and asked, "What exactly is it that you do for your father? Transcribe his notes?"

Even though Andy should have been accustomed to such belittling of a woman's capabilities, the Baron's comments still rankled. Noticing the interested look he cast at the material in her arm, however, she remembered the howling. If it hadn't been her imagination, could it have been Burne warning them of danger to the Marquess's family? After all, Dominic *was* a distant member of that family.

Perhaps it was time to practice simpering and batting her eyelids. Putting out a hand to forestall Jon, she agreed quickly. "Oh yes. How could I possibly understand research the way Papa does? My penmanship, though, is excellent. The little I help Father with allows him time for more meaningful work." She dropped her gaze modestly, peeking through her eyelashes at Phillip.

He didn't look entirely convinced and glanced at the pile of letters in her arm.

Andy simpered again and waved the material. "Occasionally, I chance upon old letters or journals I think my father might be interested in. Sometimes my hunches are correct, but more often than not, I tend to be off the mark." She ended with a self-deprecating laugh, turning limpid eyes up at the Baron, trying to ignore Emily's journal seemingly burning a hole in her pocket. She breathed a silent sigh of relief that Jon hadn't chosen to correct the impression she was giving. Her gratitude was short-lived.

Jonathon arched a sardonic brow at the other man. "You certainly didn't expect anything else from a woman who has rubbed shoulders with royalty for the last several years and perfected her waltzing techniques in Vienna. Did you, Phillip?"

Andy bared her teeth in a witless smile. Jonathon didn't have to go *that* far in supporting her masquerade. Her ire faltered. Another chill crawled up her spine when she met the speculative stare of the Baron. She struggled to retain her guileless expression when he took another look at the notes in her arm.

Finally, Phillip smiled condescendingly. "I suppose a man of your father's brilliance must have someone to relieve him of the tedium of transcription. Otherwise, he couldn't concentrate on the more analytical aspects of his work."

Andy thought of her father upstairs and hoped he wouldn't mind her interrupting his "analytical" chess game with Lady Sofia. She had to warn him and the Marchioness of the role she'd assumed. How to justify her role to Dominic, though? He wasn't aware of the diary's existence. Andy stole a glance at Simms. The butler stood with them in the foyer, watching her performance with his usual, impassive face. She doubted he'd give her away.

"According to many of my friends who have read his work,

Sir Edgar is an excellent raconteur,'' Tabitha acknowledged, her tone indicating that she, herself, rarely read. ''How is your father's work coming along, my dear?''

In other words, Andy thought, when were they expected to leave and would her daughter be facing any serious competition for the Marquess's attention? The woman was definitely a seasoned campaigner. Andy flashed them a vacuous smile and crossed her fingers, hidden in the folds of her skirt.

''Father's just finished compiling the work. It may be a while yet before he completes the annotation—Father didn't take the Channel crossing well and was a bit under the weather.''

Jonathon coughed at her understatement. Andy resisted the urge to elbow him and instead gave another vacuous smile at the company. Neither Cynthia nor her mother looked particularly pleased with the news, or with her position in the household. If only Jon hadn't referred to her as a duchess, she thought sourly.

Tabitha gave an ingratiating smile to Jonathon before turning to Andy. ''So you'll be able to participate in some of the activities the Marquess has planned for us. How lovely.'' Her pinched nostrils belied her saccharine tone.

''Of course she will,'' Jon declared. ''She should fill out the party quite nicely.''

Andy's bodice suddenly felt tight as he ran a warm glance over her and she dug her nails into her palm. Once again, she was too tall, too large, too obvious, and everyone was looking at her.

As though sensing her discomfort, Jon relented and drew the attention back to himself. ''Dominic White will also be participating in the activities.'' The statement was greeted with momentary silence. It seemed everyone was aware of Dom's illegitimate status.

Tabitha's lips thinned. ''Your secretary, I believe?''

''Not only my secretary, but also my very good friend.''

Jon's imperious tone warned his guests in no uncertain terms that he wouldn't brook any disrespect toward Dominic.

Andy couldn't help but admire his loyalty. She darted a glance at the Baron from beneath lowered lashes. The anger in his hooded expression struck her forcibly. His dandy's mask slipped back into place immediately. Was there danger to the family? Andy prayed the diary's bulk wasn't evident through her skirts.

Mrs. Simms, who had been patiently standing beside her husband, chose this moment to interrupt. "The rooms are ready, m'lord. I've placed the guests in the east wing. Perhaps the ladies would like to freshen up before tea?"

Jon looked almost disappointed at the reprieve from the building tension. "Forgive me for keeping all of you here. After such an arduous journey, I'm sure you would appreciate the opportunity to rest," he offered with a smooth bow to the ladies.

Andy walked ahead of the party self-consciously. A misstep could send her sprawling and the diary flying out of her pocket. The stairs could be dangerous to anyone who wasn't paying attention. Cheeks burning, Andy recalled how Jonathon's body had sprawled on top of hers. Safely reaching the top of the stairs, she breathed a sigh of relief when the guests were led in the other direction.

How odd, though. She glanced over her shoulder at the retreating party. She and her father were in the same wing as the family. How would Tabitha react at learning that she and the other guests had been put in the opposite wing? Andy forgot about that worry when, nearing her father's room, she met a distracted-looking Marchioness. When she informed her of the guests' arrival, Sofia was startled.

"How is it I wasn't informed? That's most unlike Simms. I shall have to have a word with that man." The flustered Marchioness frowned and picked up her skirts to hurry off.

"I'd best go and greet the ladies." Her tone indicated she didn't relish the idea.

With a fleeting thought to Sofia's unusual lack of composure, Andy's own problems overtook her. "Before you go, could I have a word with you?" Andy cast another surreptitious glance over her shoulders.

Chapter Eight

Sofia sighed. "Certainly. Let's just step into the alcove."

Banishing the memories of the last time she'd been in the same alcove, Andy quickly explained about the diary, as well as the deception regarding her role as her father's assistant.

"I really dislike subterfuge of any sort, Lady Sofia, but Helen warned me that Sir Phillip may have been searching for the diary on previous visits. Furthermore, something about his attitude made me uncomfortable. Perhaps it's just my imagination, but I would just as soon pretend to be a feather-brain. If nothing more, it will provide the perfect excuse for avoiding any pointed questions on his part," Andy ended with a rueful shrug, stopping short of mentioning the eerie sounds she'd heard.

Lady Sofia touched Andy's sleeve. Shaken, she asked in a hushed voice, "Emily's diary? You found it?"

"Yes, I have it right here." Andy patted the side of her skirt and took another careful look around. After ascertaining the hall was still clear, she withdrew the faded blue journal from her pocket and passed it to the Marchioness.

Hands trembling, Sofia accepted it. A look of infinite sadness crossed her features. After caressing its cover for a moment, she opened it at random and looked at the handwriting. "Yes, this is Emily's," she acknowledged, soft regret coloring her words. She handed it back to Andy abruptly, as though she didn't want any reminders of unhappy times. "I hope you'll find something in it—not just for the sake of my daughter's future, but also to vindicate Emily's innocence. She was one of the dearest people I've ever known."

"Are you sure you wouldn't rather read it yourself?" Andy didn't relish accepting the responsibility.

Lady Sofia stood and shook her head. "No, my dear," she said, surprising Andy with an absent pat to her shoulder. "If you're worried it may delay the work your father is doing, please don't trouble yourself on that score. You are both welcome to stay as long as need be." Sofia paused. A puzzled look crossed her features. "Truth to tell, I'm actually enjoying the company."

Refusing to meet Andy's startled gaze, she cleared her throat, the brusque Marchioness once more. "Shall I give your excuses at tea and send a tray up instead, so you can begin reading the diary?"

Andy acquiesced reluctantly. "I'd appreciate it, however, if you could find the opportunity to warn both Helen and Mr. White about my assumed role. I just can't seem to get rid of this sense of foreboding." Andy swallowed another urge to mention the howling she had heard—no, that she'd *imagined* she'd heard.

"As you wish." The Marchioness nodded and left to welcome her new guests.

Andy watched her departure with concern. Steps slow, Sofia made her way down the hallway. Her bent shoulders bore no resemblance to her usual, almost military demeanor. Something was agitating the Marchioness. Was it the guests, the diary, or something entirely different? Andy shrugged. She had to speak to her father before doing anything else and slipped into his room.

"Papa?"

Edgar was slumped in a wing-back chair by the window, his hands hanging limply from the arm rests. His entire being as he looked up was a canvas of dejection. "Hello, Andy. How goes the battle?"

Andy ignored the question. "Are you all right?"

"Yes, of course."

His shaky smile did little to reassure Andy. She recalled the Marchioness's distracted air of a few moments ago. "You didn't quarrel with Lady Sofia, did you?"

His manner altered. Testy, he replied, "Of course not. Whatever gave you that idea?"

"I'm sorry, Father. It's just that I met her in the hallway a moment ago—she seemed out of sorts as well."

"Did she now?" Edgar's features brightened and his posture straightened. "Did she happen to say anything?"

"Only that she's surprised at enjoying our company." Her father suddenly resembled the proverbial cream-licking cat.

"Any luck with the search?"

Andy darted another curious glance at him before accepting the change in subject. "And not before time, Papa. The guests have arrived." Taking the journal out of her pocket, she passed it to him together with the letters and diaries she carried. "I also found some other items which might be of interest to you for the genealogy."

He accepted all the material except for Emily's journal. "You'd best take care of that yourself. I'll have enough on my plate with this. Have you formed an opinion yet as to whether a marriage occurred?"

"I'm not sure." Andy related the correspondence between the late Marquess and Phillip's father, the Baron who had succeeded Richard. She pointed out the missing pages in the diary and explained her scheme to play the ignorant assistant, asking for his understanding. "There was something unnatural about the way Sir Phillip stared at this material. His questions regarding the status of the work made me feel cautious. Perhaps I'm seeing demons where none exist, but I'd rather be safe than sorry." Once again, she buried the memory of the imagined howling.

Edgar leaned back in his chair. Steepling his fingers under his chin, he gazed at her thoughtfully. "Your intuition is rarely wrong, my dear." He grinned, adding, "I wish you luck in your role as an ignorant chit, though. If you succeed, you might consider a career on the boards to support your father in his old age."

Andy stuck her tongue out at his insouciance. At least his morose mood had vanished. Still smiling, she turned to leave. Her smile slipped at her father's final words.

"Just be careful. I wouldn't want to see you get hurt."

Andy was still mulling over the information she'd read when she left her room for dinner. Jonathon slipped up from behind, catching her unawares. She gave him a distracted smile.

"How is the transcribing coming along, Duchess?"

"If a certain lowly Marquess isn't more careful, this Duchess may inflict some permanent damage upon his person," Andy retorted. Her haughty glare lasted only a second before she smiled again, accepting his escort. "Thank you for not giving me away earlier." Her thoughts returned to the riddles she'd read.

A moment later, Jon halted abruptly. She stumbled and grasped his arm tightly for support. "What is it?"

"Pardon me, but I'm concerned you might plummet down the stairwell again in your current state of distraction." He paused and his grin transformed into a leer. "On the other hand, that might not be such a bad thing. You *do* recall what happened the last time you slipped, don't you?"

"What sort of a gentleman would remind a lady of that?" Her rueful smile faded. Before he could answer, she apologized. "If I seem distracted, it's because I've a lot on my mind right now."

"The diary?"

Her eyes widened. "How did you know?"

His features darkened. "My aunt spoke to me earlier. It's just as well she did, although she only told me enough to give me an idea of what might be going on." Jon's lips thinned. "I wouldn't put it past my uncle to have kept the knowledge of marriage lines between Emily and Richard a secret, just to spite everyone involved. Is it possible, then, that Emily and Richard were married after all?"

Since she hadn't discussed the matter in such detail with the Marchioness, Andy could only assume Sofia had spoken with her father. She shrugged and replied hesitantly, "It's a very definite possibility . . . but I'm not sure."

"Shall we meet in the library tonight to discuss this further? Let's say about an hour or so after everyone has retired. That way we shouldn't be disturbed. I might be able to help you in some way."

Andy darted an uncertain look at him. His serious visage didn't appear to hide any ulterior motives. "Truth to tell, I could use some help unraveling the puzzle. Emily made a few cryptic references which I'm having problems deciphering. They may not mean anything at all. On the other hand, they might add up to something. Then, there's the problem of the missing pages . . ." Her voice trailed off.

"I hope you've put the diary in a safe place. If what my aunt suggests is true, and the Baron was informed of a possible marriage, then Phillip might be on the lookout for it."

"What do you take me for? Some sapskull? Of course I hid it. Knowing that my bedroom would be one of the first places someone might search, I placed it behind one of the portraits in the gallery." After glaring at him, she fell silent, once more preoccupied with trying to unravel the workings of Emily's mind.

She was still grappling with dark thoughts when they entered the drawing room. The others were already assembled. Andy caught the pleased look which passed between Cynthia and her mother at their quiet arrival. Were they hoping she and the Marquess had had a falling out? Andy's mood lightened and she swallowed a chuckle. Giving a general nod to the company at large, she went to greet her father, seated near Sir Phillip.

"Are you sure you're well enough to be down, Papa?" she asked, bending to kiss him on the forehead.

Edgar snorted. "Don't you start mollycoddling me, young lady. I won't have it, thank you very much. Can you imagine Lady Sofia allowing me down if I weren't well enough?"

Andy shook her head in rueful acknowledgment, and Edgar rewarded her with a pleased smile. Phillip stood and executed a gallant bow over her hand.

"You look charming this evening, Miss Fitzgerald." As he straightened, his gaze traveled slowly upward, pausing overlong at the décolletage of her emerald satin gown.

Andy tugged her hand free of his hold.

"Could I get you some refreshment?" he finally offered.

She swallowed the desire to pull her shawl to her throat. Instead, she practiced an insipid smile. "A sherry would be lovely."

Her gaze following him, she sat in the place he'd vacated. He joined Jon who, knowing her preference, was already pouring her drink. The two men exchanged curt nods. Andy caught herself thinking Jonathon really was the handsomer of the two. She swallowed, embarrassed—as though she'd spoken the thought she'd spoken the thought aloud—and glanced around the room.

Dom sat happily beside Helen. While plucking out a tune with one hand on the piano, she giggled at something he said. Dom looked up and his gaze honed in on the Baron, who stood watching him from the corner of his eyes. Andy noted both men turned away from each other without acknowledgment. Seated quietly on the other side of Dominic, Barbara seemed to be observing the tableau as well. The Baron returned and distracted Andy.

"Rather close, are they?" Phillip asked, giving her the sherry. Condescension laced his tone as he pointed his glass toward Dominic and Helen.

Andy's hackles rose and she dismissed the subject. "Merely childhood friends from what I understand." Her gaze returned to Jonathon, who was halted on his way to the fireplace by Tabitha's request to join them.

Tabitha patted the place on the sofa between her daughter and herself. "Cynthia, my dear, make some room for the Marquess."

"Mama, it really is unkind of you to order the Marquess about in his own home." In spite of the mild reprimand, Cynthia complied by rearranging the folds of her silk rose gown.

Jonathon's warm smile at Cynthia's demure expression reminded Andy of the need to practice fluttering her eyelashes.

"Oh fiddle," Tabitha replied. "I'm interested in hearing if he intends to return to London soon. With the Season getting under way soon, all the hostesses will want to know."

Phillip pulled up a chair and drew Andy's attention away from the Marquess. "While they speak of the Season, you can tell me about the work you're doing."

For the next fifteen minutes, it was all Andy could do to politely fend off the prying of Sir Phillip. Playing the part of a dim-witted female wasn't made any easier by the fact that Cynthia's movements distracted her. Andy had to admit the woman was a gifted flirt. She knew just when to send a man a coy glance. Moreover, Jon seemed to lap it up. In fact, he appeared to return Cynthia's flirtation in full measure. Andy's irritation grew. Her jaw clamped and she turned away from them only to note the machinations of Cynthia's mother.

Tabitha had transferred her attention to Edgar. Giving the Baron a halfhearted response to some question, Andy watched the Marchioness recoil every time Tabitha reached across the space between the two sofas to touch Edgar's arm. Andy wondered if her father noticed. Probably not. Just then, Edgar laughed at a quip of Lady Tabitha's. *Men!* Andy mused in disgust.

Simms finally arrived to announce dinner. Her manner icily civil, Sofia insisted Edgar also lend an arm to Tabitha. Andy hadn't heard such frost since their first day at the manor. Jon was already escorting a clinging Cynthia, who gazed up at him with wide, adoring eyes. Helen reluctantly left Dominic's side when Phillip extended his arm toward her.

Barbara, who had been silent to this time, stepped forward to fill the void left by Helen and slipped her arm through the crook of Dom's elbow. "It's so good to see you again, Mr. White. You were sorely missed at the routs the last several weeks." She turned her head toward Andy. "Did you know that Mr. White is as popular with the hostesses as is the Marquess, Miss Fitzgerald? Not only is he excellent company, but he's also extremely light on his feet."

Andy, on the other side of Dom, was startled by Barbara's melodious voice. "What the Town has lost, the country has gained," she replied, smiling in return. Even though she found it difficult to believe the woman's assertion because of Society's views on questionable lineage, she nevertheless appreciated Barbara's efforts to lighten the mood. As Barbara continued to chatter with Dominic, Andy took the opportunity to study her.

Cynthia's cousin, Barbara Folkstone, was about her own age. The demeanor of the quiet brunette was a pleasant change from the archness of Tabitha and, to a lesser degree, of Cynthia. Although the Marchioness claimed Barbara had suffered a major disappointment in love, Andy couldn't see any trace of bitterness toward men in Barbara's attitude.

Andy turned to Dom. "Are you as good a dancer as Miss Folkstone implies?"

Dom flushed. She and Barbara exchanged grins, in charity with each other.

It was the last time Andy smiled for the next few hours. By the time dinner was over, Andy could only sit back in awe. With incredible skill, Tabitha and Cynthia had manipulated the entire conversation to their benefit.

While unfailingly polite toward the other ladies at the table— with only the slightest hint of condescension entering their voices at times—their main focus was on the men. Neither Tabitha nor Cynthia had any problems getting the men to speak freely about themselves or their opinions on various subjects. From the figurative swelling of their chests, Andy could only assume the men loved the attention.

Andy recalled the litany uttered by her various governesses. A good conversationalist was a woman who could get a man to talk about himself. A woman of good breeding should hang on to every word the man would then utter. If it were true, then Tabitha and her daughter were extremely well-bred conversationalists. Even Barbara, in her own quiet way, exemplified the skill throughout the evening.

Unfortunately, the evening wasn't over, Andy thought as the Marchioness led the party to the drawing room. The gentlemen joined them immediately, forgoing the usual ritual of port and cigars.

Her hand on the teal drapes, Cynthia gazed out the partially open French doors. Her lids half closed, she lifted her face toward the faint, honeysuckle-scented breeze. "What a lovely evening!"

Andy caught Jon's wink. Something about it made her feel infinitely better. Perhaps he hadn't been fooled by all the attention at dinner. She smothered a grin when he turned a serious mien toward Cynthia, asking if she'd like to go for a walk. The man was not a dullard.

As he helped Cynthia rearrange her shawl, Jon glanced around the room. "Would anyone else care to join us?"

Helen, sitting at the piano with Dom, refused. "I'd like to practice some music, but thank you just the same, Jon."

Barbara stood directly behind Dom. She rested a hand lightly on his shoulder to remind him of the music sheets she held. "How kind of you to ask, Lord Baldwin, but I'm hoping Lady Helen will permit me to sing."

"In which case, the ladies will need my help turning the pages." Dom grinned at his arduous task.

Phillip yawned. "I think the journey was harder on me than I thought. I didn't rest this afternoon when I should have, so I think I'll turn in early. If the ladies will forgive me?" With a polite bow, he sauntered off before anyone could stop him.

Andy exchanged a concerned glance with her father, who was sandwiched between the Marchioness and Tabitha. Jon's almost desperate voice interrupted her.

"Miss Fitzgerald? Would you care to take a turn about the gardens with us?"

Cynthia seconded his invitation. "Oh, yes. Please do, Miss Fitzgerald. You're looking a bit peaked. The fresh air would probably do you good, I'm sure." Her innocent expression didn't change a whit as she turned to obtain the Marquess's opinion. "Wouldn't you agree, Jonathon?"

"Absolutely," he concurred with a grin.

So, he thought she looked peaked? Andy shot him a sweet smile, her eyes promising retribution. Even so, Cynthia deserved credit for the way she'd handled her campaign to get Jonathon off alone. Thanking them both, Andy politely declined. "Perhaps it would be best if I turned in early as well. Like Sir Phillip, I must have had too much excitement today." She felt safe that the reminder of the Baron upstairs on his own would forestall any protests Jon might make.

Her father agreed. "You probably should go to bed a little earlier today, Andy. I might have some extra transcribing for you tomorrow. Oh, and if it's not too much trouble," he added, "could you just tidy up my writing table tonight before retiring?"

"Of course, Papa," Andy replied. Something lurched at the pit of her stomach and she bent her head to hide her worry. The letters . . . she had left the letters in his room.

She sent Jon a sidelong glance from under her lashes. Noting his martyred expression, a grin replaced her concern. He didn't look particularly pleased about being alone with Cynthia. Andy stood and turned a guileless expression toward the couple by the doors.

"Oh, and pray have a care, Lady Cynthia. I understand the snakes are just beginning to crawl out from under the rocks." Andy shuddered and rearranged her shawl. "I would suggest you stay very close to Lord Baldwin's side." Her vapid smile covered an inward chuckle at the beginning of her revenge. It would either keep Cynthia clinging to him, or cut their walk short.

Jonathon didn't seem to mind. He cloaked a snort of laughter by clearing his throat, but didn't contradict her.

"Snakes?" Cynthia's lovely features contorted and her step faltered. Ignoring Helen's quiet chuckle, she looked to Lady Sofia for confirmation.

"Not very large ones, my dear, and certainly not poisonous." The Marchioness surprised Andy with further embellishment. "However, they do have a pesky habit of coming out at night, just as Miss Fitzgerald mentioned. Do not concern yourself, though. Their bites don't do more than sting a bit. Mind you, they have been known to give some sensitive people a bad case of hives."

Edgar patted Sofia's hand. "It must be such a trial for your gardeners."

"Quite," Sofia replied, fanning her flushed cheeks with a napkin.

Lady Tabitha clucked. "Don't stray too far from the path

then, my dear," she warned Cynthia, as if imagining her daughter covered with disfiguring spots.

"I'll take care she doesn't, Lady Tabitha," Jon said, taking Cynthia's arm to lead her out. "We shall see you later, Miss Fitzgerald."

Andy nodded at his innocuous reminder of their appointment. "Of course. Good night everyone," she said with a final smile and curtsied to the remaining company. Her smile faded as she left the drawing room. Trying her best not to run, she hurried up the stairs to her father's room. While the diary should be safe enough in its hiding place, the letters worried her.

Some twenty minutes had gone by since Phillip left the drawing room. It was enough time for him to have found them and returned to his chambers. If Phillip discovered those letters, he would undoubtedly intensify his search for the diary, or try to impede their own search for the truth.

Not stopping to think what she would do if the Baron were in her father's rooms, she burst through the door.

No one.

She wondered at the unusual darkness. Leaving the door open, she went to the low blaze in the grate. The crackle of burning wood sounded overloud, like gunshots on a hunt. All her senses tingled. She lit a taper and glanced around, rubbing her arms against the sense of foreboding which had become her companion since the arrival of the guests. Turning slowly, she walked to her father's desk and lit the brace of candles with the taper.

The letters were gone. How could she have been so careless? She should have hidden them as well as the diary. It would be easier to discover the truth about Emily's marriage if it weren't turned into a race for the facts.

Maybe I'm imagining things and Phillip was never here, she thought, striving for optimism. Sitting down with a decided thump, she began to search methodically through the material she'd brought up earlier. It appeared to be in an unusually neat pile, she noted, quite unlike her father's haphazard style. Her hands trembling, she checked everything twice, even looking into some of the journals to see if her father might have placed the letters there for safekeeping.

No. They were gone. Still, perhaps her father had hidden them?

Blowing out all but one candle, Andy made her way to the gallery to retrieve the diary, unease dogging her steps, not abating until she felt the diary's worn cover behind the portrait of the first Marquess. Relief swept through her as she removed it. At least that was safe, she sighed. Now, if the letters were in Phillip's possession, she doubted her charade of being a helpless female would hold.

Entering her room cautiously, she was relieved that nothing seemed disturbed. Apparently, if Phillip had prowled about, he hadn't dared to search more than one room this evening. She prayed her father wouldn't be long. Only then would she know for sure about the letters. After that, it would be at least another hour before she could risk meeting Jon to tell him of what had transpired.

Placing the diary on the vanity, she rummaged through her night clothes, past the silks and lace night rails she preferred, and pulled out one of her few, practical flannel nightgowns with its equally uninspiring wrap. The unappealing appearance would not only divert anyone who might meet her, but should also discourage Jon of any untoward ideas.

Andy glanced in the mirror and made a face at the unattractive picture she presented. Wryly admitting that with someone like Cynthia around, Jon probably wouldn't even notice her—never mind anything she wore—she quelled an impulse to change. Because of her apparel, no one would suspect she was on her way to a rendezvous. Appearances were essential.

All she had to do now was wait.

*   *   *

Jonathon could have taken Cynthia down one of the more private paths. The lady seemed willing, but oddly enough, he wasn't. He preferred keeping her in full view of the lighted terrace. For some reason, she wasn't as enticing as he'd previously thought. Her artful chatter, which had once amused him, was now difficult to concentrate on. Jon gave an inward shrug. Perhaps he just had too much on his mind.

Cynthia's prattle tapered off.

Jon smothered a chuckle at the occasional glances she darted toward the ground. He halted in a move so sudden that Cynthia bumped her forehead against his shoulder.

"Wh . . . what is it?" she stuttered, her voice cracking. She let go of his sleeve. Raising her skirt slightly, she looked about her feet.

Jon frowned and glanced at the bushes before apologizing smoothly. "I'm sure it was nothing. I didn't mean to startle you."

He walked a few more steps, Cynthia clinging to his side even more tightly now. He stopped abruptly again. "Did you feel that?" he asked in a hushed voice, struggling to keep the grin out of his voice. Andy would enjoy this, he thought.

"No . . . I didn't feel anything, but I do believe it's becoming a bit chilly. Perhaps you could show me the rest of the garden tomorrow, Jonathon."

Jon looked at her wide eyes and pinched features. He patted her white knuckles, visible even in the poor light. He swallowed another grin, wondering if Andy, too, was afraid of snakes. "It will be my pleasure," he agreed with a final pat to her arm, leading her back to the other guests, wondering at his sense of relief. He'd have to remember to thank the Duchess for coming to his rescue. Soon, he thought, anticipating their next encounter. Soon.

* * *

The light dimmed with a sputter, and a whiff of waxy smoke drifted over. Andy raised her head from her notes. The candle had nearly burned itself out. That meant it should be safe enough to make her way to the rendezvous now.

Her father had stopped by on the way to his rooms and, castigating himself for being too distracted to check the pile of material she had given him, confirmed her worst fears. The absence of the letters could only mean someone had taken them.

Andy noticed he didn't explain what could possibly be distracting him. After reassuring him it really didn't change the course of the investigation, she'd spent a few moments going over her notes with him.

When she informed him about her upcoming meeting with Jonathon, her father subjected her to a piercing gaze. Andy accepted his scrutiny with a steady look of her own, pleased that she didn't blush.

He finally nodded in agreement. "You're right. The weight of the Marquess's name might get faster results for any necessary searches, particularly in this area where he's well known."

He proceeded to offer Andy a few helpful suggestions which she noted faithfully in her book, valuing her father's expertise in such matters.

"Please be careful, my dear," Edgar warned with a kiss to her forehead, preparing to leave.

"I will, Papa." Andy agreed, avoiding his gaze. Was he referring to the dangers the Baron might present, or to her upcoming meeting with Jon?

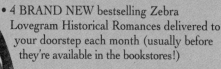

4 FREE BOOKS

These books worth almost $20, are yours without cost or obligation when you fill out and mail this certificate.
(If the certificate is missing below, write to: Zebra Home Subscription Service, Inc., 120 Brighton Road, P.O. Box 5214, Clifton, New Jersey 07015-5214)

Complete and mail this card to receive 4 Free books!

YES! Please send me 4 Zebra Lovegram Historical Romances without cost or obligation. I understand that each month thereafter I will be able to preview 4 new Zebra Lovegram Historical Romances FREE for 10 days. Then if I decide to keep them, I will pay the money-saving preferred publisher's price of just $4.00 each...a total of $16. That's almost $4 less than the regular publisher's price, and there is never any additional charge for shipping and handling. I may return any shipment within 10 days and owe nothing, and I may cancel this subscription at any time. The 4 FREE books will be mine to keep in any case.

Name _____

Address _____ Apt. _____

City _____ State _____ Zip _____

Telephone ( ) _____

Signature _____ LF0597
(If under 18, parent or guardian must sign.)

Terms, offer and prices subject to change without notice. Subscription subject to acceptance by Zebra Home Subscription Service, Inc.. Zebra Home Subscription Service, Inc. reserves the right to reject any order or cancel any subscription.

ZEBRA HOME SUBSCRIPTION SERVICE, INC.

120 BRIGHTON ROAD

P.O. BOX 5214

CLIFTON, NEW JERSEY 07015-5214

Chapter Nine

After placing the notes and diary into the pocket of her housecoat, Andy blew out the candle and opened her door cautiously, sidling out to survey the deserted passageway. Even with her slow advance, the occasional board creaked. The sound rang in her ears as loudly as firecrackers during a celebration and she couldn't prevent starting with guilt each time. The diary weighed heavier with each step she took.

She moved stealthily, without a lamp, depending on the few flickering candles left in odd sconces. The ever-changing shadows dancing on the walls made her skin crawl. Her heart pounded loudly in her ears and she clenched her fists, trying to prevent her imagination from taking flight. At this rate, she admonished herself, she'd be ready for Bedlam before ever reaching the library. The trip never seemed this long, or so harrowing, in the daytime.

Andy heaved a sigh of relief when she arrived at her destination without being detected. The door was slightly ajar. Jonathon must already be there. Thank goodness! She didn't relish the prospect of waiting for him alone in the dark. It was amazing how frightening the house seemed with its inhabitants sleeping—at least she hoped they were all sleeping. She stepped forward, reaching for the door handle.

A shadow separated itself from the wall. A large hand covered her mouth, stifling her scream. Another hand came under her breasts and yanked her back into a hard midriff.

Without hesitation, Andy bit down on the hand gripping her. Silently thanking her male cousins for educating her in the rudiments of self-defense, she slammed her elbow backward, contacting firm flesh, and was gratified by a muffled grunt. Before she could follow-up by stomping on her captor's foot, he whispered harshly into her ear.

''Duchess! Enough already!''

''You!'' Andy spun around, her fists clenched at her sides. But before she could berate Jon for playing childish games, he signaled for silence.

His shadowed scowl promising retaliation for the pain she'd inflicted, Jon ignored her unspoken question. Instead, he pressed her against the wall and peered into the library.

He glanced back at Andy and fingered her wrap's collar.

She swallowed. If the flickering flame from the solitary candle on the far wall was bright enough to highlight his sardonically arched brow and quirked lips, then it was also bright enough to reveal the frayed state of her flannel. Andy only hoped the shadows hid her flush. Once again, she forced herself to remember that the best defense was sometimes offense. She straightened her shoulders, ready to give him a piece of her mind. He halted her with the simple expedient of pressing a finger to her lips and shaking his head.

Jon took her hand and crouched down, motioning for her to do the same. His cautious movements alerted Andy and she followed suit, huddling behind him. Gradually, he opened the library door a little wider and slipped in, dragging her in his wake, not stopping until they were safely hidden behind a large armchair near the entrance. From there, he leaned over to slide the door back to its original position.

The light coming from the area of her worktable told Andy they weren't the only ones interested in visiting the library this evening. She shuddered at the knowledge and crawled quietly after Jonathon, moving along the floor, past book-filled shelves, toward the center of the room. Her hands sank into the plush carpet, and her heart beat furiously while she prayed nothing had been left out of place by a careless maid. They couldn't afford to bump into anything.

Jonathon finally halted their agonizingly slow progress behind a sofa. After thrusting her into a prone position, he lay down behind her. With little room between the sofa and the wall of books, Jon's chest pressed against her spine. The worn, thin flannel of her wrap and gown provided little protection from the rough fabric of the sofa's skirt rubbing against her breasts, and Andy shifted uncomfortably. She refrained from complaining, though, because of their unexpected guest.

From here, if they leaned over, they could see Phillip St. James without being detected. He sat at her desk, riffling through her meticulous notes.

"Transcribing for her father . . . hah!" Phillip muttered aloud. "Bloody hag thought she could fool me. She *is* a bluestocking. Knew it the moment I laid eyes on her."

Hearing his imprecations, Andy cringed. She was going to have to think of a good reason for her deception to appease him on the morrow. Otherwise, what was promising to be an unpleasant visit might turn out to be positively nasty. After that, she didn't poke her head out to look at the Baron anymore and tried not to pay any mind to his mutterings. Being referred to as a bluestocking hadn't hurt. It was being called a hag which piqued.

As the moments passed, she grew more and more anxious for the Baron to leave. At least there wasn't any trace of dust to irritate her nostrils, thanks to the tight way the Marchioness and Mrs. Simms ran the household. Even so, her position was distressing. It wasn't so much the hard floor, or the sofa in front of her. Rather, it was her proximity to Jonathon.

Where his hand had originally rested on her shoulder, it had somehow slipped down and around to the front of her belly, gliding up her midriff. Now it rested under her housecoat, just beneath her left breast. As if that weren't bad enough, Jonathon's hips were moving deeper against her buttocks. She had a sinking suspicion the hardness pressing against her had nothing to do with his bones.

The rogue was definitely taking advantage of her, and there wasn't a thing she could do to prevent it. Andy fumed, then swallowed a moan. Her anger melted. Their predicament faded from her mind when Jon tugged at the back of her gown and followed his movement by trailing silent little kisses along her nape, retracing the path with flicks of his tongue.

Phillip cursed again and she came back to reality with a start. Her cheeks burned from Jon's liberties and her reaction to them. Furious, as much with herself as with the Marquess, she jabbed his ribs sharply with an elbow. His body shook in response. Andy cringed. Knowing Jon, it was probably from silent laughter, not pain.

He tugged gently at her hair. She turned and glared at him and realized he probably couldn't see her reaction . . . no, he hadn't gotten the message at all. Instead, he began brushing his lips against her cheek.

Phillip's fresh curses stopped her from turning into Jon's embrace.

"Damn! Nothing here." Slamming down the journals he'd been perusing, Phillip made a sound of disgust. The chair scraped against the corner of the desk when he stood.

Andy finally dared to peek around the sofa. Phillip lifted the candle, turning to take a final look around the library. She drew back sharply.

"Have they found it?" he asked aloud. "Does it even exist? The letters can't prove a thing." He didn't sound convinced.

Andy shuddered as she listened to his frustration. So he *had* taken the letters from her father's room. What if he now discovered them? She tucked her chin tightly against her chest, glad that Jon was with her.

Phillip shuffled the papers on her desk.

Andy supposed he did so to erase the evidence of his search. She heaved a sigh of relief when he left with the candle, plunging the room into darkness, but followed Jon's suit by not moving immediately. There was always the chance the Baron might return.

When Jon's rough palm began inching its way beneath her wrap, however, Andy'd had enough. Baron or no, she struggled to wiggle out of his grasp—only Jon wouldn't let her go. She turned her head to berate him, unable to see in the dark.

Unfortunately, Jon had also moved and her chin cracked into his forehead with a hard thump. A sadistic sense of satisfaction at his pained grunt soothed her own aching jaw. Her skirts twisted, she succeeded in facing him. "Good. You deserved that, you lecher," she said, rubbing her chin.

"Has no one ever tried to curb your proclivity for violence? I'll probably be covered with bruises by morning."

Andy twisted again.

Jon growled and gripped her hips. "Now, kindly stop moving like that, or there will be even more damage done. My valet might never forgive me."

Andy flushed, recalling the episode with the buttons. "I'm sorry," she apologized, remembering to keep her voice low in case the Baron was still wandering near the library. "Sort of, that is," she amended after an uncomfortable pause.

He didn't respond.

"Could we please get up now? The floor is awfully hard." Jon only nudged closer.

Refusing to acknowledge the desire he awakened, she

rewarded his boldness with another blow, one which landed on his shoulder this time.

"Pax, Duchess. Honestly, though, if you don't cease that immediately, I'm going to have a word with your father. Either that, or ask Lady Cynthia to give you some lessons in deportment," Jon warned even as his grip eased.

Andy heard the smile in his voice, focusing on that instead of the heat invading her being. She stood and, leaning against the couch, adopted a wry tone. "Perhaps that wouldn't be such a bad idea," she mused. "Do you suppose Cynthia could also help me acquire a proper fear of snakes? I've always had a problem with that."

"I take it you're not afraid of the creatures?"

"Not in the least," Andy chuckled. "As a matter of fact, I had several as pets when I was a child. They had a habit of finding their way into the beds of governesses I didn't like."

"We used spiders or frogs. The frogs tended to be a problem, though, because of their tendency to croak and give warning." Jon suddenly gripped her shoulders.

Andy could almost feel him peering down at her in the dark.

"Does this mean I'll need to check my bed from now on?"

"You're not my governess," Andy pointed out before envisioning how he might retaliate. An oddly delicious shiver rippled through her.

Jon's voice lowered. "Perhaps not, but I'd like to think there's still a thing or two I might be able to teach you."

Andy's heart fluttered at the innuendo, and at his nearness. She made a halfhearted attempt at thrusting him away. He still wouldn't let her go. Her hip brushed against the sofa and the diary in her pocket dug into her, reminding her of their purpose for meeting in the dead of night. She turned her head away, trying to ignore the way his breath tickled her sensitive ear. "Enough of this."

"Could I have just one little kiss before we get down to business?"

"No!" Andy exploded, no longer caring if they were discovered. She shoved at him and jerked backward, lurching into the globe near the sofa. Quickly, she spun round, barely managing to steady the globe on its stand.

"Be careful," Jon laughed without offering any assistance.

"Will you kindly get over here and help me?"

"All right, all right," he grumbled. "You're certainly no fun to be stuck with in a dark room. Wait there before you do any more damage. I'll get a light."

Material rustled as he patted his pockets. A moment later, he held a lit candle. The sputtering flame accented his devilish grin.

Andy crossed her arms in front of herself. "Vexing man! You had a light with you all this time? How long were you going to let me stumble around in the dark?"

"Until you tumbled into my arms asking for aid."

Her innate sense of humor came to the fore. Grin wry, Andy informed him, "You really are a hopeless bounder, you know."

Jon merely smiled at her assessment instead of arguing. Seating her at her desk, he sat facing her on its corner, barely resisting an urge to brush the tumbled hair back from her face. As much as he enjoyed their playful repartee, it was time for some serious discussion. "What exactly was Phillip referring to when he spoke about the letters? My aunt mentioned something to me, but just in passing."

Andy explained the contents of the letters. "Unfortunately, while I had realized the importance of hiding Emily's diary, I'm afraid I forgot about the letters. They were stuck between the correspondence I gave my father. When I went to check his room after dinner, the letters were gone. Apparently, Phillip got there first. I wouldn't make a very good agent, would I?"

He comforted her chagrin with a quick kiss to the cheek. "It's true, I'm afraid. Wellington would have appreciated your beauty and your intelligence, but he'd be less than pleased with your skills in covert operations." He leaned back, absently rustling through her papers. "Did the letters contain any definite reference to a marriage?"

Lips pursed, Andy paused. Her gaze wandered over a far bookshelf while she considered her response.

Jon could almost see her visualizing each letter in her mind. His fingers curled around a jade paperweight on her desk. It was a match to one on his own desk—a carving of Burne. He struggled to concentrate on the statue instead of the worried lines on her face. He was tempted to smooth away her fears with kisses—a temptation which surprised him. He wasn't accustomed to concern for women who weren't members of his family. He wasn't accustomed, either, to women capable of thinking beyond the next rout or their wardrobe. Andy's words brought him back to the present.

"No, there wasn't," she finally answered, her tone decisive.

"There wasn't what?"

Andy stared at him as though he were a simpleton.

"Oh . . . the marriage lines. . . . You might not make a good agent, but there certainly doesn't appear to be anything wrong with your memory—unlike mine." Jon tweaked a loose strand of her hair.

Andy withdrew, frowning, ready to take umbrage, but he forestalled her. "What about the diary? Have you had a chance to learn anything from that?"

"There was an exchange of vows between the two. But whether the vows were the sort made privately between lovers, or in a way recognized by law, I'm just not sure."

Andy passed him the journal. "Lady Emily seems to have been a very sweet soul. Unfortunately, the clarity of her writing leaves a lot to be desired. She didn't even bother dating all of her entries. Yet it's evident from the slant of her writing and color of the ink that these, for example, were made at different times."

Jon glanced at the entries she pointed to. When he looked

up, her features were even more pensive. "Did you finish reading all of it?" She nodded. "Would it help to reread it?"

"Possibly, but I don't really think so. Although I'm not a particularly good agent, I'm a fairly decent sleuth. Emily left a number of hints—whether inadvertently or intentionally, I don't know." Her voice devoid of pride, she held out some scribbled notes together with the diary.

Jon turned the key in the lock before accepting them. "I'd just as soon not have any interruptions, or invite any eavesdroppers." Taking the papers from her, he leaned down to whisper in her ear, "Besides, with the door locked, I can have my wicked way with you, Duchess, and no one will be able to rescue you from my clutches," he teased, unable to remain serious with her for too long.

Andy gave an unladylike snort as he stood back. Jon grinned and dropped a fast kiss on her shoulder.

She turned and picked up a heavy encyclopedia with both hands, her intent obvious. Her own smile faded and she dropped the book with a resounding smack. "This is not a joking matter."

Jon winced at the reminder. "You're correct as usual," he sighed. Putting down the diary and notes on his own desk, he lit the lamp.

Andy followed him and fixed him with a pointed stare. "By the way, before we continue, would you mind explaining why you had to attack me like that in the hallway? You nearly frightened me out of my wits. You knew Phillip was here. Wouldn't it have been more sensible for you simply to walk in and disturb his search? You could have done so without raising any suspicion."

"Correct again, Duchess," he agreed, "and I apologize most profusely for startling you. But, however reasonable it would've been for me to walk in on the good Baron, it simply wouldn't have been as much fun. Didn't you find the experience even a touch exciting?" He wiggled his eyebrows.

Andy groaned. "I once had a governess who tried to teach me that there was a time and place for everything."

"Was that one of the governesses who found a snake in her bed?"

Andy tapped her chin. Her thoughtful pose lasted less than a moment. Her nose wrinkled and she grinned. "As a matter of fact, it was. She was truly horrible . . . but that's neither here nor there." She pulled a chair closer to his desk and sat down, shuffling through her notes. By the time he'd seated himself, the papers were reorganized into several piles.

"Father went over these and made a few additional suggestions as to how we might pick up the trail, even after so many years. I also took the liberty of penciling in page numbers as I went through the diary. If and when Dominic gets his mother's journal, I hope he won't mind." Andy looked up in question.

"I'm sure he won't," Jon responded.

Andy nodded and pointed to one pile of sheets. "These notes contain all the references Emily made in regards to her possible marriage. Where no dates were indicated, I tried to approximate. She and Richard seemed to move around a fair bit before they went to the Continent. Sometimes she mentioned the actual places, but most times she didn't—so I also had to guess at some locations."

Sighing, she sat back. "For the moment, I'm assuming Emily and Richard married in England, if at all. Once we hear from the various sources, we'll know if we need to look farther afield. We have to keep in mind, though, that they might have married in Europe. If so, it could delay our investigation significantly."

While she spoke, Jon read through the notes she'd indicated. When she paused, he looked up. "The diary's missing pages?"

Andy shrugged. "They might have proven invaluable. However . . . ?" she said, her palms spread upward in a helpless gesture.

"Damn shame." He shook his head, his lips twisting as he

recalled his spiteful uncle. He reached for the second pile of papers. ''And these are in regards to . . . ?''

''People whom we'll need to contact for information. I'm afraid that's where you come in.''

At her hesitation, Jon sat forward and met Andy's intent gaze with a steady one of his own. ''You should know that Dominic is probably the closest friend I've ever had. If there's anything I can do to smooth his way in life, I am more than willing to do it. Just tell me what.''

Apparently satisfied by his sincerity, she nodded. ''The work is actually more tedious than difficult. It will be necessary to initiate a tremendous amount of delicate correspondence. Since you make your home in the same area as Emily and the Baron did, letters in your name will carry more weight than if my father would write them. Those should go as soon as possible, probably by special messenger—especially if we're to stay ahead of Phillip. Of course, I'm willing to assist you.''

Jon gazed at her, taking in her serious features, knowing he shouldn't be as surprised as he was at her competence. He'd known for a long time that she was different from other women. For a moment, he struggled with his conscience, cursing himself for his tendency to act the rogue in her presence. He was too attracted to her by half. Finally, he nodded. ''Very well. Where do we start?''

''If you're planning any activities for your guests away from the manor, you might consider something which would allow us to visit nearby parishes, particularly those in the vicinity of a lake. . . . Emily made several references to a body of water in conjunction with their vows. When we stop for tea, one of us could slip away to view the parish registers. Thankfully, the marriage occurred relatively recently—speaking in historical terms, that is—and registers are easier to read now.'' Andy placed her elbows on the desk with a theatrical sigh. ''God bless Lord Hardwick for introducing the Marriage Act.''

Jon returned her impish grin with one of his own and leaned

forward. He was actually enjoying a meaningful conversation with a woman. "I thought that was a long time ago. Besides, how would it affect us?"

Andy rested her chin on her hands and rolled her eyes. "It wasn't *that* long ago. It was in 1754 and it most certainly does affect us. Without Hardwick, there still wouldn't be standard printed forms used to record marriages." Her forehead wrinkled, and gnawing on her bottom lip, she mused, "Hopefully, none of the local registers are missing or destroyed. Otherwise we'll be saddled with more correspondence, double-checking with the diocese for any annual copies of registers submitted by incumbents."

She took a deep breath and shot him a hesitant look. "Of course, you realize that, if a marriage took place without the reading of the banns, it would be considered void—even if it were performed by a chaplain."

Jon leaned back, absently stroking his jade carving of Burne, beginning to realize just what a maze the search could lead them into. He felt a sudden chill and put the carving aside. "Yes, I know. Unless, of course, they went to Scotland or the Channel Islands, where consent to a marriage before witnesses would suffice. Or they could've obtained a special license from a bishop, thus dispensing with banns."

"Exactly," Andy agreed. "In which case we need to figure out which bishop they might have approached for a special license. The Bishop for Kent will need to be contacted if they married in this area. Since both Emily and Richard were residents here, he could have granted them one, but only if they were to be married in his diocese." She proceeded to further muddy already murky water by explaining what would happen if they were married outside the jurisdiction.

Jon's head spun as she rattled off the names of Canterbury and York's Vicars-General, and the Archbishop of Canterbury's Master of Faculties. When she added that politics could also have played a part in deciding whom Richard would approach, he held up his hands. "Good lord! Let's hope it doesn't come to that. What else needs to be done?" He picked up a quill to take notes.

"We might as well request information on the probate of any will Richard might have had, or the administration of his estate at the same time. As distasteful as the idea might seem, it could have serious repercussions in this case."

Jon brushed the quill against his chin, musing, "You're absolutely correct. Since Richard died at sea, we'd have to contact the Prerogative Court of Canterbury, wouldn't we?"

Andy gave him an odd look. "That's right."

Jon assumed an affronted mien. "I'm not exactly a useless fribble, you know. I do have some grasp of technical legal matters. I even know that the Archbishop could grant letters of administration to the heirs if Richard didn't have a will."

Andy's slight giggle at his schoolboy manner was quickly followed with a shudder. "What if Richard were declared to have died in England as opposed to at sea? It would mean a minor temporal court could probate his estate, potentially resulting in tremendous mismanagement. The legal ramifications are frightening."

Jon leaned back in his chair. His fingers steepled under his chin, he shook his head. "I can't imagine someone in Richard's position, or anyone who owns something for that matter, not having a will. However, if one is considering possibilities, his will could have been destroyed, giving the Archbishop the authority to divide Richard's property amongst his closest surviving family . . . in other words, Phillip and his father."

"Ugh!" Andy exclaimed with a moue of distaste. "In other words, the type of machinations one would expect of Italians."

Jon's brow rose. "On behalf of all Englishmen, I take exception to that," he shot back. "Our penchant for intrigue is no less than that of the Italians. It's just that we tend to be more sportsmanlike about it," he added in a pompous tone.

"But of course. I forgot Englishmen tend to spare the women and children. Is that what you mean?"

Jon inclined his head. "My compliments on your superior powers of deduction."

Her impish grin was replaced with a thoughtful look. "What will happen to Phillip if Dominic proves to be legitimate?"

"The legal work will be incredibly tedious, as I'm sure you're well aware of. Phillip's estate books and records of bank accounts will be closely scrutinized. Once Phillip relinquishes the baronetcy to Dominic, it will be up to Dominic to decide whether or not to seek additional reparation through the courts—though I doubt he will."

Jon paused and shrugged. "As for Phillip, he should survive his change of circumstance. His mother was quite wealthy and he inherited the bulk of her estate. How he will deal with the unavoidable scandal is another matter. He's always been quite conscious of his position in Society." Jon's lip curled, unable to hide his disdain.

"Well, so long as he won't be left out on the streets to fend for himself. I honestly wouldn't feel very comfortable with that happening either," Andy admitted.

Jon silently agreed, even though he'd never really cared for Phillip. He gathered the papers into one neat pile. "If the amount of correspondence you've indicated is necessary, then it will be quite a while before we need to concern ourselves with that. Is there anything else I should be made aware of?"

"You mean other than the fact that nothing might ever be proven and that all of this work may be for naught? Or that we might need to expand the search to the Continent?" Andy sighed. "I think that about sums it up for now."

Jon grinned at her glum tone. He struck a self-righteous pose. "You really don't have any sense of adventure, do you? Have some faith, Duchess. Besides, I believe in the power of positive thought." He ducked to avoid the crumpled sheet of vellum Andy hurled at him in response.

Jon picked up Emily's diary. All traces of levity vanished. "If you don't mind, I'd like to read this and keep it together with the notes you've made."

Andy's relief was obvious. "You're welcome to it. I would just as soon not have the responsibility of its safekeeping," she admitted and stood to leave.

Jon put the items in his jacket pocket and placed his hand under her elbow. His glance sober, he asked, "We're agreed that Dom should know nothing of this just yet?"

Andy nodded.

"Very well, then. Will you be able to help me initiate the correspondence in the morning? With your training, you'll know precisely what must be said. I'd hate to delay our investigation by leaving out pertinent questions or details."

"Certainly," Andy affirmed in a quiet voice. She avoided his gaze by tugging at the belt of her disreputable wrap, looking unaccountably shy.

She isn't accustomed to being praised, Jon realized. Hadn't anyone besides her father ever complimented her on her skills? He thought about the circles they both moved in. His grip on her tightened and he shook his head. Probably not. Her voice interrupted his thoughts.

"We could meet after breakfast. Hopefully your guests aren't the type to rise early and require entertaining immediately upon doing so."

"I believe it's against their religion," Jon drawled. His good humor restored, he offered a formal bow. "May I escort you to your room, Miss Fitzgerald?"

Andy's shyness vanished. She pursed her lips and shot him a prim glare. "Your escort to my *door* would not be amiss, Lord Baldwin."

Jon chuckled. Leaning to extinguish the lamp, his glance raked over her outfit. "By the way, Duchess, I may have forgotten to mention it earlier, but I must say your current apparel puts me in mind of some of the more intolerable governesses I've had.''

''Exactly as it should.'' The twinkle in her eyes belied her frosty tone.

Jon swallowed another chuckle and blew out the candle, not at all put out by the tart response.

Chapter Ten

Andy couldn't help being grateful for Jon's escort as they slipped through the darkened mansion. Most of the lights in the hallways had long since sputtered out. Unfamiliar as she was with the surroundings, it made the trip back to her room not only eerier, but also more dangerous.

Jonathon, apparently, had no such qualms and led the way without hesitation. Either the man was gifted with the eyes of a cat or he had honed his nocturnal skills by lurking around the darkened bedrooms of his paramours. Banishing that particular thought and the painful twist it caused somewhere deep inside her, Andy concentrated on putting one foot in front of the other without stumbling.

When they reached their wing without incident, Jon stopped, dug a candle out of his pocket, and lit it. "It should be safe to have some light now," he whispered, taking her hand once more.

Ghostly dancing shadows now flickered along the murky gloom of the walls. Andy shivered. She clung to Jonathon, almost preferring the darkness they had just emerged from, and she didn't breathe easily until they reached her room. Jon eased open her door and she nodded gratefully. All appeared well. Her gratitude, however, quickly disappeared when he tried to follow her in.

"I just want to make sure Phillip didn't find his way here while we were gone."

Andy rounded on him with a snort. "What a cropper! Don't you think that rather unlikely, considering Phillip would have expected me to be in here sleeping? Sounds more to me like an excuse to gain entrance to a woman's bedroom."

Instead of accepting her dismissal, Jon dipped the wick of his candle to light the one in the sconce by her door. Extinguishing his own taper, he appraised her with a frankly sensual look, and a roguish grin illuminated his features. "All I want to do is to make sure you're safely tucked into bed," he coaxed.

Andy studied Jon's now guileless expression, not trusting it *or* him a whit, and tried to ignore the fluttering in her stomach as well as the small voice in her mind urging her to damn propriety to perdition. "I think you'd better leave now," she said, silently cursing the quiver in her voice.

"But I know some excellent bedtime stories."

Andy wasn't proof against his wheedling, boyish tone even as she refused his offer. "Thank you, my lord. Perhaps you could give me a copy of the tales. I'm sure my young cousins would appreciate hearing them the next time I visit." She stifled a yawn and slumped against the door frame, her arms crossed protectively in front of herself. "Forgive me. It's been a hectic day . . . and night, for that matter. I am truly tired, Jon." She looked longingly at the inside of her room to avoid the gaze stirring forbidden heat within her and hoped she sounded convincing.

Immediately contrite, he apologized softly. "I'm forgetting the debt my family owes you. My apologies. Go to bed then, Duchess. After all, we've another full day ahead of us tomorrow." Then, seemingly as loath to leave as she was to see him go, he glanced downward at her disreputable robe and frowned, fingering its frayed lapel, moving it slightly to reveal the equally plain, worn-out gown the robe hid. "Good lord, Andy! Those things should have been exiled at the same time as that governess of yours."

Andy merely grinned but her smile faded as she met his suddenly inscrutable gaze. Her breathing faltered. It was as though he was waiting. But waiting for what?

"Madam?" he whispered as his fingers found their way to her hair, rearranging the tresses so they fanned out over the collar of her robe to frame her face and neck.

Unsure of what the question was, Andy remained silent, worrying he might hear the increased staccato beat of her heart against her ribcage.

"Even more beautiful than I imagined," he murmured, still threading his fingers through her hair, his voice tinged with wonder.

She forgot about her fatigue. She forgot about the work to be done tomorrow. She forgot about the possibility that someone might chance upon their tryst. All she could think of was that no one had ever been as fascinated by her as Jonathon appeared to be. He made her feel so ... beautiful. Her lips, moistened by her nervous tongue, parted.

He lowered his face toward hers and whispered, "Now, how about a good night kiss for your faithful nanny?" Before she could protest, his warm mouth pressed against her throat.

She made a halfhearted attempt to push him away. His fingers crept, stroking from her collarbone to the curve of her shoulder. The arms Andy had meant to push him away with instead found themselves wrapped around his neck, urging him closer, the heat of his fingers against her skin shocking her. Her eyes widened, then shut. Frantically, she tried to remind herself of the propriety she'd just damned. However, when he pressed his firm body against hers, she forgot about modesty, her exhaustion, and everything else, and simply whimpered in longing.

Jon groaned and suddenly, much to Andy's consternation, he leaped away from her. "No, Duchess. You're not going to seduce me . . . at least, not tonight." He shot her another boyish grin.

"You!" Indignant, Andy swung a clenched fist at his shoulder.

He jumped back, safely out of reach, his grin widening, his palms out in self-protection. "I like to play games as much as the next person, but they will have to wait, my dear. It's past your bedtime." Then, rubbing his hands together in obvious pride, he asked, "Well, what do you think, Duchess? Wouldn't I make a wonderful nanny?"

Still confused by his unexpected about-face, Andy felt a soft smile tug at her lips. She couldn't make any sense of his actions, but the turmoil of the long day had taken its toll and she was suddenly deeply fatigued. Her eyelids drooped and she opened her door wider, ready to go in. "I don't think so," she mumbled sleepily.

"Pardon me?" Jon asked, halting, about to extinguish the candle in the sconce.

"You wouldn't have made a good nanny at all. You don't even know how to kiss like my nurse did," she murmured past another yawn, entering her room.

"I can always practice—anytime you're ready, love."

Jon's roguish grin was the last thing she remembered as she closed her eyes and allowed sleep to claim her.

"Can I help you with anything in particular today?" Dominic asked as he prepared to leave the breakfast table.

Jon shook his head. "There's only some minor correspondence to do . . . nothing overly demanding. As a matter of fact, anyone with a few basic transcribing skills could do it."

Smirking, Jon turned to Andy. "Miss Fitzgerald, perhaps I could impose upon you? I'm sure Dominic has more important things to do."

Andy's foot connected to Jonathon's shin with a decided and very audible thump.

Dominic didn't even attempt to choke back his laughter, wagging a finger at Jon's muffled oath. "Admit it, Jon. You deserved that."

"I have yet to meet another woman with such aggressive tendencies," Jon groaned before adding, "Thank heavens!"

Dominic turned to Andy. "Actually, there are a few things I'd like to catch up on. Would you mind terribly giving up your morning to help Jon?"

Directing a saccharine smile at Jonathon, Andy batted her eyelids. "Are you sure, my lord, that I'd be capable of handling the work?" she asked, her voice breathless.

Jon sat back, clasped his hands across his stomach, and studied her. After a short pause, he replied pompously, "I'm sure you could. Besides, I'll be there to supervise, in the event you encounter problems."

"Oh, you're too kind, my lord," Andy gushed, her lashes fluttering demurely.

"Very well, then. That's decided," Dom interrupted their exchange with a grin. "I shall leave the two of you to it, then. I only pray you won't come to blows."

With Dom out of earshot, Jon rose. "I thought I did that rather well, don't you? Dom didn't suspect a thing," he said, escorting her from the room.

"My congratulations on your subtlety," Andy shot back. Their levity faded once they entered the library.

"What now?" Jon asked, seating her at her usual place.

"I'll start on the letters. The one to the Archbishop of Canterbury will be the most involved. You may have the pleasure of making a list of parishes within a hundred-mile radius, noting which ones are near a significant body of water . . . I'm sure you can handle that, my lord,'' she added with a condescending smile. ''But if you should run into any problems, don't worry. I shall be here to help you.''

Jon's lips quirked as he rolled up his sleeves, ready for the work ahead. ''I was afraid you wouldn't forget that line.''

When Andy leaned back in her chair a few hours later to massage the crick in her neck, she was surprised at what they had accomplished. A pile of neatly sanded, stacked correspondence attested to the fact that she and Jonathon worked well in tandem.

''I'm glad that's done,'' Jon uttered, brushing back his hair from his forehead, echoing her relief. ''Not exactly the most exciting aspect of your work, is it?'' He went to ring for Simms.

Andy nodded. She slumped forward, resting her cheek on folded arms. ''It's like being an archeologist. When people look at something like the Elgin marbles, they never consider the countless hours and labor spent to dig them up, clean, and then assemble them.''

''M'lord, m'lady,'' Simms greeted upon entering the room. ''You rang?''

''These letters need to be sent out by special messenger.'' Jon exchanged a glance with Andy.

Andy looked at the devoted butler for a moment, then nodded at Jon. She knew they could trust Simms with their purpose.

Jon explained the search briefly before adding, ''Absolutely no one must know these are being sent. When the replies come, they are to go directly from your hands to either Miss Fitzgerald or myself. Under no circumstances are they to be left unattended on a desk or a table. I'm sure you realize the sensitive nature of this inquiry. May we count on your discretion?''

Indignant, Simms huffed, ''Have I ever let you down before, sir?''

Andy looked on amused while Jonathon spent the next several minutes smoothing the butler's ruffled feathers. Nevertheless, it was obvious that Jon genuinely appreciated the man, even though they were from different classes. Her breath stilled and her smile faded. For some odd reason, his loyalty brought a lump to her throat. Simms departed and they settled back to work.

Her stomach was rumbling by the time they went for tea. She and Jon had worked their way through luncheon, barely touching the contents of the tray which Simms had personally brought them. Her stomach growled again, only more loudly this time. Andy flushed and pressed a hand against it.

Jon's eyebrows rose a notch. "Mmm," he purred into her ear. "I just love a woman with a strong appetite."

Andy clenched her jaw, trying to tame the proclivity toward violence that Jon had accused her of having. "I'm sure I have mentioned this to you before, but it obviously bears repeating. You are nothing more than an old incorrigible bounder!"

A footman moved to open the door to the drawing room for them. Andy noted his lips twitching as they passed by and she groaned. He must have heard her quiet accusation.

Jon assumed a hurt expression and whispered back, "I'm not that old."

Andy looked back at the footman. She caught his grin widening as the door closed behind them.

A stiff-looking Lady Sofia greeted them with what appeared to be considerable relief. Andy glanced at Tabitha, who was resting her hand on Edgar's sleeve, seemingly hanging on to every word he uttered. Could that explain the Marchioness's mood?

Preening, Cynthia was emulating her mother. She leaned toward Phillip in reward for his obvious attentiveness. Barbara, Helen, and Dom were at the piano. If this kept up, Andy mused, Helen might become an accomplished musician—if only she could learn to keep her eyes on the notes instead of on Dom. And she'd need to use more than just a couple of fingers from her right hand!

Andy's inward smile faded. She sensed the same strong

loyalty in Helen that she had in the Marquess. She knew Helen interpreted any slight toward Dom as a slight toward herself. That probably explained why they didn't sit closer to the Baron.

Cynthia brought her head up sharply when Jon greeted his aunt. Sending Phillip for another cup of tea, she invited Andy to join her. "May I call you Andy? Or perhaps you'd prefer that silly name Jon has for you?" she asked, her gaze narrowing. "What was it? Countess? No, that wasn't it. Oh, I remember now. It was Duchess." She brought a hand against her thin smile.

Sensing the upcoming interrogation, Andy gritted her teeth and recalled several Latin declensions before politely replying, "Andrea will suffice."

Her nails were pressed firmly against her scar by the time Jon finally bowed over Cynthia's hand some ten minutes later, ending the pointed grilling. The blonde cast her a dismissive glance, signifying the interview was over. Glad to escape, Andy gave a brief nod and excused herself, cringing at Cynthia's opening comments to Jon.

"I feel so sorry for her, don't you, Jonathon?" Cynthia's voice assumed a false compassion. "So tall, you know. A pity, really. Her looks are passable, I suppose, but that height . . ."

Jon's gaze followed the sway of Andy's hips as she went to her father. The woman at his side might be the current toast of the Ton, but the woman walking away was far more enticing. He schooled his features into a polite expression without deigning to reply.

Cynthia placed a delicate hand on his arm and wisely dropped the subject. "I just don't know how you can bear to be buried out in the country, especially when the weather is so unpredictable, Jonathon," she complained, her lips puckering into a petulant bow. "That horrible mist just won't go away, and here I was, so looking forward to the stroll you promised."

"The gods must be conspiring against us," he replied, striving to keep his voice smooth.

Andy, still near enough to overhear them, arched her brow. He winked at her grimace. She looked away and he turned back to Cynthia.

"I promise to make it up to you as soon as possible." He continued on in a similar vein, soothing Cynthia with his suave manner. It was like being back in London. The feeling stifled him and he was relieved when Phillip returned with her tea. "Let's hope the weather is less inclement in the morning so we can go riding. If the country has nothing else to recommend it, one can at least enjoy a bruising ride, quite unlike the restrained canters about the parks in Town. You should enjoy that, especially since you're such an excellent horsewoman."

"You do have the right of it, Jonathon." She inclined her head, accepting the compliment with another touch to his arm.

Jonathon was reminded of the tentacles of an octopus and he blinked at the image. It really didn't fit the lovely Lady Cynthia.

Unaware of his thoughts, the lady blithely continued. "I just love the feel of all that hard muscle pounding away beneath me." Her gaze lowered. Her tongue darted out, brushing against her lower lip in blatant invitation.

Jon glanced at Andy. He swallowed a groan at her quiet snort. She turned her head away quickly. His nostrils flaring in disgust, he looked back at the beauty by his side, trying to maintain a cool fascade. *I never realized how brazen the hussy is. Now what have I gotten myself into?* he thought. At the same time, he noted Phillip's eyes glaze over at her shockingly bold innuendo.

However, other than a slight smile, Jon once more avoided responding to Cynthia's comments. Instead, he proposed the ride be followed up by an expedition to one of the nearby towns. Including the company at large in the invitation, he insisted Tabitha join them. He glanced at Andy again. She didn't look particularly thrilled even though the town contained one of the parishes from the list they had drawn up. *Now, what was wrong with her?*

Andy had enough of watching Cynthia and Jon flirt with each other. She'd noticed how his nostrils flared at Cynthia's overtures. Disgusted, she turned away, taking another sandwich. Finally replete, she stifled an urge to belch. She looked up from the few remaining crumbs on her plate and caught Phillip's malevolent glare. It was the third such she had noticed this afternoon. She would to have to find an excuse for misrepresenting herself, and soon.

When Helen waved at her, Andy gladly made her excuses to her distracted father and escaped to the piano. Relieved at being safely out of range from both Cynthia's conversation and Phillip's barely concealed suspicion, she plopped down on a nearby armchair with a total disregard for ladylike behavior. "I do believe I've had enough for today."

Helen stifled a giggle. Dom shot her a reproving look.

"It isn't that bad, is it?" Barbara asked with an understanding smile.

Too understanding. Andy swallowed a groan at her transparency. The two women were so different, she'd forgotten Barbara was Cynthia's cousin. She stumbled for an excuse for her irritation. "It's just that I was up early, helping the Marquess with correspondence."

"Really?" Barbara shook her head in disbelief and glanced toward her cousin.

Andy's gaze followed hers and saw Jon slide a finger along his collar.

Barbara chuckled. "You forget how well I know Cynthia."

Helen's eyes twinkled. "Jonathon looks a little warm, doesn't he?"

Dom grinned. "Perhaps I'd best go over and see if I cool him off a trifle."

Helen laid a hand on his arm, trying to halt his departure. "Wouldn't you rather stay with us for a while, Dom?"

Dom removed her hand gently and shook his head. "Duty to one's friend and all that, you know. Besides which, I might learn something from him on how to fascinate women. You must admit, Jon has a talent for it."

Andy frowned and opened her mouth.

Dom circumvented the tart rejoinder she was about to make. "You're grinding your teeth, Miss Fitzgerald. Didn't your nurse ever tell you how unhealthy that is?" He shot the women a hasty smile and beat a retreat.

A sudden vision of Jon offering to play nanny the night before popped into Andy's mind. She shook her head to clear the disturbing memory and turned to Helen and Barbara, whose undemanding chatter finally soothed her.

The next day dawned clear and warm. Cynthia separated Jonathon from the crowd during the morning ride without any difficulty and they were already some distance ahead.

Andy decided she wouldn't let Cynthia's maneuvering bother her. After all, what difference did it make as to whom Jonathon showered his attentions upon? She patted her quiet, steady mare on the neck, trying to banish the hurt feeling budding somewhere in the region of her heart. Lifting her face to the fresh breeze, she gave herself up to the pleasure of the slow ride. Her satisfaction didn't last long.

Phillip cantered up alongside her. Barbara, Helen, and Dom fell behind. Phillip gave her a curt nod before asking snidely, "How is the transcribing coming along, Miss Fitzgerald?"

One look at his suspicious gaze and Andy decided it was time to practice her feminine wiles. Reaching out a hand to slow his progress, she looked up at him, struggling to keep her expression free from guile. Her mind working furiously, she noted the Baron was actually quite attractive in a shallow, if shifty, way.

"I hope you'll ride with me for a few moments, Sir Phillip," she invited, assuming a grateful smile at his condescending nod. They rode together silently. She wondered what to do next. The Baron was obviously not going to make this any easier for her.

"May I confide in you?" Andy finally asked, her voice breathless. Phillip gave her a blank look. *He's forgotten I exist.* So much for her feminine wiles. Still, she didn't give up. Casting her gaze demurely to her hands holding the reins, she sucked in a deep breath and began to weave a hesitant tale. "I'm afraid I haven't been totally honest with you. You're *so-oo* different from the normal fribble of Society that you've probably already caught me out."

A sidelong glance assured Andy she now had his full attention. He looked pleased with himself, as though assuming she had just complimented him. She wasn't about to point out he was unusual because most gentlemen didn't go skulking around libraries in the dark of night to ferret out secrets. He looked at her expectantly. Andy cleared her throat.

"Yes ... I actually do more for my father than simply transcribe his notes. In truth, Papa depends on me to do much more." She held up her gloved hand as he made to interrupt her. "Please let me finish, Sir Phillip. The deception has weighed heavily upon me. I must make a clean breast of it."

Andy sighed and looked up at him sadly, regretting she wasn't practiced enough to summon up some tears. "You see, my lord, it's really all my father's fault." She bit her lip, silently begging her father's forgiveness, and paused for effect. Straightening her shoulders, she stared off into the distance, as if ashamed to meet his gaze.

The Baron cleared his throat expectantly and she glanced back at him. "My father ..." Andy paused again. Suddenly, inspiration struck. "My father always wanted a son. He was sorely disappointed with my birth, particularly when the doctor informed my parents that Mama couldn't have any more children. Father chose my name so he could call me 'Andy' for short. That way, at least, he could pretend I was a boy," she carried on, crossing her fingers under her skirt for the lies. In fact, she'd been named after her grandfather, Andrew. It really was a shame she'd never learned the art of weeping spontaneously. A few tears would help embellish the tale at this point.

"Then, Papa saw to it that I was given an education more suitable for a male, expecting me all the while to do well at my studies. My mother was unable to sway him." *Of course, Mother didn't want to, feeling as she did that women were undereducated and undervalued.* However, Andy wasn't about to share that with Phillip.

"When Mama died, my father grew to rely on me more and more." That much was true. "Unfortunately, if people knew the extent of the work I do for my father, I would be ostracized. I wouldn't be able to go anywhere in polite society and I'd have to give up the routs and balls completely."

Andy turned a mournful gaze upon him. "There are very few people who know of my secret burden. Even the Marquess and his family aren't aware of just how much my father depends on my help."

"Really?" Phillip asked. He returned her gaze with more charity.

Andy breathed more easily. He hadn't asked her about the stolen letters yet. The remark about his knowing more than Jonathon must have struck the right chord. She stretched out a hand in supplication. "Thank you so much for allowing me to unburden myself. Do say you won't give my secret away."

"Truth to tell, I knew something about you didn't fit, right from the beginning. Was aware of it all along, you know," Phillip informed her pompously.

"Yes, I could tell you were," she replied quietly. *If you hadn't seen my notes, you never would've guessed.* She hoped her limpid smile successfully hid her thoughts.

Phillip rewarded her with a condescending nod. "I've heard

of other fathers who are cursed with only female children and
end up making life very difficult for them.''

Andy's smile didn't waver even though she ground her teeth.
She swore to consider her father's suggestion of a career in
acting after all this was over.

''Not only that—''

Helen's anguished scream cut Phillip off.

Chapter Eleven

Andy yanked on her reins, earning a pained whinny from her mare. She turned and her heart gave a sick thud. Not far behind them, Dominic was sprawled out on the ground, motionless.

After shouting over her shoulder for Jonathon and Cynthia, Andy urged her offended horse into a gallop, reaching Helen and Barbara well before the Baron—a major feat in itself, considering she was a poor rider.

She leaped off the sidesaddle, ignoring her hat as it tumbled back. Her ankle twisted and she tripped over the hem of her riding habit. With a muttered curse at her clumsiness, she picked up her skirts higher than acceptable and rushed to Dominic's still form.

Barbara cradled his bleeding head in her lap while Helen frantically dabbed at the wound with a frivolous scrap of lace which passed as a lady's handkerchief. Andy pulled out her own handkerchief from her sleeve and added her efforts to Helen's, demanding, "What happened?"

"I'm not really sure." Helen gulped, biting back her tears.

"We were riding along quietly when Dom's horse stumbled." She gave Phillip a distracted nod when he dismounted and joined them.

Andy ignored him and looked at Barbara, but Barbara could only shake her head helplessly. Her face a pale sheet, her eyes widened in shock as Dom's blood pooled in a spreading stain on her turquoise habit.

Trying to calm both women, she adopted a brusque manner. "The cut doesn't look too serious." She wiped away most of the blood and glanced up. Neither Barbara nor Helen looked convinced. Phillip was beginning to look ill and stepped back. Andy swallowed her frustration. "Remember, head wounds are notorious for bleeding prodigiously."

A soft moan escaped Dominic's lips. "You should see it from my side, Andy. You wouldn't be quite so droll about it," he groaned without opening his eyes.

Andy smiled grimly. At least he was alive. She looked over her shoulder at a thundering sound. Jon's roan stallion ripped up the turf as man and beast hurled toward them. The vibrations from the earth rippled through Andy's body. Cynthia was far behind, failing to keep pace despite her vaunted ability as a horsewoman.

Jon looked far more graceful leaping off his mount than she had, Andy was sure. In his concern for his friend, he missed her nod. He brushed the women aside and moved his hands deftly over the fallen man's body, checking for broken bones. "Dom, are you all right?" he asked, his voice hoarse.

"Ouch! Easy, old chum!" Dom complained when Jonathon pressed his hip. He sat up and, still groggy, held the useless scraps of lace against his forehead. "I'm all right . . . a bit shaken and bruised, but no permanent damage done," he said, trying to reassure the gathered company.

Helen brushed the grass from his jacket in nervous swipes. Still sitting, Barbara twisted her hands in her lap, her apprehensive gaze fixed on his forehead. Jon supported Dom by the shoulders and helped him to his feet.

"Honestly," Dom added, with a rueful grin at everyone's patent disbelief. "Didn't check the saddle properly, I guess. Cinch came loose," he continued disjointedly, shaking his head in an attempt to clear it. The movement made him wince.

"That will do for now, Dom," Jonathon ordered, taking charge. "We've got to have that wound taken care of. Are you well enough to ride by yourself?" His friend nodded, more cautiously this time.

Andy heard Cynthia muttering in displeasure, probably at having the morning ride cut short. Glancing back, she saw the frustrated beauty standing beside a visibly shaken Baron. A perfumed slip of silk twisted against his lips, Phillip looked decidedly unwell. "Sir Phillip?" she was moved to ask.

"Terribly sorry. It's the sight of blood. Never could handle the stuff," he admitted, somewhat sheepishly. He inclined his head in Dom's direction. "Will he be all right?"

"He'll do," Andy replied, surprised at the Baron's uncharacteristic nervousness. She knew many women fainted for less reason than a bit of blood. She'd also heard of men being squeamish when it was spilled. However, she had yet to see anyone quite as skittish as Phillip. He looked even more agitated than either Helen or Barbara.

"Could you see the ladies back, Phillip?" Jon interrupted curtly. "I had better ride with Dom." He retrieved Dom's mare, which was now placidly munching on grass, together with the other horses.

"I'm going back with you," Helen quickly declared, refusing to leave Dom's side.

Andy helped a still-dazed Barbara stand. "I'll ride with Barbara."

"Thank you. I'm afraid I'll need the company," Barbara whispered, placing a shaking hand on Andy's arm.

Phillip turned and bowed to the petulant blonde, now tapping her foot. "Lady Cynthia, then? If I may have the pleasure of escorting you back to the house? Perhaps you'd join me for a turn about the garden to complete the exercise we've missed this morning. It might help us forget this misfortune."

She placed her arm on his. "The pleasure would be mine, Sir Phillip."

Andy's brow arched at the overly warm smile Cynthia bestowed upon the Baron. The woman was probably put out that Jon would rather assist a bastard up on his horse than her. Cynthia's cooing and outrageous flirting when Phillip gave her a hand up confirmed Andy's suspicions.

Cynthia caught her glance and pursed her lips before calling to Jon. "Will the afternoon excursion need to be canceled as well?"

"I doubt it, Lady Cynthia," Jon replied with a dazzling smile. "I've been anticipating displaying my charming guests to the village. I wouldn't want to delay that pleasure. Mr. White will have to remain behind, however," he added with a stern look at his companion.

Apparently mollified by his pretty words, Cynthia nodded and once more turned her charms on Phillip.

Disgusted, Andy shook her head, watching both Cynthia and Phillip preen in mutual admiration. She glanced ahead to Jon. There was definitely no comparison between the two men. She shrugged at Cynthia's inconstancy and tugged at Barbara's arm.

"You'll feel better once you've had a cup of tea," Andy offered her pale companion with gentle smile.

"Thank goodness the parsonage is just around the corner from the inn!" Andy exclaimed as Jon seated her at a table with several ledgers. "My feet are killing me! Lady Tabitha should have offered her services to Wellington as a scrounger. There wasn't a shop she didn't drag us into."

"And here I thought an ability to shop was a skill women

were born with, or at the very least, had drummed into them as a ladylike accomplishment—not unlike watercolors,'' Jon teased.

"Yes, well, I happen to fall short in a number of so-called accomplishments. My watercolors are abominable, my flirting skills are nonexistent, and so on. I won't bore you with the rest of the list.''

At the wicked glint in his eyes, Andy's hand shook ever so slightly. Determined to ignore him, she opened up the first register. After watching Cynthia flutter between both Jon and Phillip all afternoon, she was not in what one would call a playful mood.

"When reading the registers,'' she said, assuming a pedantic air, "don't be misled by the spelling. Their clarity depends very much on the literacy skills of the recorder.'' Darting a glance at him, she noted the glint was still there. Her affected nasal intonation hadn't dampened his humor at all. She'd have to work harder at boring him to distraction.

"This was a problem during the Commonwealth, in particular, when illiterate laymen were often appointed,'' she droned on, mimicking one of her despised governesses. "I remember seeing an entry made once regarding the 'dooke of bookingham.''' Andy resumed her normal attitude and covered a soft laugh. She propped a hand under her chin. "So, don't be surprised by anything you might read.''

"Yes, ma'am,'' Jonathon replied piously, his hands folded like a polite schoolboy's.

Andy arched her brow at his apparent meekness.

He shot her a grin. "It should be fairly easy to pick out 'St. James,' although I suppose we could run into a number of variations with 'White,''' he mused. His humble façade disappeared, and with a final wink at her, he pulled another ledger toward himself.

They settled down to work quickly. There really wasn't much choice. Their excuse of looking for a book for Edgar gave them only a minimal amount of time. Andy fervently hoped Helen was successful in keeping the guests entertained during their tea. She feared their absence being questioned.

The silence was interrupted briefly when Jon remarked that it must have been a particularly cold winter, if the number of births registered in the summer were anything to go by. Andy glared at him.

"There's no need to stare down your nose at me, Miss Fitzgerald. It was just an observation." Jon's eyes twinkled before he turned another page and resumed his work.

A short while later, Andy slammed shut the last register. "Well, that's it for this parish. I presume you had no luck either?" Frustrated, she swept back a few loose tendrils of hair from her face and looked up.

Jon was staring at her speculatively. She swallowed. The wicked tilt to his mouth sent a tingle down her spine. Unaccountably, visions of their encounters in the library, the gallery, and outside her bedroom flashed through her mind. Was he recalling those times as well? She shivered and lowered her gaze.

He leaned over and tipped up her chin. Her tongue darted out to moisten her dry lips. The ball of his thumb brushed along her tongue's path and he shook his head.

"No, I didn't have any luck."

It took Andy a moment to realize he was responding to her question. She grabbed the ledgers and stood. "Then we'd best hurry back, or Helen and Dom will have our heads."

After leaving the ledgers at the rector's cottage, Andy turned to Jonathon and smiled. "I'm so glad Dom wasn't seriously injured and could come along. Otherwise, Helen would've been too distracted to keep up her end of things at the inn."

Jon made a noncommittal sound without returning her smile. If anything, he became more pensive.

Andy's smile faded. "What is it?"

He tucked her arm through his and hugged it closely to his

side. His silence sent a shiver of alarm through Andy and her steps slowed.

Jon finally looked at her, his features taut. "You might as well know. Fred, the head groom, spoke to me just before we left this afternoon. He had personally saddled Dom's horse—and when Fred saddles a horse, there's no question it's been done properly. He takes a lot of pride in his work. He's been doing it too long to make a careless mistake like not tightening a cinch."

Andy shook her head at the implication. "You think Phillip . . . ?" she asked, afraid to complete the question.

Lips thinned, Jonathon shrugged. "Phillip was waiting for us at the stable. He certainly had the opportunity."

An abiding sense of fair play forced Andy to declare, "You can't hang a man for being prompt." Even so, she recalled how preoccupied the Baron had seemed during their ride. Dozens of unasked questions tainted with dread spun through her mind as they arrived at the inn.

A tense Helen greeted them when they entered the private parlor. "Were you able to find the book, Andy?"

Andy looked at her apologetically. "I'm afraid not. Perhaps I'll have better luck elsewhere." Helen's crestfallen features indicated she understood the marriage lines hadn't been discovered. Andy nodded toward the other company and sat for a hurried cup of tea. Both Dominic and Barbara were noticeably absent.

Jon looked around the room and voiced her observation. "Where's Dom? He isn't ill, is he?" Concern laced his voice.

Cynthia turned from Phillip with a petulant toss of her head and glared at Andy, as though she were somehow at fault for Dom's absence. "He decided he needed some fresh air. I don't see why he didn't offer to escort Miss Fitzgerald to the bookstore in the first place. Barbara decided to accompany him in the event he might feel faint after his fall."

Cynthia's gaze traveled from Andy to the Marquess and her

tactics changed midstream. Eyes widening, she smiled sweetly. "But of course, I'm sure you feel obligated to assist Miss Fitzgerald."

Andy was amazed at the rapid about-face and shot her own vapid smile in return, thankful once more for the confidence she'd gained in dealing with subtle barbs. Fluttering her eyelashes demurely, she spoke up before Jon. "Yes, I'm sure I haven't thanked you properly for all your help, my lord."

The innkeeper put down another tray of food. A maid poured him some tea. Seated at Andy's side, Jon used the distraction as an excuse to offer Cynthia a mere nod in response to her cattiness. Then, leaning over, he whispered in Andy's ear, "As a matter of fact, you haven't thanked me properly, Duchess. We could remedy that later if you like."

Andy's jaw snapped shut and she turned a cool shoulder to him, deciding to watch Cynthia and Tabitha instead. But there was something about the innocent way Andy raised the cup of tea to her full lips which Jon couldn't quite trust. Just as he wondered if he was about to suffer for his impertinence, her shod heel crunched against his foot.

Jon choked on his drink, much to the consternation of everyone around him. "It's nothing," he assured them, clearing his throat. Thank goodness Andy wasn't wearing sturdy riding boots, he thought with a silent chuckle. He slipped his hand under the table and gripped her thigh, warning her of retaliation.

His hand felt comfortable resting against her leg and he wished he could leave it there. Out of the corner of his eye, he noted Andy's polite smile and attention waver. What would she do if he massaged her thigh with light, feathering strokes?

Her smile became positively fixed. Her hand trembled and she nearly spilled her tea.

Jon's grin widened. Regretfully, though, he removed his hand instead of inching her skirt up until it bunched above her knee to touch her—*that* was what he really wanted to do and he suspected she knew it.

"Lord Baldwin!"

Lady Tabitha's cross voice brought him back to reality with a crash. "I'm sorry. I was thinking of other potential amusements. Could you repeat the question?" He shot Tabitha a rueful smile which succeeded in mollifying her.

No such success with Andy. She stomped on his foot yet again. So, she had felt the attraction. Jon's smile deepened before he joined in the desultory conversation.

For the journey home, he and Dom rode their horses alongside the open carriage. Jon alternated keeping a sharp eye on Phillip, who chose to ride with the ladies, and on a pallid, bandaged Dominic. Fortunately, nothing untoward occurred.

As he helped Andy from the carriage, he tightened his grip on her hand ever so slightly. "I do hope you enjoyed the afternoon," Jon said, keeping his tone innocuous. "I know I did."

"If you'll excuse me, I must see to my father."

He couldn't prevent his chuckle when she marched off with only a curt nod, her heated cheeks giving her away. He wondered if she, too, had wished the company at the table to perdition. It could have been such a pleasurable interlude.

A harried-looking Sofia slipped into the room. "Please don't let anyone know I'm here, Edgar." She closed the door, leaning against its support. Her eyelids fluttered shut and she took a deep breath. Opening her eyes slowly, she started at the sight of Andy in the corner. "Oh dear . . . I'm sorry. I didn't realize anyone else was here. Am I interrupting?" She turned her anxious gaze up at Edgar, who was already at her side.

He patted her hand and gallantly escorted her to a chair. "Of course not, Sofie. You should know you're always welcome," he admonished. "As a matter of fact, Andy was just leaving. Weren't you?"

Andy took one look at the way her father hovered solicitously

over the Marchioness and promptly decided she was *de trop*.
She put her notes down, nodding, "The work can wait. Besides,
I was hoping to have a few minutes to visit with Helen. I'll do
that now."

Sofia hesitated. "Are you sure? I'll only be here a short
while. I just needed some quiet place to catch my breath.
Preparing for this evening has taken more out of me than I
thought."

Andy stood and agreed, "Yes, it has been hectic." So hectic,
she thought, that she hadn't seen much of Jonathon during the
last few days. Her father's unusually gentle voice interrupted
her chagrin.

"Here, put your feet up." Edgar pulled up a footstool for
the Marchioness. He kept up a steady, mild chatter as he went
to pour Sofia some tea—the tea which had been brought up
for Andy.

Andy paused at the door, studying the tableau. A soft, warm
air enveloped the older couple, making both of them appear
much younger. Her father stood straighter than she'd seen him
do in years, and the lines around the Marchioness's mouth were
no longer quite so obvious.

How very interesting, she mused, quietly closing the door.
Her smile was tinged with a combination of hope and melancholy. It would truly please her if her father were fortunate
enough to find love twice in his life. Her smile faded. Would
she even find it once?

Andy halted at the top of the stairs. Simms was just coming
up. "If you're looking for Lady Sofia, I believe she's otherwise
occupied at the moment . . . My father's busy, too," she added
hastily, in case the butler was seeking Edgar. Hopefully, there
wasn't an immediate crisis which had to be dealt with.

Simms quirked his bushy eyebrows.

Was that a glimmer of understanding in his eyes? Had he,

too, seen the budding relationship between Edgar and Sofia? It wouldn't surprise Andy in the least and she permitted herself a small smile. Simms had a way of keeping his finger on the pulse of everything in the manor. She clasped her hands in front of herself, waiting.

The butler merely cleared his throat. "I see, miss. Actually, I was looking for you." Simms paused, checking over his shoulder to make sure no one else was about, and shot her a meaningful look. "I believe Lord Baldwin has some correspondence he'd like to discuss with you."

Andy's knuckles whitened. Like Simms's, her gaze darted around. Voice hushed, she asked, "Some word has arrived then?"

"There were several letters addressed to his lordship in this morning's mail. He is expecting you in the library, at your earliest convenience," he ended with a bow.

Andy bit back her questions.

Understanding, Simms shook his head. "I'm afraid I'm unaware as to the contents of the letters."

With a hurried smile, Andy nodded her thanks to the butler. Picking up her skirt so she could make her way down the stairs more quickly, she prayed for positive news. Nearing the library, she childishly crossed her fingers for good luck. She was about to enter the library when a footman brought her up short.

"If you're looking for Lord Baldwin, miss, he just left. . . . I think he stepped out into the garden." Unusually nervous, he evaded her gaze by tugging at the length of his sleeves.

She studied him, curious. The servants in this household normally carried out their duties in a prompt, but easy manner. When he bent to straighten an already perfect floral arrangement on a hallway table without further comment, Andy shrugged and entered the library to make her way outside via its French doors.

It was going to be a lovely evening for the party, Andy

mused as she walked down the path in search of Jonathon. The warm, round bits of gravel massaged her slippered feet. The sweet scent of roses filled the air. . . .

Cynthia's cajoling voice came over the stone wall.

All thoughts of the bucolic scene fled Andy's mind.

Casting aside the admonitions her nurse had made about eavesdropping, she moved closer to the old structure. Her arms crossed in front of herself, she kicked at a stone, wishing it were Cynthia. Or Jonathon.

Cynthia's squeals came through loud and clear, as did her moaning of that reprobate's name. Andy's vision blurred at Jon's soothing sounds . . . sounds resembling those he had used with her during their intimate encounters. *The bounder!*

She wasn't about to wait to have her meeting with him— nor did she have any desire to hear more of the same. Seething, her hands balled into fists, Andy marched into the walled garden, only to stumble at the sight which greeted her.

Hair disheveled, Cynthia leaned against Jonathon. Clinging to him, arms wrapped tightly about his shoulders, her head settled against his chest.

Since Jonathon's back was to the entrance, Cynthia alone witnessed Andy's arrival. Her eyes narrowed in acknowledgment, but before Andy could speak, Cynthia lifted her face to Jon's.

"You have no idea of how happy you've made me!" Cynthia followed her breathless exclamation by clasping his head and giving him a long, drawn-out kiss. She stepped back, ever so slowly, without releasing her grip on his shoulders. "Promise me you won't tell anyone about this just yet . . . I'm so embarrassed, even though I know I shouldn't be," Cynthia pleaded with a pretty pout. She lowered her eyes demurely, repeating her request. "Will you promise?"

Andy's thin patience diminished rapidly. Nevertheless, she too, awaited his reply. It wasn't long in coming.

"If it will make you feel better, then of course. I promise."
Jon patted Cynthia's shoulder.

"Word of honor?" Cynthia asked, peeping up at him.

"Word of honor. There really isn't any need for you to be
embarrassed, though."

Andy had enough. Clearing her throat loudly, she excused
herself. "Pardon me, but I was given to understand you wished
to see me, Lord Baldwin."

At Andy's frigid tone, Jon thrust Cynthia back as if she were
a viper, nearly pushing her off her feet. He swung round,
meeting Andy's tempestuous gaze, and flushed a darker red
than the roses around him. "I can explain," he gulped in the
face of her silent fury.

Was he truly surprised at her anger, Andy wondered. Sternly,
she told herself it didn't matter. Jon's affairs were his own
concern. She stiffened against the niggling pain and spoke, her
voice cool. "I don't believe you can explain, my lord. Didn't
I hear you give your word of honor?"

"That's true, Jon," Cynthia confirmed.

Andy saw Cynthia's sly smile which, from his position,
Jonathon couldn't.

"You did give your word as a gentleman. This will be our
little secret for now." Cynthia smoothed the lapels of his jacket.
"I'll leave you to your business with Miss Fitzgerald. We shall
see you later, Jon." She reached up on her toes and brushed
another light, familiar kiss against his cheek. All traces of
coyness vanished when she looked at Andy. She didn't even
try to hide her triumphant expression. "Miss Fitzgerald," she
nodded in a dismissing tone.

"Lady Cynthia." Andy was equally remote with a stiff nod
of her own. She stared expectantly at Jonathon when the other
woman departed. "Well?"

Jon folded his arms against his chest and glared at her, his
frustration evident. "Well what? You already told me I'm not
allowed to explain because I gave my word of honor."

"That wasn't what I was referring to, *Lord Baldwin.*" Her tongue tripped acidly over his title. "You had something you wished to discuss with me, I believe."

"Yes, I'm sorry. I forgot." He ran his fingers through his hair and tucked his hands into his pockets.

Kicking at the soft dirt, he looked like nothing more than a repentant schoolboy—again—and Andy's anger and pain faded. "Obviously," she offered dryly, moving closer to allow for greater privacy. She fought the urge to brush back an unruly lock of dark hair from his forehead.

"I'm so sorry for what you must be thinking." Gently putting his hands on her shoulders, he dropped a light kiss on her lips before she could protest.

His gaze lifted and searched her features. "Do you trust me, Andy?" he asked after a moment.

"I suppose so," she admitted, albeit grudgingly.

"Then, please believe me when I tell you that what you just saw isn't what it appeared to be. It was really very innocent— on my part, at least," he clarified.

Andy's nostrils thinned. She took in his flushed cheeks and recalled Cynthia's heated, familiar embrace. She snorted and stepped away abruptly, wiping her mouth with the back of her hand at the same time. "If you say so."

Jon accepted her rebuke with another regretful sigh. "If I would've caught you out in a similar situation, I'd probably be just as suspicious." Resigned, he took her arm and escorted her back to the manor. "We'd best have our discussion in the library. Our privacy should be assured there."

Andy allowed him to lead her away. Mentally, she replayed the scene with Cynthia, a niggling doubt planted in her mind. Was Jon innocent? The sophisticated Cynthia could have manipulated him into holding her so intimately. It wouldn't be that difficult to do.

On the other hand, Andy fumed, Jon hadn't appeared too

unhappy embracing Cynthia. She glanced up to see him studying her and looked away from his silent entreaty. "Well, what have you heard?" she asked, forestalling any other protestations he might be about to make.

His features altered and she stiffened.

Chapter Twelve

Jonathon couldn't help his sardonic grin. Her stance marshal, Andy fairly bristled with self-righteous indignation. He wanted to shake her, and then, kiss her. But would that suffice to soften the sharp edges of pain Jon suspected Andy was hiding?

Devil take it, he thought, still cross at how Cynthia had taken him in. He really was innocent this time, yet there wasn't a thing he could do to prove it. Andy's anger and hurt bothered him and he rued his hastily given promise. However, it didn't mean he couldn't bait her . . . just a bit. The corners of his eyes crinkled.

"You aren't jealous by any chance, are you, Duchess?" he drawled.

Andy's full lips thinned. She picked up her skirts and turned on her heel.

Expelling a long, frustrated breath, he admired her trim ankles. "I was just teasing, Duchess."

She shot him a fulminating glare over her shoulder. The threat was obvious. Either he would cease, or she would leave.

He shrugged, accepting defeat. "All right, all right." Going to an intricately carved panel on the far wall, he pressed on a scrolled leaf and a section sprang open to reveal a hidden cache. He pulled out the letters Simms had given him earlier and passed them to her. His touch lingered, reveling in the vitality and warmth of her hands. How very different she was from Cynthia. When she didn't open the letters immediately, he tipped up her chin. "Wouldn't you like to read them?"

Andy dropped into a chair, still holding the letters in her lap, and stared up at him in mute question.

He shook his head and went to his desk. "There's nothing there. Not really. One of the clerics double-checked his journals and found reference to a young couple going through his parish at about the time Emily and Richard eloped. According to his notes, there was something unusual about them. Unfortunately, he didn't elucidate when he made the entry. Now he can't remember what it was."

Andy's head cocked to the side, suddenly alert. "What could've been so unusual about them? And were they seeking to get married?"

Jonathon shrugged. "I'm not really sure about the answer to either of those questions, and by all appearances, neither is the vicar." He pointed to one of the letters in her hand. "It's the next letter. He explains briefly that their community isn't accustomed to strangers passing through. That's why he might have made note of them."

Andy checked the address on the letter Jon indicated. She waved the envelope, smiling. "Of course strangers would stand out. This is from Land's End. Cornish smuggling communities are notorious for being tightly knit." Her smile slipped. "It could've been any one of several hundred couples eloping that year."

"Unfortunately, that's true. It really isn't any sort of a lead at all." Personally, Jon was ready to consign the letter to all of their other negative responses.

"On the other hand . . ." Andy hesitated, tapping the envelope against her cheek. Without finishing her thought, she stood and, pacing the confines of the library, read the short letter. She paused and sent him a speculative look. "On the other hand, it could have been them." Coming back toward him, she stopped in front of the desk. Putting both hands on it, she leaned forward and stared at him intensely. "You do realize where Land's End is, don't you?"

Jon looked askance before grinning widely. He'd just been enjoying watching the sway of her hips. "As a matter of fact, I do. One of my tutor's had a particular love for geography. He drilled a plethora of trivia into my mind, including the location of Land's End."

"Be serious!" She smacked her hand against the edge of the desk. "What is on the other side of Land's End, you slow top?"

"A large body of water?" His flippancy faded. The significance dawned. "The large body of water which Emily referred to in her diary? The large body of water which one can cross to reach the Channel Islands . . . the Islands of Scilly—Guernsey and Jersey, just to mention a few—where no banns or special licenses are needed for a marriage to be considered legal."

"Well done, sir!"

Jon focused on the excited gleam in her eyes. He put up a palm. "Slow down, Duchess. This is pure speculation on our part." Even as he warned her, he struggled to quell his own widening sliver of hope.

"So, let's speculate. There really isn't any other choice." Andy held up a hand to tick off the few facts at their disposal. "We know they spent time on the Continent. Before going to the Continent, Emily gives the impression they exchanged vows in an area with a lot of water. We know you can reach the Continent via Cornwall—smugglers have been doing it for generations. That's why we wrote to Land's End in the first place. And as you pointed out, the Channel Islands happen to lie between Cornwall and the Continent.''

Andy turned to pace again, her arms now hugging her body. Her voice was as agitated as her steps. ''If it turns out no special license was granted or banns read, we know they could have married on Jersey, for example, without any questions. Furthermore, the Scilly Islands are only a few days' journey from here, much closer than Gretna Green.'' With that, she ran out of points and returned to her seat. Plucking restlessly at the other letters, she watched him, awaiting his response.

The leather of his chair squeaked as Jon leaned back in his chair. He propped his feet up on the corner of his desk and clasped his hands together on his stomach. For a long moment, he gazed out the French doors as he reconsidered the few facts at their disposal. Finally, he turned to a fidgeting Andy, now alternating between sitting on her hands and fiddling with the carving of Burne.

''It's a long shot, you know.''

Andy shrugged and silently nodded her agreement.

His feet dropped to the floor, thudding lightly against the carpet. Bracing his elbows on the table, he propped up his chin on a hand and pinned Andy with a hard gaze, finally acquiescing with a curt nod. ''There's something in what you say. Unfortunately, with the guests here, it's impossible for me to get away. However, I think I could entice our vicar, Taddeus Green, into taking a short . . . holiday. I'm sure he'd love to go to the Channel Islands. They have fabulous bird sanctuaries and he's an avid bird watcher. As a matter of fact,'' Jon mused, ''I could reward his hard work in the parish by lending him my yacht— it would greatly speed matters up.''

''Forgive me for asking, but is your vicar trustworthy?''

''Absolutely. Taddeus has been here practically forever. He even knew Emily from her short stay with my aunt. Not only is he discreet, but he's also familiar with both church records and searching out genealogies—perfect for our requirements. .

Furthermore, it's unlikely his taking a holiday, even if it's on such short notice, would arouse any suspicion. Of course, if you prefer, I could get a Bow Street runner from London." He paused. With her experience, Andy deserved the option of choosing.

She shook her head. "We'd lose too much time. I know the information, if any exists, has been there for years and should be safe for another few weeks—as long as Phillip doesn't find out about it. Therein lies the rub, you see. We'll have to send your vicar. The locals there would recognize a Runner without any trouble and close ranks, just on principle."

Andy paused to give him a pointed glare. "Besides, I'm sure Mr. Green could use a holiday, particularly considering the amount of time he must spend on his knees praying for some of his more sinful parishioners."

"Hah!" Jonathon snorted. "If Taddeus spends any time on his knees at all, it's more likely to thank God that no one interferes with his passion for research and bird watching."

Some of the starch slipped from her posture and Jon caught a glimpse of her unwilling smile. She stood quickly and turned to the door.

"If that's all you have to report, then I look forward to meeting the vicar tonight."

He shot out of his chair and was at her side before she could open the library door. Maneuvering his way around, he leaned his back against the door and loosely cupped Andy's shoulders, preventing her escape. "Say you trust me, Duchess," he asked, unable to keep the whimsy from his voice. She had no idea how important her answer was. How could she? Even he was having trouble accepting it.

Andy rolled her eyes. "I do trust you—in some things, anyway." She brushed the front of his shirt, her shaking hand belying the light response.

Jon stared deeply into the kaleidoscope of turbulent emotion revealed in her hazel eyes. Unaccountably cheered by what he saw, he asked, "What does 'for a while' mean to you?"

"Pardon me?" Perplexed at his sudden change in topic, Andy frowned. "I suppose that's quite relative, isn't it? Why do you ask?"

"Oh, I'm just curious. If you asked me to keep a secret for 'a while,' accepting my word as a gentleman that I would, how long would you expect me to keep my silence?"

"You scoundrel!" Andy choked back a laugh before pretending an earnestness. "Mmm . . . probably until the evening at least." The angle of her brow informed him she expected a good explanation for the scene she'd witnessed earlier.

"So it shall be." Jon nodded, accepting her decision with equanimity even though he was ready to tell her now—gentleman's honor be damned. "I suppose I can keep my word that long. But I need something from you first, to tide me over until then." His lips curved slightly and he lowered his head.

She didn't fight his kiss. Had she forgiven him? Jon forgot everything as her lips parted. He bent slightly, pleased when her arms wrapped around his neck and her fingers slipped through his hair.

Jonathon hugged her tighter against his chest and groaned. Immediately he wished he'd kept silent. The small sound was enough to recall her to time and place and she pulled back abruptly.

Still, her gaze remained soft. She smiled and raised a finger to his lips. Bringing that same hand to her own mouth, she gave him another small, secret smile and stepped away.

"We'll see you this evening, my lord." Her words came out as a throaty promise.

Jon opened the door and she walked away without a backward glance. He could have sworn, though, that she deliberately exaggerated the swaying of her hips.

* * *

Andy slammed her hair brush on the dresser. The impact pressed the rosewood handle against her scar. She turned her hand over and stared at that scar, unseeing, until a log crashing in the fireplace startled her into awareness. She frowned, both at her distraction and the events of the last few hours. For an evening which had started out so well, it had ended particularly poorly. Frustrated, Andy stood and began pacing.

Everyone remarked on how the Marchioness virtually glowed with pleasure. Her smile came easily and she walked among her guests with a confidence bearing no relation to her former rigidity. A special softness entered her eyes whenever she happened to glance at Edgar, a tenderness which only mirrored Edgar's own.

Obviously something had been resolved when Sofia visited her father earlier in the day, Andy mused. If nothing else came of this visit, at least her father had found some pleasure, perhaps even something more permanent. Hopefully, neither of them would allow old memories to prevent a chance at happiness with each other.

After the dinner, local musicians entertained the small party of about three dozen. Jonathon started off the dance with Cynthia. That really hadn't bothered Andy. After all, the invited house guests were the main reason for the gathering.

Andy looked out at the dark garden with a small, gloating smile. At least Cynthia's efforts to goad her when they'd met in the retiring room had been in vain. She recalled how Cynthia had looked up at her entrance.

Curtly dismissing the maid, she straightened her dress and invited Andy to join her. For a silent moment, the blonde studied Andy's gown, all the while waving an exquisite hand-painted ivory fan to cool her flushed cheeks. Cynthia's expression tightened imperceptibly, and Andy felt a sudden surge of confidence.

She knew her deceptively simple gown, without any of the frills or flounces currently in vogue, reeked of the sophistication of the Continent. The high-waisted, deep green silk had been dyed unevenly to create intriguing shadows when a woman moved. A few rows of tiny gold beads, stitched into folds, radiated out from the right shoulder, subtly drawing attention to Andy's full, firm curves as well as to the length of her body. The only concession the dressmaker had made to current fashion was to slash the short, slightly puffed sleeves.

It was a bold dress—one Andy never would have dared to wear years ago. She really did look her best tonight, she thought complacently. She leaned toward the mirror, pretending to fix her hair. Her fine, white cambric wrap slipped off her shoulder slightly, revealing the low cut of her gown even more. Watching Cynthia's inspection out of the corner of her eye, Andy couldn't help her slight smirk when the other woman's gaze narrowed. She needed all the artillery she could muster to fight Cynthia's own beauty and the way it was finely robed.

If Cynthia's determined smile was anything to go by, however, she detested women who carried themselves with any degree of assurance. When Cynthia suddenly turned that fixed smile upon her, Andy braced herself. Had she been overconfident? Her nails dug into her scar, but her smile didn't slip.

"I do hope Jon kept his word." With a satisfied sigh, Cynthia smoothed a nonexistent wrinkle from her long white gloves. When Andy didn't respond, she looked up, lips pursed. "He hasn't told you of our little secret, has he?"

Andy turned wide, innocent eyes at her companion. "Of course not! You should know better than that. There isn't *any-thing* more important to a gentleman than his honor!" She didn't add Jonathon felt his honor would be upheld by keeping his explanation until later in the evening.

Cynthia's gaze returned to the mirror. She patted her perfect curls before darting another look at Andy. Quickly, she looked demurely back to her hands, turning them this way and that, in front of herself. "I'm so glad. You've absolutely no idea how much that means to me. I want to savor the secret a bit longer. . . . Jon simply made me the happiest of women."

"Congratulations are in order then?" Andy asked dryly. Experience told her she was being baited.

Cynthia's wide smile exhibited the perfect teeth she had been gnashing a moment ago. She ignored Andy's question, completely missing the sarcasm. When Andy's gaze remained unclouded, her expression soured. Cynthia was the first to look away, leaning forward to pinch some color into her cheeks.

"Actually, I don't expect an announcement to be made for some time, but you know he's mine, don't you?" Cynthia declared, astonishing Andy with her boldness. Without awaiting a response, she rose, giving Andy a curt nod. "I'd best go. Jon is waiting for me."

Andy stared at her reflection after Cynthia's departure. In spite of her faith in Jon, Cynthia's broad hints of an engagement did not sit well. She took a couple of deep breaths. Surely, if Cynthia were so sure of Jonathon, she wouldn't wait for any announcements to be made—would she? Seething with curiosity, Andy shook her head. She owed Jon her trust, at least until tonight.

If nothing else came of the evening, however, at least she'd met the vicar. He had been sitting in one of the side rooms with her father, discussing genealogical research. The pair appeared to get on famously. After quietly explaining the vicar had agreed to assist them with their search, Jon had taken her over for an introduction.

Andy liked the lively little man. Short and lean, his keen intelligence shone through clear, sharp eyes and his entire manner invited confidence. No wonder Jon trusted him.

"I understand you enjoy bird watching, sir," Andy said when Jonathon introduced her.

A beatific smile greeted Andy's comment. "With a passion, my dear. As a matter of fact, I've just heard of a very rare species which might be found on Guernsey. I intend to go and see for myself after church tomorrow. Have you ever been to the Isles of Scilly?"

When Andy shook her head, he began to reminisce about the last visit he'd made many years ago. "They have the most spectacular natural sanctuaries I've ever seen. I have a cousin on the island with whom I stay whenever I am there. She thinks I'm quite mad, you know. But that's the way of it . . . people have a tendency not to appreciate the beauty which surrounds them, seeking it elsewhere instead."

Andy met his sharp gaze, acknowledging the information he had family on Guernsey with an infinitesimal nod. Jon hadn't mentioned that. Considering how closed some of the island communities were to strangers, it would certainly help their cause.

The rest of the evening sped by in a blur. Jon danced with her twice. Unfortunately, it seemed everyone conspired against their meeting privately. Every time they tried to escape onto the terrace, or walk in the well-lit gardens, either Cynthia, or Barbara, or Phillip, or one of the guests interrupted them.

Coming back to the present, Andy sat at her dressing table. Resting her chin on her hand, she closed her eyes and recalled how she'd felt in Jon's arms and the way his muscled body had moved against hers. Perhaps it was just as well they *hadn't* been able to catch a few private moments. She shivered and her elbow slipped. Startled, she opened her eyes with a groan. How disgusting—she was actually mooning over the Marquess like a schoolroom chit!

Still, she really had been curious to hear Jon's explanation. Grudgingly, she accepted it would have to wait for another time. Forcing the matter from her mind, she took a candle to her bedside, deciding to read for a while.

Andy had no idea of how long she'd been staring blindly at

a page of *Pride and Prejudice* when something made her look up.

Jon.

He was leaning against the door frame, holding a bottle of brandy in the crook of one arm. Two glasses were in the hand at his side. His smile could only be described as satiric.

Andy slammed her book shut and glared, but his composure didn't crack.

"Hello, Duchess, he said, and sauntering into her room, raised the glasses. "Where should I put these?"

"Perhaps in the library where Simms or one of the servants could see to their removal?" Andy retorted, hoping the dimly lit room hid the heat flooding her cheeks. "Really, my lord! Have you no sense of decency, entering a gentlewoman's chambers?" she asked, clutching the bedcover to her chest.

"Have you no sense of adventure?" he shot back, grinning before assuming an injured pose. "Besides, I'm merely trying to keep my promise to speak with you privately—impossible to do earlier. Would you have a gentleman go back on his word?"

"Heaven forbid!" Andy bit out.

"Well?" he prodded, the two glasses clanging dangerously against each other.

"Oh, all right . . . in the sitting room. I'll be there shortly. You dratted man," she added under her breath as he turned to follow her instruction. Only the curse lacked conviction, unable as she was to summon any true indignation. She simply was not as appalled by his audacity as she ought to be. If only she weren't so curious to hear his explanation. At least he was fully clothed, she consoled her conscience. Surely a man bent on seduction in the middle of the night wouldn't be.

Of course, she wasn't about to take any chances and hastily riffled through her dressing gowns to find the disreputable flannel one. Knotting it with shaking fingers, she entered her sitting room with what she hoped was a *blasé* air, assuring herself it was all the rage for gentlewomen *en dishabille* to entertain men in their chambers.

Jonathon was already seated at the sofa, the brandy poured into the glasses. He patted the place beside himself and passed her a goblet. Andy accepted the drink and sidled to the corner of the couch, striving to appear as casual as she could. She didn't trust him *that* much.

"I really can't believe the efficiency of the Simmses. Do you realize the door didn't make a sound when I opened it?" he offered, adopting her casual air.

His wicked grin made Andy wonder just how long he'd been watching her. "If I recall correctly, the sound is normally made when one knocks," she pointed out.

"Knew there was something I forgot." He lifted his glass in a silent toast and took a sip. After that, he folded his arms against his chest and continued to silently observe her.

"Well?" Andy asked, unnerved by his appraisal. She took a gulp of the brandy to avoid looking at him and nearly choked when the liquor scalded her throat.

"It's meant to be sipped, Duchess," he explained patiently, stretching his long legs out, crossing them at the ankles.

With the back of her hand, Andy wiped the tears from her eyes and grit her teeth. "You can stop toying with me anytime now, Jon."

Sighing loudly, Jon put down his drink on the low table near the candle he'd lit. He sank deeper into the sofa and clasped his hands behind his head. "We really do need to work at your sense of adventure, Duchess. However, as I said, I merely stopped by to have the discussion which everyone seemed determined to prevent this evening."

He sat forward suddenly with an intent look. "That is, of course, if you're sure it wouldn't be dishonorable?" His tone slipped into a lazy drawl. "Or perhaps you're no longer curious?" He picked up his glass and swirled the brandy around.

His eyes twinkling, he tilted it up and took a slow sip, watching her over the rim of the glass.

Andy muttered, "No sense of adventure? Hah!" In spite of his teasing . . . in spite of his compromising presence in her room . . . she couldn't help a rise of pleasure.

Attempting to imitate his insouciant manner, she glanced at the glass now cupped in the palm of her hand and shrugged. "I doubt there will be any harm done to your honor—such as it is—so, since you're here anyway, you might as well tell me about it." She certainly wasn't going to tell him that, if he didn't satisfy her curiosity, one of his precious Simmses would be forced to clean up a glass which was about to be smashed against the wall in another moment or so.

His quiet laugh as he studied her nearly prompted Andy to change her mind. Perhaps she should simply toss her glass with its contents at him instead? No. No point in wasting good brandy. She took another sip, fighting to bide her time.

"Snakes."

The comment was so unexpected that Andy choked on her brandy again. "Pardon me?" she sputtered, wiping the droplets of fine cognac from her chin.

"Our tender Lady Cynthia is afraid of snakes," he explained, as if that clarified the situation.

Andy glared at him. "We already know that," she said, careful to enunciate each word. Was Jon foxed?

He poured himself another drink after topping up her glass. She was convinced that, if he wasn't already several sheets to the wind, then he would be soon. So might she be, for that matter, and warned herself to go more slowly with this drink.

"It's really very simple. Cynthia decided this morning would be the perfect time for me to show her the gardens. I wasn't sure if Simms would find you occupied and I couldn't refuse her request outright—being the gentleman I am, you see," he added with a lecherous grin.

Andy pursed her lips, allowing the comment to slip by.

He winked. "I begged pressing business, allowing I'd only have time to show her my aunt's rose garden, and stepped out with her." Drawing out his explanation, he took another drink of brandy and heaved a theatrical sigh.

Irritation mounting, Andy turned and punched the pillow at her elbow.

Jon understood her silent threat, grinned, and continued. "As we were walking, she claimed she heard something moving in the bushes. Thinking it was a snake, she leaped into my embrace. I assured her the gardeners had, that very morning, irradicated the entire population of vipers. *That's* the knowledge which supposedly made her the 'happiest of women.' Those were her words and, I believe, where you came in."

He pointed an accusing finger at her and placed the blame for the whole episode on Andy. "If you hadn't mentioned snakes the other night, none of this ever would've happened. So, you see, it's really all your fault." He placed a hand to his breast. "*I* was perfectly innocent."

"Snakes?" Andy repeated. Her features twisted. Taking a closer look at Jon to make sure he wasn't funning her, she shook her head in disbelief. Her gaze narrowed, recalling how Cynthia had tried to mislead her. "And she had the gall to bring *your* honor into question?" Andy shook her head again, this time in disgust.

"You'd be surprised at the various tricks women employ to gain attention." He shrugged off her comments with a cynical twist to his lips before moving nearer. Tenderly, he brushed a hand against her cheek.

Instead of scooting away, she looked at him, thinking of the tales Helen had told her. How the women pursued Jon. She almost felt sorry for him. Almost.

"Thanks for trusting me, Duchess, and for giving me the chance to explain." His fingers trailed down from her cheek, along the path of her shoulder, to the hand which held the cognac. His touch moved, glancing off the seductive satin of her pearl-colored night rail peeping through the top of her dressing gown. His features lightened. "Mmm, much better than that . . . thing you borrowed from your governess, my dear," he said as he took the brandy from her nerveless grasp. "A pity, though, that you haven't as yet discarded that wrap."

Andy tried not to reveal the effect his nearness had on her. Surely the reason she didn't back away from his touch was because she had nowhere to go? Oh, she could leap off the sofa, but she'd only make herself look like a fool.

Escaping his hypnotic gaze, she focused on a point beyond his shoulder. "Shouldn't you leave—now that you've given your explanation? Being such a gentleman and all, of course."

"There's a difference between being a gentleman and being a saint, you know. Would you really banish me, Duchess?" Jon put his hand under her chin and tipped her face toward him. He searched her features. "I'm really not ready for sackcloth and ashes and I don't think you are, either."

After an endless moment, Andy lifted her gaze. She sucked in her breath at the heat in his eyes and admitted truthfully. "No, I'm not. . . . However, a bit of sackcloth and ashes probably wouldn't hurt either one of us." She fought to quell the fluttering near the pit of her stomach. She couldn't."

After a breathless pause, her gaze dropped from his. Her teeth worked her bottom lip. "That's why I'm asking you to leave now, Jon." It wasn't just a question of propriety, Andy knew. She choked back a strangled laugh. There wasn't a room large enough anywhere which could house both propriety and Jon at the same time.

That wasn't it at all. It was her feelings. However, she wasn't about to admit the depth of them to someone as experienced as the Marquess. She felt so exposed, a feeling which had nothing to do with her lack of clothing. Never had she felt more like the "Awkward Amazon" than now.

Jon grazed her trembling lips with his fingers. He moved closer and trapped her shoulders in a silken grip. "You're right.

I should leave.'' His gaze hovered over her for a brief second. Then, his mouth descended.

The kiss was brief. Too brief.

Andy moaned in disappointment when he lifted his head. He ran his fingers through the hair streaming over her shoulders. After tugging on it lightly, he drew back, his regret obvious. He stood and bent, giving a brotherly peck to her forehead. Silently, she watched him walk away.

His hand on the doorknob, he paused and turned. ''The next time we write to the Archbishop of Canterbury, perhaps we could add a post script, asking him about the requirements for canonization.''

Andy echoed his sentiments with a rueful grin.

His grin matching hers, he added, ''Speaking of the church . . . I forgot to ask what you think of our gentle vicar.''

Grateful for the change in subject, Andy stood, preparing to extinguish the candle. ''He's perfect. I'm glad you thought of him.''

Now it was Jon's turn to be silent.

She glanced at him. He didn't move. All he did was stare, his expression hungry. Her gaze dropped and she felt a flush blossoming along her cheeks. Her wrap had slipped to reveal a shocking amount of bare shoulder, highlighting her skin with beckoning shadows. Andy groaned inwardly and tugged her wrap into place like some protective armor.

The action mobilized Jon. He grinned and blew her a kiss. Without giving her a chance to even say good night, he turned and left.

Chapter Thirteen

Lily bustled in with a tray and deposited Andy's morning coffee and croissant on a table near the window.

Andy heard her, but didn't want to wake up. She snuggled deeper into her pillow, wanting just one more moment to savor the last flicker of a blisteringly warm dream.

Lily drew closer.

Rising consciousness frayed the last strands of her sensual fantasy. Suddenly, Andy froze. The dream totally forgotten, she was sure her face was flaming.

I'm in the suds now, she thought. *The glasses . . . Jon had forgotten to take the brandy and glasses when he left last night.* Unable to face the garrulous maid just yet, she pretended sleep and turned on her other side.

"Miss . . ." Lily started through to the bedroom to wake Andy according to their established routine.

Andy waited for her to continue, but all the maid said was a quiet, "Oh my . . . oh my goodness me . . ."

A soft tinkling indicated Lily was removing the traces of her late-night meeting with Jonathan. Andy burrowed her head farther into the pillow, grateful for its protective shield. She heard the decanter follow the glasses.

Lily picked up the tray without making another attempt to wake Andy. Her crisply starched apron rustled as she turned to go. Andy's shoulders collapsed against the bedding. Her relief, however, was short-lived.

"I'll say I found these in the hallway, miss," Lily said, the grin in her soft voice evident. "Simms will just think it was from the house party."

The episode had so shaken Andy's faith in her ability to keep a clear mind around Jonathon, that she passed several difficult days assiduously avoiding him. She simply couldn't deal with how he upset her equilibrium. The only time she spent with either Jon or his guests was when she accompanied them to neighboring villages.

Since no word had come from Taddeus Green yet, Andy owed it to Helen to continue assisting with the search. But whenever she slipped away to read the parish registers, she made a point of doing so either alone or in the company of Helen. Cynthia and Barbara became unwitting allies. They managed to distract both Jon and Dominic whenever Andy and Helen supposedly went off in search for Edgar's books. Barbara really seemed happy whenever she was with Dom. Such a shame she didn't have her own beau, Andy thought. An attractive, intelligent woman like her deserved better than a borrowed suitor.

At the same time, Cynthia kept Phillip's attention from straying—not that Andy minded. In fact, she was sincerely grateful to be spared the Baron's notice. Phillip had made a few weak attempts to flirt with her, but he'd left Andy feeling cold. She couldn't help it. She really didn't like him very much. At least he didn't try to prod more information from her, or mention the stolen letters. There weren't any further attempts to injure Dom either, at least not as far as she knew. Andy prayed they had nothing more to fear from Phillip and that she hadn't been lulled into a false sense of security where he was concerned.

The following day would bring a brief respite from the current uneasy truce. Tabitha, Cynthia, and Barbara were going to visit the older woman's cousin for a week. Phillip was escorting them part of the way before going on to his estate to tend to some unexpected business. All too soon, however, the entire party would be returning—much to Andy's dismay.

She needed some privacy—a quiet place to relax. Since her father didn't need her, she slipped out of a side door and strolled toward the man-made lake. Thinking about the visit, Andy grinned, recalling the barbs cast between the Marchioness and Tabitha since the party. Oh, they were subtle. One could expect nothing less of two proper Society matrons. The veiled insults could easily be missed by anyone who wasn't paying careful attention. It didn't make the insults any less deadly.

It was obvious Sofia had captured Edgar's interest. The reality didn't sit well with Cynthia's mother, who wanted his attention for herself. Andy noticed her father, caught in the middle as he usually was, seemed torn between wanting to come to Sofia's defense whenever Tabitha was being particularly catty, and having to act the gentleman in order to keep the fragile peace.

As she walked down a tree-lined path, Andy remembered automatically catching Jon's eye during some of the more cuttingly polite exchanges. His features had reflected her silent laughter. She sighed deeply, wondering if their ability to communicate without having to say a word troubled Jon as much as it did her.

She reached the old elm trees near the pond. Turning her head between the gazebo and the inviting grass beneath her feet, Andy decided to stay where she was. Propriety be damned! Her muslin was the same color as the lawn, so stains wouldn't show.

It was a glorious day. She sank to the ground and removed

her wide bonnet. Her shoes and stockings followed. Raising her face, she enjoyed the heat of the morning sun for a moment before shading her eyes and observing the courtship antics of the ducks swimming on the pond.

Her thoughts returned to Jon and her growing attachment to the irrepressible scoundrel. She brushed a finger lightly over her scar. She ought to know better than to become involved with someone of his ilk. *Think of him only as a handsome, amusing companion—nothing more.* It didn't work. The declaration left a hollow feeling in her chest.

Concentrating on the sparkle of the sun reflecting off the water, Andy's thoughts drifted uneasily. She lay there, unaware of the passing time until voices from the gazebo startled her out of her reverie.

Cynthia and Phillip, she groaned and sank against an elm, thankful for the additional cover provided by the small bushes growing alongside her. She had no desire to visit, but if she moved to leave, she'd be detected. Perhaps she'd be lucky and they wouldn't stay long. Unfortunately, by the sounds of the conversation, it appeared they would be there for some time. Andy peered through the bushes.

Seated on a bench just outside the gazebo, Cynthia rearranged her skirt and glanced over her shoulder, giving the Baron a pretty pout. "It's very flattering to have been invited to visit the Marquess, but honestly Phillip, if it weren't for your company, I know I would've been totally bored during our stay." Her gaze dropped to her hands. Her tone low, she added, "I hope you don't think it too forward of me to say."

Off to the side, Andy nearly snorted at the flirting invitation evident in the other woman's voice. She could just imagine Cynthia fluttering her eyelashes right about now.

"On the contrary, my dear," Phillip declared, breaking into Andy's thoughts.

Andy snuck another peek through the shrubs. The Baron was now standing directly behind Cynthia. He placed a hand on her shoulder, playing absently with the fringes of her pine green shawl. Feeling guilty, Andy looked away.

"Actually, I'm honored you even noticed my humble self amid the exalted company we're keeping. I feared my attention might disgust you."

"Oh no!" Cynthia promptly contradicted. "How could you even think something like that? Every woman needs the attention of a worldly man such as yourself. Otherwise, how could she maintain a sense of well-being?"

Was that why Andy had been feeling unwell as of late? Cursing herself for prying, she peeked again.

Cynthia's hand rested on Phillip's. The Baron preened and slipped his hands onto her shoulders, drawing Cynthia toward himself. Her back pressed into his hips, the skirts of her pale sienna gown wrapping around his knees.

"I would be happy if I could give you even more pleasure," Phillip added slowly.

Andy was ready to cast up her accounts. Obviously, he'd read the invitation in Cynthia's voice.

His fingers slipped beneath her shawl and the fabric slid to the ground, unnoticed by either of them. Cynthia made no demure at his caress. Andy slumped back.

Not hearing anything for a few moments, she wondered if they had left without her realizing it. She peered cautiously through the bushes once more and gasped.

Phillip was taking shocking liberties with Cynthia's person. The blonde's pleasure was obvious. Eyes closed, her neck arched back. Her fingers clung to the Baron's head for support, faint moans escaping her lips.

Andy shot back into hiding and clapped her hands over her eyes. Ever so slowly, she dropped her hands, seeking an avenue of escape. There wasn't any. *What a coil!* She had no desire to stay. Not only did she find Cynthia's manipulation of Phillip unpleasant—particularly in view of her previous attempts to capture Jon's interest—but the unfolding scenario made her feel extremely uncomfortable.

She buried her head in her hands again to block out the nearby sights and sounds, only to be inundated by memories. She recalled how Jon had touched her. She remembered sliding her hands through the rough texture of his dark hair. The taste and scent of his skin.

The mallards on the lake called out to each other and her eyes shot open. Gracious! Gritting her teeth, she knotted her fingers in a tight clasp, not daring another glance at the couple. It was impossible, however, to totally block out their sighs. It was all she could do not to imagine herself locked in Jon's embrace.

Whatever was she thinking of? Her color escalated. It would be nothing more than a dalliance for him. Angrily, Andy brushed away a tear which threatened to spill through her lashes, telling herself it was caused by the glare from the sun.

She wrapped her arms around her knees, frustrated. Cloth rustled. The couple must have been rearranging their clothing. The process took longer than she had expected. If the moans and sounds of kissing were anything to go by, they had spent as much time caressing each other as they did repairing their appearance.

Andy hugged her knees harder. She turned away from the gazebo to avoid the temptation of looking at them. How could she have been so brazen as to watch them at all?

No, that wasn't what really worried her, she admitted. It was the fact that she kept envisioning herself and Jonathon enacting a similar scene. *That* was the problem.

Restlessness still dogged her the next morning. Andy paced her room, reliving the events by the gazebo. The void she felt after leaving the lake had been reinforced when she'd met her father and the Marchioness.

Hands clasped, they were just returning from a walk in the

woods. The sated expressions on their faces changed abruptly to flushing embarrassment. Her usually urbane father lost his legendary way with words. Sofia snatched her hand away from his, self-consciously hiding it behind her skirt. Neither could look Andy in the eye and she assumed they had probably been doing much the same as Cynthia and Phillip. At least they looked happy, Andy thought.

She tried to shrug off her gloomy mood, but couldn't. Grabbing a shawl, she escaped her room. Surely it was time to make her way downstairs and say goodbye to the departing guests.

Andy's steps slowed at the foot of the stairs. There was Cynthia, standing between Phillip and Jonathon in a dazzling concoction of storm blue silk, fairly glowing from the attention of both men. She extended her hand and thanked her host prettily. Her eyes widened at Jon's touch.

Andy caught the surreptitious gaze Cynthia darted between the Baron and Jonathon. Was Cynthia still interested in capturing Jon's attention? Andy studied Jon. His jacket clung to the expanse of his broad shoulders; he was tall and ruggedly handsome, loyal to those whom he cared for, and had a wicked sense of humor. Her breath caught. How could Cynthia *not* be interested?

"You simply have no idea how much we've enjoyed our stay, Jon." Cynthia stroked his arm. "We'll see you in a week."

Andy nearly tripped. Fortunately, her unladylike behavior was covered by the forced seconding of Tabitha. Barbara was busy talking with Helen and Dom. Jon glanced away and greeted Andy. Her gaze darted to Cynthia's unrelenting grasp on his arm and her eyes narrowed. Jon grinned.

Cynthia shrugged when Jon failed to return her warmth. She inclined her head toward Andy and turned away, placing her hand on Phillip's. The Baron covered it solicitously.

Phillip added his thanks for Jonathon's hospitality. "Kind of you to offer to put us up for a few nights on our way back to London." He shot a sideways glance at Dominic and his lips tightened. The Baron's gaze reflected a stormy uncertainty before his lids hooded the expression.

Nevertheless, Andy had seen it. Had anyone else been as chilled by it as she? The memory of an eerie howl flitted through her mind. This time, she was sure it was just a memory. Even so, her scalp tingled.

"Is your research complete, Miss Fitzgerald?"

Andy started. She hadn't expected the question. Phillip's thin smile worried her. While the words alone were innocuous, he looked tense, as though awaiting her response with more than a passing interest.

"Yes, it is. Until my father finishes his writing, there's really nothing more for me to do." She was pleased her tone matched his in blandness.

Having learned the tale from the Baron, Lady Tabitha harrumphed. "I still don't know what Sir Edgar was about, raising you in such a fashion."

"Personally, I think he did a fine job," Lady Sofia remarked with a kind nod at Andy. She turned back to Tabitha. "And speaking of Sir Edgar, he apologizes for not seeing you off. He's in the middle of a difficult passage and couldn't leave his work. He asked that I tell you how very much he enjoyed your company."

Andy filed away the fact that her father was too busy to make his goodbyes, but he had obviously made time for the Marchioness. *Hopefully* . . . Cynthia broke in on her thoughts.

"Such a pity you won't be going to London for the Season." She glanced at Andy with feigned compassion. "I suppose you'd probably find it uncomfortable. No doubt it's troubling to be labeled a bluestocking, making it even *more* difficult for you to get along."

Andy's fingers curled into a fist, her growing nails digging into her scar while her mind raced for a suitable reply. Actually, Cynthia's unspoken reference to her age was almost laughable, particularly in light of the fact that Cynthia wasn't much younger. The thought relaxed her. It was time for her to unsheathe her own underdeveloped talons.

"You're right," Andy smiled agreeably. "It is difficult after a while. You're not finding any problems? No, you shouldn't be yet. . . . It's only your fourth season, isn't it?" she asked innocently, standing her ground in the face of Cynthia's glare.

"It's my third." Cynthia's chin tilted and she turned her back on Andy.

Andy caught Jon's wink and swallowed a grin. Her glance fell upon Barbara and her smile fled. What an ill-mannered baggage she was. It was Barbara's *fifth* season!

Pale, Barbara clutched Dominic's arm. Andy felt awful. She'd never meant to insult Cynthia's cousin. Only, there wasn't any opportunity to explain or apologize. With a flurry of activity, the footmen removed the last of the baggage.

And then, the guests were gone.

After everyone had departed, Andy wandered about the grounds, searching for something to do. Unaccustomed to idleness, she finally made her way back to the manor to visit with her father.

Edgar looked up from his work when she entered. "Bored, are you? Just think how bad it would be if you were in London, gracing the sidelines with the other ape leaders." He grinned, the corners of his eyes crinkling.

Andy swatted his arm. "I see the Marchioness has already related the put-down I suffered."

Edgar nodded, then grumbled, "Mmm. . . . She won't accept the fact that I've recovered totally and nags me to have a care for my health. Wanted me to rest. Can you credit that?"

"While I must agree the Marchioness is not one to be gainsaid, I'm not convinced she came only to nag you."

"Yes, well. . . ." Edgar stumbled over his reply, his gaze avoiding Andy's. He waved his hand vaguely before burying his face in a book and muttering, "She mentioned something about taking another walk this afternoon."

"Another walk? . . . Of course!" Andy smote her forehead. "The very thing to help rebuild your strength." She slanted a sideways glance at her father, remembering how he and Lady Sofia had looked when she'd met them the other day.

Her father shifted in his seat and massaged the back of his neck. Taking pity on his discomfort, Andy knelt at his feet and clasped his hand. "I don't mean to plague you, Papa. I'm sorry."

"It's no more than I deserve for having mentioned your advanced age," a rueful Edgar admitted, accepting her apology with an affectionate pat to her shoulder.

Andy paused. She chewed on her lip, wondering how to continue. "Lady Sofia's a very special person, isn't she?"

Edgar drew patterns on the desk with a finger. His manner seemingly detached, his tone conversational, he asked, "Do you think so?"

Gathering that he wanted to hear her opinion about the Marchioness, Andy spent the next few minutes singing the woman's praises. Edgar rewarded her with an oddly shy, but pleased smile. "I suppose, though, what's really important is what *you* think of her, Papa."

He raised troubled eyes to her. Forehead knotted, he glanced away. "You've obviously guessed that I hold Sofia in very high esteem. Unfortunately, I'm having problems convincing her as to the sincerity and depth of my regard." He glanced back at Andy with a half-hearted smile, defeat written in the way his shoulders slumped. "Any suggestions?"

An indescribable feeling of happiness for her father enveloped her. He had found another chance at love. Choking back her emotion, she rose and tugged him from the chair. "First things first, Papa. I think you're looking a little pale. You could probably do with some fresh air. Shall I ring for a footman to escort you?" she asked, her hand already on the bell pull. "I wouldn't want you to fall into a faint while you're walking through the woods alone. It might take *forever* to find you."

Edgar wagged a finger at her. "Doing it a bit too brown, my dear. Too brown by half." Suddenly, he moaned softly and slumped back in the chair. "On the other hand, perhaps you're right. Fresh air might be the very thing, but I daren't go by myself. You don't suppose I could convince Sofie to join me this early, do you?" The twinkling in his eyes belied his apparent weakness.

Andy tapped her chin. "I'm not really sure. The last I saw of her, she was with the housekeeper, reviewing household accounts. It might be difficult to tear her away."

Edgar sputtered. "But she hates doing accounts!"

"Truly?" Andy asked, her gaze innocent although she, too, knew Sofia considered the accounts a dreadful bore. She hid a smile. At least now, her father knew where to begin his search for the Marchioness.

Looking immeasurably cheered, Edgar asked, "Would you mind taking over the writing for a few hours?"

"I would be happy to." Andy seated herself in his place at the desk.

Edgar opened the door.

"Oh, and Papa," she added without turning.

"Yes?"

She paused to sharpen the end of a quill. "If the walks don't work . . . you could always try compromising her." She shot a grin over her shoulder.

Edgar's initial shock at her bold suggestion faded quickly. "For shame, child."

In spite of the admonition, Andy caught the way his eyes gleamed before he left.

Chapter Fourteen

Dinner was a distracted affair that evening, the conversation coming in fits and starts. If nothing else, at least the conflict between Helen and Dom seemed to be a thing of the past. They spent the entire meal exchanging warm, emotion-laden glances, the depth of which made Andy ache with unfulfilled longing.

The expressions flitting across the Marchioness's face, on the other hand, alternated between a hesitant pleasure and a quiet pensiveness. Andy wondered why. Was it due to Sofia's concern for her daughter's future? Or was it somehow related to her own relationship with Andy's father?

Almost automatically, Andy shot Jon a sidelong look. It seemed he, too, felt the tension. Brow furrowed, he nodded toward Sofia and Edgar. Andy's gaze followed his, intercepting the Marchioness's glance darting in Edgar's direction before it quickly skittered back to her plate. A fork steadied in her hand, Lady Sofia stared at the honey-glazed baby carrots as though they were some exotic creatures.

Andy and Jon turned toward each other again. From his imperceptible shrug, Andy gathered he couldn't understand what was happening, either. He motioned his glass of burgundy at Helen and Dom with a grin, as if to say that chapter closed with a happy ending. Andy smiled over the rim of her glass.

Her smile faded and she sipped her wine slowly. It was happening again. The troubling, silent communication. Suddenly, the trifle now in front of her didn't look quite so appetizing anymore. She refused to look at Jon for the balance of the meal. She *had* to put a stop to her growing regard for him. It was too akin to love. Once dinner was over, she intended to escape immediately to her apartment, forgoing the routine gathering in the drawing room.

She counted the minutes until the meal finally ended. Chairs scraping and material rustling as everyone moved from the table muffled Andy's sigh of relief. Only her relief proved to be short-lived.

"No port today, Simms," Jonathon directed. "We'll be joining the ladies for tea right away," he added, stopping to confer with the butler. Whatever it was that he said creased the giant's face with a smile.

Shortly afterward, Simms entered the drawing room, followed by a pair of footmen bearing fluted glasses and iced buckets of champagne. Mrs. Simms, who usually retired about this time of night, trailed in behind them. Dismissing the footmen with a nod, Simms uncorked the fine wine and poured it into the glasses. Andy accepted her glass, biting back a grin when, after distributing the drinks, Simms poured champagne for himself and his wife.

The reason for the occasion quickly became obvious. Helen blushed furiously while Dom's shoulders were squared. Sitting side by side, they gripped each other's hands tightly.

Andy's spirits rose. *That* was Jon's unspoken message at dinner. She looked at him in anticipation and her breath caught. His gaze was already fixed on her. How long had he been studying her? He shot her a rakish wink before looking at Helen and Dom, and Andy drew a shaky breath.

Glass raised, Jon's voice resounded with warmth and sincerity. "To my two dearest friends, who have finally agreed to get leg-shackled. May your union be blessed with much happiness." So saying, he drank deeply from his glass as the others, including the Simmses, added their good wishes.

"I never cry, yet here I am making a cake of myself." Sofia dabbed a handkerchief to her moist eyes.

Edgar took advantage of her blurred vision, edging closer until his side pressed firmly against hers. Instead of demurring, Sofia leaned her head on his shoulder. He reciprocated by wrapping his arms around her in comfort. Andy suddenly felt lost and lonely.

When Sofia spoke again, it was more to Edgar than to anyone else. "They asked me earlier for my blessing, but it's only beginning to sink in now ... my babies are actually going to be married," Sofia said in wonder, knotting her handkerchief, her unusual display of emotion all the more poignant for its rarity.

Although Helen wouldn't release Dom's hand, she at last brought her blushes under control and turned a shy gaze at Andy. "It will be a small affair, here in the family chapel, near the end of the summer. I would be honored to have you as a bridesmaid. You'll still be in England then, won't you?"

Andy glanced at her father for confirmation. They had planned to remain in England, going on to visit her uncles once the Marquess's genealogy was complete. However, she wasn't sure he hadn't changed his mind. At his nod, Andy gave Helen a delighted smile. "The honor is mine. And I'll make sure that Papa's next assignment isn't too far away from here. I don't know about him but *I've* had enough traveling for a while." She shuddered at the memory of their uncomfortable journey upon their return from the Continent.

Then, prompted by some inner demon, Andy peeped slyly at her father. "Who knows, I might even be able to get Father to settle down in one place someday."

The comment appeared to please Edgar. His gaze lowered, hiding his merriment. When he finally raised his head, his features had assumed an unusual, troubled thoughtfulness. He darted a glance at the Marchioness and, clearing his throat, responded slowly, as though giving serious consideration to Andy's comments. "I expect we'll still be in England—at least until the fall."

Andy hid her own smile by sipping on champagne. She knew her father had no intentions whatsoever of returning to the Continent.

"As for settling down in one place, it's too early to tell. It would be lovely to return for the wedding." His brow rose. Without bothering to conceal his grin this time, he teased the young couple. "That's assuming, of course, that I'm to be invited to the wedding as well?"

Interrupting the reassuring laughter of her daughter and Dominic, Sofia twisted in her seat to observe Edgar's once more innocent expression. Her own features were a study in conflicting emotions. "But you'll still be here, working on the genealogy, won't you?"

"Oh heavens, my dear," Edgar demurred. "It's actually quite rare for Andy and myself to remain in any one place as long as we have this time. My illness is responsible for that, of course," he said, patting Sofia's hand in a familiar fashion. "Normally, we simply collect the data and go off to a quiet home base to do the actual writing." He paused, waiting for the Marchioness to assimilate the information.

Sofia frowned. "But . . . I'm sure your health won't permit you to leave before the wedding," she insisted.

Edgar squeezed her hand. "On the contrary. My health is fine. Thanks to you, I feel better than I have in years."

Sofia's gaze slipped away from his to focus sightlessly on a nearby particularly fine Meissen bowl. Edgar, his smile complacent, winked his thanks to Andy for setting the bait.

And no wonder, Andy thought, watching how he pressed even closer against Sofia. The confused woman forgot to shy away from his flagrant display of affection. Obviously Sofia hadn't considered the possibility they'd be leaving anytime soon, and the knowledge didn't sit well with her.

Several more toasts to the upcoming nuptials followed. Simms did a fine job in keeping the champagne flowing. No one commented when he kept refilling both his own glass as well as that of his wife's at increasingly frequent intervals.

Andy's vision was getting fuzzy. Jon moved to sit with her, draping his arm loosely behind her on the couch. She couldn't help a lopsided grin and felt herself leaning toward him. He grinned back at her and tugged her hair. Instead of arguing, she yawned, barely managing to cover it in time. "I'm sorry, but I think I should be off to bed now," she apologized, suddenly sleepy.

Jonathon held her back. "How about a picnic at the lake tomorrow—to celebrate the upcoming wedding?" He turned to include the others.

"It's such a lovely spot," he added before turning to whisper into Andy's ear, "and there are so many private places where one can sit to enjoy the view." He brushed back another loose tendril of her hair.

Private places? Andy recalled Cynthia and Phillip. It roused her from her alcohol-induced stupor like nothing else could. She pulled away from Jon. Her shaking hand combed through her untidy hair. She remembered sitting in helpless fascination under the elm, and felt another telltale blush stain her cheeks. Surely Jon couldn't know about *that*. She darted a worried glance at him from beneath her lowered lashes.

Andy waited only long enough for everyone to agree to the picnic and promptly escaped to her room. Jon's last, wicked leer worried her even as she put her head on the pillow.

* * *

It was a heavenly day for the outing. Andy inhaled the heady perfume of the roses she was cutting for Lady Sofia. Clippers in gloved hand, she bent to snip a pink blossom for contrast to the red.

Unexpectedly, the gravel crunched behind her, sounding like a gunshot. Startled, she dropped the shears.

"Sorry if I surprised you, Duchess," Jonathon offered.

Andy ignored his mocking apology and berated him. "Look at what you made me do." She stepped back, waving at the petals strewn about, damaged by her falling clippers. Her tone was probably harsher than it need be, but how could she admit to the thrill of pleasure at seeing him here and alone?

Jon's grin faded as he took in her flustered beauty. He couldn't remember having been affected by anyone like this before. Without a doubt, he desired her physically. But he also *enjoyed* her company. That was definitely a first for him, he acknowledged silently. His gaze was hooded to hide his thoughts even as he brought a fingertip to her forehead and slid the hair from her face. When he dropped a kiss on her up-turned cheek, upon which the sun had graced a faint sprinkling of freckles, her eyes widened, but she didn't protest.

He wished he could slip his hands to her shoulders and draw her against himself, to settle his mouth on her parted lips and drink in her sweetness. However, she was a gently bred lady, not someone's mistress. Reluctantly, he retreated, reminding himself that he was getting too close to her. It was that innate fear of his growing attachment which, more than anything, prompted him to lighten the mood with a jest.

His brow angled with lecherous intent even while his tone remained gracious. "What a wonderful way to wish me good morning, Duchess. I honestly wouldn't complain if you made a habit of it."

He expected a blow for intimating she was the one to initiate their intimacy and it wasn't long in coming. He accepted it in good humor, bussing her cheek affectionately with an admonishment, "Such violence, Duchess. How am I going to explain my bruised body to my valet? It was difficult enough to find excuses for the buttons you made me lose."

"Jonathon . . ." Andy said with quiet warning.

He chuckled. Obviously, she didn't appreciate a reminder of that episode. Nevertheless, she permitted him to lead her to the stone bench. Jon allowed himself a moment to enjoy the reflection of the sun on her hatless head, highlighting the auburn strands shooting through her heavy chestnut hair. His hand reached up to touch it before he realized what he was about. He swallowed hard and quickly drew back. He didn't want to start something which might be difficult to conclude.

Struggling to appease his desire, Jon pressed a fast kiss to her left palm. It's unexpected texture distracted him. He shot her a curious look. "How did you get this?"

When Andy tried to pull her scarred hand away, he tightened his grip. She fidgeted and glanced away. He unclenched her fingers, studying the puckered skin. The crescent-shaped scar wasn't all that large. He touched Andy's averted cheek to remind her of his question. She flinched, as though struck, but didn't respond. He accepted her reticence and kissed her palm again, this time with a gentle smile.

"Personally, I'm rather pleased to find you have at least one flaw, slight as it might be. It will give me something to focus on whenever your intelligence and strength are particularly daunting." Jon tugged at her hand, trying to coax her out of her pensive mood.

"Oh, I have more than *one* imperfection, if that will add to your peace of mind." Her wry comment lacked even a smidgen of the strength he'd just complimented her on. Her lips twisted in the semblance of a smile and she turned toward him with a rueful gaze. "Shall I enumerate?"

Jon felt her pain as if it were his own. He squeezed her hand.

"You, my dear Duchess, are an Amazon. Amazons are as close to perfection as is humanly possible."

"Amazon?" Andy choked back a strangled laugh. She plucked at the burgundy folds of her skirt with her free hand. "Yes. You're right . . . an *awkward* Amazon."

Her derisive snort surprised him. If such a minuscule imperfection bothered her, there must be a good reason. Andy wasn't a typical, shallow female to hide behind curtains at the appearance of an unsightly blemish. He hesitated. "Duchess?"

"Awkward Amazon . . . my sobriquet when I came out." Andy shot him a halfhearted smile. "It seems my height intimidated a number of people. I *was* clumsy. Sometimes, I still am." Her smile chilled. "A few *good* friends were kind enough to explain why others withdrew at my entrance. Those same friends also suggested I might try tempering my conversation with more flirting and less philosophy."

Jon ran his fingers along her clenched jaw. She shrugged off his touch. Her stare fixed on one of the shrubs climbing the wall.

"Unfortunately, I couldn't master the art of batting my eyelashes." Andy's lips curved at some memory. The stiffness slid from her shoulders. "Every time after that, whenever I entered a room, I would tilt up my nose. They changed my name to the 'Arrogant Amazon.' No one ever knew my nails dug into my palm. Since few asked me to dance, no one ever noticed the spot or two of blood on my glove, either."

A melancholy smile shadowed her features and her gaze drifted downward. "I went through quite a few pairs of gloves in those few weeks. Mama was the only one who ever wondered at it, but she never said anything about the stains."

What could he say? Unable to think of anything, Jon lifted her chin and gently brushed her cheek. Distracted, she didn't demure. Were there more painful memories for her to discard? Had he ever been so attuned to another's feelings before? He didn't think so. Andy's voice interrupted his musings.

"Mama fell ill before the Season ended. As horrible as it sounds, I was almost relieved since it spared me further humiliation. . . . Yet, I never thought she'd die." A few slow, silent tears slid down the sides of her face.

Jon wrapped her in an embrace, stroking her damp cheeks, trying to comfort her with soft sounds. After a few moments, she looked up at him with a watery smile.

"Thank you for listening. I've never spoken of that time to anyone, not even to my father or dear cousins. I hadn't even realized how guilty I felt about Mama's death."

Andy was startled by her boldness. Just the same, she felt incredibly cheered. She really hadn't realized before that it wasn't the taunting which had bothered her so much as her relief at escaping from London. Her mother's death had altered that sense of relief to guilt.

"I doubt you came here simply to listen to some childish woes." She scooted to the far side of the bench. Oddly, in spite of the distance between them now, she still felt close to him, closer even than when he'd kissed her all those times before.

However, that didn't mean she trusted him.

His sudden, boyish innocence could only mean trouble. Jon reached for her elbow and tried to pull her back. In typical fashion, the corners of his eyes crinkled in amusement. Andy resisted. His smile widened.

"Come, come, Duchess. This is no time for any childish game of tug-of-war. If you insist on playing something, I can think of a few games more suitable for our age."

Andy stared straight ahead, battling the urge to accept the suggestive invitation. Her lashes fluttered and she bit her lip against the temptation. "You came out here for some reason other than to simply torment me, didn't you?"

Jon traced her lips with a finger. Her tongue flicked against the rough pads of his fingertips. She swallowed and repeated, "Your purpose, my lord?" Her voice cracked. She met his gaze and forgot her question.

Fortunately, Jon hadn't. "My purpose, Duchess?" Still grinning, he riffled through his pockets. "I thought you might like to look at these." He pulled out some letters and passed them to her.

Andy quickly flipped through the correspondence. The Archbishop of Canterbury had written that there had been a duly executed will, dated about two years prior to Richard's death. The administration of the estate appeared to have been handled properly. A copy of the will was enclosed together with the Archbishop's promise to provide any additional information which the Marquess might require.

There were also a few other letters from the various parishes they had written to. Unfortunately, the correspondence had nothing to add to their inquiry. Disappointed, Andy looked up. "Doesn't look too promising, does it?" she asked, dejected. "Nothing from the vicar yet?"

"Oh, didn't I give you his letter?" Jonathon asked with a straight face. "I was sure I had. It must be here somewhere." He made a show of rummaging through his pockets once more, not holding back his laughter at her mounting irritation. He finally pulled out the missing letter from his breast pocket.

"It doesn't really say much. Seems to be mostly about bird watching," Jon told her. His manner offhand, he pointed out the second paragraph. He shrugged and shook his head in apparent defeat. "Perhaps I made an error in asking him to help out with our search."

Andy glared at him and grabbed the letter, wanting to see the contents for herself. The first paragraph dealt primarily with how his cousin had welcomed him. Nothing there. The second paragraph, she read twice before looking up at Jonathon, her eyes shimmering. She quoted aloud as if to convince herself of its contents.

"The brother of my cousin's husband visited today. He's from Jersey. When he heard of my search, he reported a rare species which may have nested on his island. I intend to return

*with him tomorrow. Perhaps I'll find some traces for myself. . . .
The islanders definitely prefer the company of each other. Out-
siders have a hard time blending in. The man's sister-in-law
is married to Jersey's vicar, a man who was also raised on
these islands. Nevertheless, I'll drop in and have a short visit
with him. As a fellow man of the cloth, he ought to welcome
me."*

The letter fluttered onto her lap. Andy looked up at Jonathon.
"He's found something, hasn't he?"

Jon's response was cautious. "It really is too soon to say."

Andy saw her hope reflected in his eyes, but he quickly
broke the mood.

After bending to pick up her basket of cut flowers, he
extended his arm. "It's time to get ready for the picnic. Come
along, I'll escort you back."

Andy allowed herself to be led off, still pondering over the
vicar's letter. She glanced up only when Jon passed the flowers
to Simms.

"I'll be taking Miss Fitzgerald for a walk now," he informed
the butler. Seeing the question in her gaze, he offered a solici-
tous explanation. "It should aid you in working off some of
your ill-temper, my dear."

Andy snorted. No doubt he was referring to the bruises she'd
inflicted upon him.

"A good long walk might even help you sleep better at
night." Jon's eyes gleamed wickedly.

How would the rake know she had problems sleeping? Andy
tried tugging her hand from his grasp.

Jon wouldn't let her go and concluded his instructions to
Simms. "If you could let the others know we'll meet them at
the gazebo?"

"Certainly, my lord."

Andy caught the hint of a chuckle as Simms cleared his
throat and flushed. "Rather dictatorial, aren't we, m'lord?"

she asked in a furious whisper even though Simms had already walked away.

Jon only winked. He dragged her along the path, distracting her with talk of inconsequential matters until they reached the lake on the opposite side from the gazebo.

Andy had never been on this side and looked around. They were on a slight rise which angled away from the gazebo. The hill was shielded by an old growth of elms, yet both the pier and the quaint structure could be seen clearly from where they stood. This spot really *was* private. Anyone sitting below wouldn't even know if someone were there.

Her gaze fell upon the spot where she had sat observing Cynthia and Phillip. At the recollection, a slow heat rose from the pit of her belly. The flush reached her cheeks and she turned away from Jon, hoping he wouldn't notice. Her dreams of that afternoon returned to plague her.

"It's a lovely view from here, isn't it?" Jon's attitude seemed a shade too virtuous. He appeared vastly amused, as if he were laughing at some private joke.

The footmen had arrived at the gazebo to prepare for the picnic. Andy tried focusing on their activities. The servants' voices carried over the water clearly. Had anyone besides herself heard Cynthia and Phillip?

"Did you notice how familiar Cynthia and Phillip became during their visit?" Jon asked, reading her thoughts.

Had he any idea of just *how* close the two had become? Andy didn't dare look back at him. She struggled not to trip over her thickening tongue and answered obliquely, "Rather." Her father's voice carried across the water, making her jump.

"Don't worry, Duchess," Jon assured her. "This really is an excellent spot. One can see the most *interesting* things from up here and never worry about being observed."

That secret amusement again. Worrying, Andy hurried ahead of him to join the others. His wicked chuckle echoed in her ears. Where had Jon been that day? Visiting tenants in the southwest corner of his property.

Her steps slowed. That meant . . . that meant he could have come home this way. He could have witnessed not only Cynthia's interlude with Phillip, but her own reactions to that episode as well. Mortified by the thought, Andy picked up her skirts and ran the rest of the way.

For the balance of the week, Andy found herself constantly mulling over her growing attachment to Jon. She dreaded the thought of having to leave when her father's work was done. And yet, she almost looked forward to the escape. Her relationship with Jonathon mirrored an inner struggle—a contradicting push-pull feeling. Even when she was at ease with him, there was always a hint of tense awareness.

His recent behavior, however, puzzled Andy. Ever since he'd sent a private letter to the vicar by special messenger—just after she'd related her disastrous Season—Jon appeared to withdraw from her. Oh, he was still scrupulously polite. But he hadn't made any attempt to seek her out the way he had earlier. Was he truly as weighed down by estate matters as he claimed? Or was he avoiding her the way she had avoided him not that long ago?

She intercepted an occasional intense look on his face whenever she caught him gazing at her. Had her admission of guilt over her mother's death given him a disgust of her? She simply didn't know what to make of the change and greeted the return of Cynthia's party with relief. At least they would provide some distraction from her disturbed thoughts.

Chapter Fifteen

Andy's teeth gnashed. Why ever had she anticipated the return of the guests? Their tea was now a stage on which Cynthia was exhibiting the art of seduction. How could the woman be so gifted?

In truth, Cynthia's flirting skills lay more in her mannerisms than her actual words. She had a particular ability to give an innocently alluring smile. And her touch ... that especially light feathering touch on an arm undoubtedly aroused men's primeval instincts. Cynthia would have made a wonderful courtesan. Andy swallowed back not only her disgust, but her regret at lacking similar skills.

Even more amazing, though, was that Cynthia held Phillip's interest at the same time as playing the coquette with Jonathon. Obviously, the woman still entertained hopes of capturing the Marquess's attention. It seemed her nanny had taught her well about keeping the bird in the hand.

Cynthia clung to Jon's arm, gushing, "I'm *so* looking forward to returning to London. Have you changed your mind yet about returning soon?'' A soft, inviting smile played about her lips before she lowered her lashes.

Some of Andy's irritation eased when Jon made a noncommittal reply about estate matters still keeping him busy.

Cynthia pouted and turned to Phillip, who was seated comfortably on her other side. ''Isn't he positively dreary, Sir Phillip?'' The Baron nearly panted some nonsensical response.

Andy looked away and found Barbara watching her study the couple. Barbara winked. Feeling immeasurably cheered, Andy hid a smile, glad Barbara hadn't held any grudges over her inadvertent insult on age the previous week.

Sofia announced the upcoming nuptials of Helen and Dom. Lady Tabitha looked pityingly at Helen. The Marchioness noticed and stiffened. Cynthia and Phillip's stilted congratulations were accepted coolly.

The unsettled mood affected even the well-mannered Barbara. Her gaze darting about the room, she was evidently at a loss for words. Andy felt a stab of sympathy. Had Barbara harbored hopes of a relationship with Dominic? It took a moment, but Barbara collected herself enough to embrace the betrothed couple.

Phillip pointedly turned away from them. ''How is your work coming along, Miss Fitzgerald?''

Andy gratefully acknowledged the change in subject, even though she knew he had an ulterior motive for asking. ''Everything is progressing smoothly. Nothing new has come up.'' Well, it was only the truth, she told herself. After all, they hadn't heard anything definite from the vicar yet.

Satisfied, Phillip put down his cup of tea and stood. ''I don't know about the others, but I would welcome a chance to stretch my legs after all that riding. Would anyone care to join me for a walk?'' While he'd asked everyone present, Cynthia earned a particularly heated glance.

Andy snorted, wondering as to the sincerity of his invitation. Everyone else must have, too, since only Cynthia accepted.

The two of them walked out the French doors, Cynthia laughing up at some comment of Phillip's.

As Andy watched them go, she wondered about Phillip. It was hard to believe he had tried to injure Dom. He didn't seem like a bad sort. Not really. Not when he was like this—a typical London dandy, more concerned about the cut of his coat and the opinions of pretty ladies and Society. While that was definitely not the type of company she enjoyed, it didn't make him evil. Was it all a façade? She shook her head, reminding herself nothing had happened to Dom. Her worries were groundless.

All things considered, the Baron was actually a good match for Cynthia. *I wonder if they're going to the gazebo.* Heat washed up her face at the thought of what they could do there. She took a hasty sip of her tea and nearly choked at the sight of Jon's knowing eyes taking in her awfully warm cheeks.

Her father spoke up, distracting Jon. "Why don't we go out and blow a cloud, gentlemen?"

"Edgar! That's the last thing you should be doing," Sofia argued. "It's a filthy habit and I'm convinced it isn't good for you."

"Now, now, Sofie." Edgar patted her shoulder. "It will give you ladies an opportunity to have a comfortable coze about the wedding."

A hint of melancholy tugged Andy's heart. Even while their relationship wasn't resolved, their communion still resembled Helen's and Dom's. She saw Dom share a caring glance with Helen before he joined Jonathon and her father on the terrace ... That was what Andy missed, having someone look at her like that.

Once the men had left, Sofia engaged Lady Tabitha in a conversation of scandalous Society weddings they had attended in the past. Feeling unaccountably lonely, Andy joined Helen and Barbara, hoping their company would lift her spirits.

"Well, I'm glad they're gone for at least a few moments," Helen said. "We haven't had much of a chance to ... visit lately.'' Her cheerfulness faded and she darted a hesitant smile at Barbara.

''If we haven't been able to visit, it's probably because you've been otherwise occupied. ''Andy covered her slip, smiling. They couldn't exactly discuss the progress of the search in Barbara's presence.

The diversion worked and Helen blushed. Her gaze filled with joy, she watched Dom standing on the terrace with the other men.

''Oh my,'' Barbara chuckled, albeit somewhat forcedly, at Helen's distraction. ''So tell me, Lady Helen. How long have you and Dom had an understanding?''

Helen's flush deepened and her gaze fluttered to her hands folded so carefully in her lap. ''It seems like forever.''

Andy glanced away from Helen's animated features and stared out the French doors. Her father was just lighting a cigar in obvious pleasure. Beside him, Jon propped an elbow against the balustrade. Jon—lean and tanned from riding in the sun. For some reason, Andy's attention faded.

After lighting the cigars, Jon blew out the match and watched the cloud of smoke dissipate. Edgar drew deeply on the first puff and exhaled in satisfaction. A moment of silence passed.

Finally, Edgar spoke with a self-deprecating grin. ''You've probably noticed the feelings I have for your aunt, gentlemen.''

A declaration? Jon exchanged a knowing look with Dom. He returned Edgar's grin in equal measure and nodded.

Edgar cleared his throat while they waited patiently for him to continue. Taking another puff on his thin cigar, he leaned against the balustrade. One foot between the rails, he gazed into the distance. ''I consider myself the most fortunate of men. I've had the privilege of knowing two very special women in my life—the first being Andy's mother. The second, Sofia. The problem is, that while I know Sofia returns my regard . . .''

Edgar paused to tug at his collar before rushing on, "She won't let me make an honest woman of her."

Jon choked on the smoke he'd just drawn in. He hadn't expected such frankness. Tears streaming down his face, he let out a burst of laughter. Dominic, struggling to contain his own merriment, pounded on his back. Edgar blushed, waiting for their hilarity to subside. Before long, he, too, chuckled.

His lungs finally clear, Jon wiped the last of the tears from his eyes and asked, "What do you propose to do then?"

Edgar turned to face them, no trace of mirth left. Calmly, he told them. "Andy once suggested that if all else failed, I could always compromise Sofie."

Dom hooted. "That sounds like something Andy would say."

Jon grinned. "How true."

"Yes, well," Edgar stammered. He cleared his throat again. "After all, if Sofia were well and truly compromised, she really wouldn't have any choice but to marry me. Wouldn't you agree?"

Jon glanced at Dom before studying Edgar through another billow of smoke. With a smile, he nodded for Edgar to go on.

Edgar patted his breast pocket. "I have a special license here—doesn't hurt to have a bishop as one of my brothers, you know. And I'd like to use it as soon as possible."

Jon's brow rose. Smothering a chuckle, he strove for a self-righteous tone and pressed a hand against his chest. "While we're pleased your intentions are honorable, I'm somewhat concerned. Is this where you bring us into the dastardly plot to ruin our aunt's good name?"

"As a matter of fact, yes," Edgar replied bluntly. "Furthermore, I'd appreciate any suggestions as to how I might achieve the deed. Not that I expect either of you to speak from *personal* experience, of course," he added with a grin of his own.

Jonathon chanced a glance over Dom's shoulder and noticed Andy staring at them. He hushed his companions with a warning. "Perhaps we'd best make sure we're out of earshot before we continue."

They made their way around the corner of the terrace and stepped into the privacy of the library. After pouring out a generous measure of whiskey for each of them, Jon took a long sip of the mellow liquor, enjoying its smooth flavor. "Better than tea, wouldn't you say?" he asked with a crooked grin. They sat quietly for the next few moments, considering the various options open to Edgar.

Dom tipped back his chair, rocking it slowly. His gaze narrowed thoughtfully. "Jon, do you remember when we used to play at being noble savages?"

"And poor Helen usually ended up either being scalped, or tied to the stake? I remember." A wince quickly replaced his smile. "I also recall the time we were caned for ending up with more than a handful of her hair."

Dom grinned at the memory before falling serious. "After our games, do you recall how we'd go to the old gamekeeper's cottage—the one which was never used, but always kept in good condition because your uncle wanted to have a place to stop for a drink after fishing the stream?"

Jon grimaced at the reminder of his despised uncle. He nodded without further comment.

"The cottage is still in good repair. The Simmses have seen to that. Don't you think it would make a wonderful spot for another picnic? The ladies might like to pick flowers while we catch their dinner," Dominic suggested. He paused to stroke his chin. "If I remember correctly, there's even a rough sort of partition which hides a bed—quite useful should one of the ladies become fatigued from either the work or the heat."

Jon agreed, "That certainly has possibilities. In fact, I'm rather impressed." He looked closely at Edgar. "Are you *absolutely* sure about your feelings for our aunt?"

"Yes," Edgar answered simply. He spread his hands helplessly. "What choice do I really have? Even though I've been going as slowly as I possibly can, my work is almost completed. I'm running out of excuses to delay it. Without Sofia's firm commitment to our relationship, I will not be able to justify remaining here, yet I cannot imagine leaving without her.''

Pleased with the answer, as well as with the look in Edgar's eyes, Jonathon nodded. ''All right. Do you know where the cottage is that we are referring to?''

''Sofie has shown it to me during our rides,'' Edgar acknowledged.

''Good.'' Jon propped his feet on the desk and folded his hands on his stomach. His fingers steepled against his chin, he began, ''Speaking of rides . . . why don't we have dinner set forward this evening so that we might take the ladies out. If we happen to become parted . . . well, these things happen.'' He grinned to himself, knowing who *his* companion was going to be.

Dominic picked up on the idea. ''Of course, we'll probably come back at different times. And if the men are too tired to stay for tea afterwards, I doubt the ladies will remain without us. There won't be a chance for them to compare notes, so to speak.''

''Therefore,'' Jon drawled, ''if some of us wouldn't come back at all, who would ever know? We could simply agree beforehand to meet at the cottage in the morning. The *al fresco* breakfast could be followed by a fishing expedition.''

Not to be outdone, Dom interrupted with another suggestion. ''Mrs. Simms is quite the hand with herbs. She might make a special tea for anyone who needs to take a flask for their ride this evening. Very innocuous stuff. Not harmful at all. Quite the relaxing concoction, in fact. Hard to believe, but some people have even been known to fall asleep after having just one cup of it. . . . Of course, it would mean explaining matters to the Simmses, but they're both romantic souls. They'd be thrilled at the thought of Lady Sofia finding some happiness.'' Dom glanced at Jonathon for confirmation.

Jon picked up the carving of Burne. Stroking the dog's jade back, he thought over the plan for a moment. Finally, he turned to Edgar. "It really is a good idea. Both of the Simmses are devoted to our aunt. I doubt she would otherwise willingly 'go missing' for the night. However, the decision to involve them should be yours."

Edgar didn't hesitate. "I need *all* the support I can get to achieve my goal. I like your housekeeper, and your butler truly is a gem. If they can help, then so be it. I'll leave the details of arranging the *refreshments* to you, then."

After agreeing that only the Simmses should know of their scheme, they shook hands and returned to the drawing room.

"If you don't mind, I'll just have a spot of tea and then retire. You go ahead, though, my dear," Tabitha urged Cynthia when their early dinner was over. She shot a coy look at Jonathon. "It's a perfect evening for a ride."

Her meaningful glance at Cynthia as she said good night reminded Andy of the conversation she'd overheard between the two of them earlier. After the suggestion for the outing had been raised, Tabitha quietly instructed Cynthia to do her best to get separated from the others in Jon's company. Unspoken was her hope that Cynthia could still snag the Marquess.

Andy glanced around to see if anyone else had caught the silent exchange, but the others were busy leaving the table, having agreed a short ride would be just the thing on such a beautiful evening.

Dom and Helen disappeared quickly, Barbara trailing closely behind them. The balance of the party stood in the foyer waiting for the arrival of Lady Sofia. Outside, several stable boys held anxious horses who, by the sounds of their whinnying, were as eager to be off as the company.

Andy noted the stately Simms hovering again. He didn't do it often, but when he did, it was impossible not to notice. This time he seemed particularly nervous, nearly dancing as he was, from foot to foot.

Phillip offered his arm to Cynthia with a gracious bow. "If I might help you mount, Lady Cynthia?"

Cynthia cast one last look over her shoulder at Jon. When he didn't intervene, she shrugged and gave the Baron a particularly warm smile. "How very kind of you."

Andy felt Jon tug on her arm as that couple departed.

"Ready?" he asked.

Andy nodded. Sofia and Edgar were just behind them.

Simms suddenly called out to her father. "Sir Edgar, I believe you forgot something."

Jon turned and asked his aunt for her advice on an estate matter while Edgar went back to Simms. Andy glanced over her shoulder. Her father accepted a pocket flask from the butler with a wink and rushed to rejoin them.

Since when had her father made a habit of drinking?

Any questions about the scene flew out of her mind when Jon helped her up on her mare. The Lothario used the pretext of rearranging her skirt to subtly caress her ankle. Shivers traveled from her leg up her spine. She swallowed hard and stared straight ahead. Had it not been for the presence of her father and Lady Sofia, she might have been tempted to swat Jonathon for his impertinence.

Phillip and Cynthia were at the crest of a hill, nearly out of view. Helen, Barbara, and Dom were nowhere in sight. Andy was confused, unsure of where to go, not wanting to intrude on her father and the Marchioness. She allowed Jon to hold her back while the older couple passed them.

"It looks like everyone would like a little privacy this evening. Why don't we let them have it?" he asked without looking at her directly.

Feeling hollow at the reminder, Andy agreed with a half hearted smile. They rode quietly for a while, Jon seemingly at ease. Andy used the time to try and come to grips with her dejection. Surely she hadn't expected Jon to be interested in getting her off on their own?

She followed him quietly when he veered off the path and stopped on a high ridge. In awe, she looked at the valley below them. The slowly sinking sun set the vista aglow and made the distant creek sparkle with dancing imps of light. "How very beautiful," Andy said softly.

Just outside a quaint cottage near the creek, a pair of horses were tethered to a tree. A couple was walking toward the water, but at this distance, she couldn't see clearly who they were. Turning to comment to Jon, she paused at his imperceptible nod and decided against saying anything.

"Yes, it is beautiful," he agreed. An oddly pleased look crossed his features. He motioned toward the cottage and stream. "That's where we'll be having breakfast tomorrow and, if we're lucky, where we'll be getting our dinner from as well."

"Do you expect it to be quite a battle tomorrow then?" Andy asked, summoning a smile. Jonathon choked and she darted an anxious look at him.

"That's entirely possible. Some fish are simply more difficult to catch than others." He grinned and led Andy away from the hill. "Would you care to canter out to the gazebo?"

Considering what could happen in the privacy of the oncoming darkness, Andy abruptly refused. "I don't think so." Besides which, the gazebo wasn't all that private, she thought, recalling the view Jon had shown her.

His brow rose at her hasty reply. Andy flushed in the shadow, qualifying her refusal. "It's getting late." Unable to meet the knowing look in his eyes, Andy's gaze dropped to her hands lightly holding the reins. She envied her mare's calm, plodding ways. If only she could remain as even-tempered.

Before they got too much farther, Jon reined in his horse. Andy's mare followed suit. He stilled Andy's question with a signal. Grinning, he pointed to a small clearing off to the side.

Phillip and Cynthia leaned against a tree. Locked in an embrace, they were lost to all propriety.

Andy stared, jerking with a start when Jon picked up the slack in her reins and led her away.

"Now, where have I seen that before?" Jon mused.

Andy tilted her chin with more confidence than she felt. Ignoring his mock leer, she stared straight ahead, primly stating, "I'm sure I wouldn't know." Actually, she *wasn't* sure. Was he referring to the times the two of them had embraced or had he seen Cynthia and Phillip entwined before this? She certainly wasn't about to seek clarification.

"You wouldn't care to refresh my memory?" he prompted.

Andy glared at him and nudged her mare into a gallop. Jon took her up on her unspoken challenge and gave chase.

Breathless by the time she arrived at the stable, Andy felt wonderfully relaxed. Although it wasn't any contest—Jon was there well ahead of her—the race had done much to dispel her earlier discomfort. She gave a final rub to her mare's head before the groom led the horses away, then she smiled up at Jon. "It was a wonderful race—even if you did win."

"A pity we didn't make just a small wager on the outcome," Jon said, his sigh soulful.

"It's just as well that we didn't." Andy grinned as they walked up the steps to the manor. Simms opened the door for them and took her cape. "Has anyone else arrived?"

"Miss Barbara arrived earlier, some time before Lady Helen and Master Dom. Other than Lady Cynthia and Sir Phillip, everyone else has been accounted for." Simms darted a look at the Marquess.

Nodding, Jon gave him a wink. "We passed them on the way home. They seemed quite wrapped up in their ride. All is in order, I'm sure."

Andy held back a chuckle at Jon's choice of words. "My father and Lady Sofia?"

"I believe they've already retired for the night." The butler changed the subject, assuming one of his benevolent airs. "Could I bring you any refreshments, Miss Fitzgerald?"

"Is there anyone left in the drawing room?" When Simms shook his head, Andy covered a small yawn. "In that case, no. I'm for bed as well. Must get my rest, especially since Lord Baldwin promises a battle royal tomorrow."

"He *what?*" Simms croaked.

Puzzled at his apparent shock, Andy could only stare at him for a moment. "The fishing, Simms. He expects the trout to put up a good fight," she finally explained, enunciating her words carefully. She frowned at his sigh of relief.

Simms folded his hands and bowed at Jon. "The fishing . . . of course."

"Are you all right, Simms?" Andy asked, concerned. His behavior was definitely abnormal.

Jonathon's shoulders shook. "It's the violence, you see. Simms abhors it. Comes from all those years in the ring. Your mention of a fight must have thrown him off. Isn't that correct, Simms?"

The butler straightened his shoulders. His chest puffed out and his crooked nose reddened. "My fighting career was much better than his lordship implies!" Simms looked darkly at the Marquess. "Except for that last year when my age caught up with me . . ." His words sputtered to a sudden halt. He nodded meekly. "You're right, of course, sir. That last year of fighting really did me in."

If anything, his actions denied Jon's claims, Andy thought, but Jon distracted her before she could comment.

"Good night, Simms." Taking her by the arm, Jon led her down the hallway. "Are you sure I can't interest you in a game of cards before we retire? Perhaps with a friendly wager on the outcome this time?"

She arched an eyebrow and removed her hand from his arm. "I don't think so, but thank you just the same." She tempered her refusal with a cool smile.

Not put off, Jon recaptured her arm and led her up the stairs.
"The least I can do, then, is to see you safely to your room.
Wouldn't want you to get lost. Unless . . ." he added, his eyes
dancing wickedly.

Andy tugged to free her hand.

Jon sighed. "Oh, very well. I'll behave."

In spite of her actions to the contrary, Andy was pleased to
have this teasing Jonathon back. It had been too long since
he'd behaved so naturally with her. She had missed his innuen-
does and flirting.

Jonathon paused at the top of the stairs and looked over his
shoulder. Simms was still in the foyer, watching their progress.
"Thank you again for everything, Simms," he called down.
"Be sure and thank Mrs. Simms, too, for a job well done. The
butler bowed at the compliment, in charity with his master once
more.

When they reached her door, Jonathon prevented her from
opening it. "I think I should come in—just to check that everything's in order," he declared, his hand on hers. He'd assumed
his infamous, innocent expression while stroking the inside of
her wrist.

Andy tried to focus on the bland face he presented, struggling
to control the fluttering in her stomach at his touch. Looking
into his eyes, she saw the dancing light she knew would be
there. Breathless, she whispered, "I don't think it would be a
good idea."

Still covering her hand with his, Jonathon moved closer,
grinning when she backed away as far as she could. "But what
if there's an intruder in your room?" he murmured into her
ear.

Andy turned her head away from his descending mouth. "I
might be safer with an intruder than with you," she replied.
Finding a resolve she didn't believe she had, she gently pushed
him away.

Jon brushed a quick kiss against her cheek and apologized.

"I'm just not proof against your charms. Good night, then, Duchess. We'll see you bright and early in the morning. If you find any intruders, or if you can't sleep, come down to the library," he invited, stepping back. "I need to finish off some work before the morning."

Andy returned his jaunty wave with a sigh. She entered her room, her steps slow. If only she could have invited him in. Dispirited, she lit a candle and dropped her hat on her bedside.

Suddenly, she froze. That eerie howling again.

Andy dashed to the door and yanked it open. Jon was gone. She glanced back at her chambers. Perhaps, she'd imagined the sound?

No. She shivered. It was impossible to imagine anything so sad and laden with warning. Reluctantly, she reentered the room.

Chapter Sixteen

Smooth walls absorbed the last echo of the ghostly wail. After a moment, only stillness remained. Jon's breath returned and he recalled the eerie sound he'd imagined the night he returned from London. Had Andy heard it, too? He was too disconcerted to find out.

While swearing it must have been his imagination again, he nevertheless walked about the family wing to make sure everything was all right. Nothing seemed out of place and he shook off a feeling of impending trouble.

By the time he made it down the stairs, most of the servants had retired for the night, and the main floor was in semi darkness. He halted a few feet from his destination. The only exception was the library. A light shone from under the door.

Not again! He raked his fingers through his hair. He had no intentions of sneaking in on his belly this time—besides, it wouldn't be any fun to do so without the Duchess. Swallowing a smile at the memory, he opened the door and stepped in.

Phillip sat at his desk, riffling through the drawers.

Jon recognized the vicar's distinctive letterhead crumpled in the Baron's hand. How in the name of all that was holy had he forgotten to hide the letter with the diary and other correspondence? So much for thinking its contents were innocuous. It seemed they had aroused Phillip's curiosity.

Clearing his throat to announce his presence, Jon stepped forward and adopted a languid pose against his desk. "Looking for something?" he drawled before placing both hands on the desk top and leaning forward. "If it's a wedding invitation, Helen and Dom haven't had time to have them printed just yet." His menacing stance belied the innocence of the question.

Phillip pushed himself away from the desk, his eyes darting back and forth. There wasn't any avenue of escape and his shoulders slumped.

"Speaking of the young couple, they're both very special to me. I wouldn't want to see anything happen to them. You know what I mean, don't you, *Sir* Phillip?" Jon continued, every inch the Marquess now. "I would be particularly unhappy should either of them meet with, let's say, a *riding* accident or some such."

Phillip flushed. He stood and held his hands up, backing slowly away from Jon. "I might be guilty of much, but not that. It wasn't me, honestly. I didn't do anything—can't stand violence, you know," he sputtered in self-defense.

Jon's eyes narrowed as he studied the Baron carefully. Was that a guilty stain washing up his face? Or was Phillip telling the truth? He'd heard of Phillip's squeamishness back in London. The fellows in the club often joked about it. However, desperation could drive even the weakest individual to commit a crime. Was Phillip that desperate? Perhaps. Jon hoped he'd never find out.

Phillip broke into his thoughts. "It's the diary, not my half-cousin, which concerns me. No doubt you're aware by now, that documentation might exist which could deprive me of any claim to the baronetcy—I'm sure the capable Miss Fitzgerald has discovered evidence of it already. Can you imagine the potential scandal?'' He sniffed in distaste, as though he'd just stepped into a less than pristine stable. ''I was merely hoping to destroy any traces. Honestly. It isn't Dominic, nor even the wealth. It's the *scandal* which frightens me.'' The distraught Baron covered his face with his hands.

''You'd survive,'' Jonathon responded, his voice edged with steel. He sat down in his favorite position, feet propped up and fingers steepled under his chin, motioning for Phillip to sit as well.

Phillip slumped into a chair. He gazed up at the ceiling, as though seeking inspiration, and sighed. ''You're searching for the marriage certificate, aren't you?''

Jon didn't see any point in denying it. He nodded.

Phillip paused. ''I realize I have no right to ask how the search is going after the behavior I've exhibited,'' he finally said. ''However, I hope you'll let me know when something positive is found—I'd hate to hear of it from someone at the club during a card game.'' Phillip's nonchalant laugh was contradicted by his knuckles, whitely gripping the arms of his chair.

Jon rubbed the back of his neck, surprised by the pity he felt for the younger man. He studied the braced shoulders and squared chin. Phillip looked as if he were expecting a beating, yet wouldn't run from it.

Jon turned his gaze to his own hands. His fingernails needed trimming. He offered a reluctant, quiet warning. ''You'll likely want to get your affairs in order fairly quickly.'' He looked up and added, ''That way you'll be free to batten down the hatches and weather out the oncoming brumblebroth.''

Phillip sucked in his breath and squirmed. ''Would it be at all possible to be forewarned in some way? Just enough time to allow me to convince Lady Cynthia to elope and escape to the Continent for our honeymoon? That way, we'll be gone before the news breaks. Otherwise, both you and I know her well enough to realize she'd cry off if the knot isn't firmly tied—and in the long run, I'm probably the best man for her, you know. Then, by the time we return, the scandal will be old news.''

"Very well," Jonathon agreed and stood abruptly. "You have my word."

Andy's head turned in frustration between the two gowns. Which would be the most suitable for the picnic? The yellow sprigged muslin or the azure jonquil? Did it really matter? Still, her hand wavered before making a decision. Finally, she shrugged and donned the blue gown. Jonathon probably wouldn't have time to notice her anyway.

A hesitant knock sounded on her door, and her chagrin at the foolish worry faded.

"Helen? What is it?" She looked on in consternation when the obviously troubled younger woman slipped in.

Eyes red-rimmed, Helen's hands pressed against her breast. She hiccuped and slowly outstretched a hand.

Andy's breath caught at the sight of what she held. So, it *had* been Burne howling in warning last night. She took Helen's free hand and led her to the sofa. "When did this happen?"

"I don't know," Helen sobbed, her fingers clenching convulsively. "I didn't notice until this morning."

"When was the last time you'd seen it?"

"Just before the ride yesterday, when I had gone up to change."

Phillip? Andy wondered, spending the next several moments calming Helen. She hadn't thought the Baron could be so malevolent. He'd definitely fooled her. Anyone malicious enough to attempt murder—Dom's riding accident could be construed as nothing less—would consider mutilating a portrait child's play.

Andy took another glance at the destroyed miniature of Dom. "Have you spoken to Jon about this?"

Helen nodded. "I just came from the library. He suggested I waste no time in warning you."

Andy wanted to say she'd already been warned, but bit her tongue. The last time she'd raised the specter of Burne, the servants had gone into a tizzy. In such a fragile state, Helen might collapse at the mere mention of Burne.

"Jon said we should carry on, as if nothing's occurred." Helen gulped back a sob.

"He probably has the right of it."

"But how can we?" Helen whimpered, her sobs renewed.

Andy sighed and passed Helen a handkerchief. She put herself into Helen's position. If she'd had a miniature of Jon slashed, no doubt she would be just as upset. She hugged Helen closely and patted her back until the sobs ceased. "We'll just have to make sure Dom isn't left alone at any time, at least until the guests leave."

Helen rewarded her with a watery smile. "That's exactly what Jon said."

"Then, let's follow his advice and take care of those tears. You wouldn't want to overset the prospective groom now, would you?"

Somehow, she managed to calm Helen and sent her off to prepare for the picnic. Andy quickly completed her own toilette, all the while wondering what was going on. She was still puzzling over events when she went outside. The others were already there.

Lady Tabitha's shrill voice carried from the open landau all the way to the front of the door. "You really mean to leave *all* the servants behind?" Although her parasol was open, she had to shade her eyes with a hand against the bright sunlight. She darted an anxious look at Cynthia's fair complexion while awaiting the Marquess's reply.

"Have you no faith in me, Lady Tabitha?" Jon asked with a grin, handing Cynthia in before turning to Andy. "The men under my command during the war had no complaints." He took Andy's hand and squeezed it lightly. His serious gaze at her contrasted with the balance of his flippant comment to Tabitha. "Just imagine how good it will feel to order the four of us men about instead of servants."

"Four?" Tabitha looked around. "Yes, where is Sir Edgar?"

"He and Lady Sofia went ahead to prepare for our arrival."

Jon's deceptively innocent expression prompted Andy to forget about Dom's portrait. *Now* what was the dratted fellow up to? Glancing over Jon's shoulder, she noticed Dominic exchange an unreadable look with Simms as the butler passed him two large hampers. Something was going on. She nodded absently to Helen and overheard Simms wish Dominic a quiet "Good luck."

It reminded her once more of the trouble. Had Dominic been warned about the portrait? But then, that wouldn't explain Jon's sudden lightheartedness. Dominic didn't look particularly worried, either.

Tabitha's mouth pinched into a thin line. "How can a hostess leave without her guests?"

Barbara set about soothing Tabitha. Phillip joined them in the carriage while Jonathon and Dom got up on the box to drive. By the time the carriage entered the woods, the good spirits of Barbara, Cynthia, and Phillip dispelled Tabitha's dour mood.

As they neared the cottage, Dominic and Jon began singing. Phillip joined in, adding a surprisingly pleasant tenor in harmony. Andy exchanged a curious glance with Helen. Soon they were all chuckling at the chosen ditties. Not to be outdone, the women managed to add a few verses of their own before they finally drew up to the small lodge.

Jon stopped the landau and Dominic leaped from his seat to hold the horses' heads. Phillip helped the ladies down. Two horses were already tethered in the shade.

Tabitha's expression soured again. "It seems the Marquess was right. Lady Sofia and Sir Edgar are already here."

Jon grabbed the hampers and dashed to the door, barely managing to get there ahead of Tabitha. Dropping the hampers at his feet, he bowed with a flourish. "After you, my lady."

Tabitha twittered at his gallant nonsense. Holding her skirt, she lifted a foot to step over the portal. She screeched and halted, tottering on the spot.

"Sir Edgar," she uttered in shock. Her eyes darted about and she clenched a hand to her breast. One more weak moan and she collapsed in a faint.

Jonathon almost didn't catch Tabitha in time.

The party instantly sobered. Concern etching her features, Cynthia dashed to her mother's side. Phillip rushed after her. Jon transferred Tabitha to him, and the Baron dropped to his knees. Helpless, Phillip waved his handkerchief under the nose of the unconscious woman.

A very disheveled Edgar stepped to the door and motioned for Phillip to carry Tabitha into the cottage. Andy and Helen stood back in stunned surprise. A moan from inside galvanized Helen.

"Mama," she cried and ran in, nearly tripping over the hampers.

Andy followed, hesitating beside her father, who studiously avoided meeting her gaze. She took in his rumpled appearance and her brow rose. Looking about the inside, she took in the open-beamed room large enough to house a party of hunters. The foot of a bed was visible from behind a paneled screen and the covers on the bed shifted. The rustle of material was accompanied by another moan.

Helen dashed to the screen. Her frantic voice carried back to the others. "Mama, are you all right?"

More rustling movement on the bed. Finally, after a long pause, Sofia groaned, "I'll be fine."

Recovering, Tabitha moaned in competition with Sofia.

Finally realizing what her father was about, Andy fought back an urge to giggle. The stage was as well set as for any

Greek tragedy. So *this* was what had distracted Jon and Dominic. No wonder they sang those outrageous songs during the drive. They needed to warn her father of their imminent arrival.

"Lady Sofia may decide that boiling you in oil would be too quick and kind a death," Andy whispered to her father.

"I know." Grinning ruefully, he shrugged. "However, since this was all *your* idea, I'm counting on you to save me."

"Oh, no, Papa!" Andy threw up her hands, trying hard not to laugh. "You made your bed—now *you* sleep on it—no pun intended," she added, looking to the screen when Sofia uttered another moan.

Groaning, Sofia attempted to get up. "Could you please lend me your shoulder, Helen?"

Andy's humor faded. The Marchioness sounded as if she were truly suffering. What had her father done? She looked askance at him. He winked.

"Oh, lord! What happened to your leg, Mother?" Helen exclaimed. "Are you in terrible pain?"

Now Andy was really curious. She leaned against the back of a chair and glanced at her father's cohorts, Jon and Dominic. Although they looked as puzzled as she did, they, too, struggled to keep straight faces. Andy snorted. They'd never walk the boards with any measure of success.

When Sofia whimpered again, the two men exchanged careful sidelong glances with Edgar. His slight nod apparently reassured them. Andy chanced a look at Tabitha and her companions, hoping they hadn't noticed anything out of the ordinary. Except for Barbara, who looked amused, they were otherwise occupied and Andy breathed a sigh of relief.

Although unsure of what exactly had happened, Andy was determined to add her efforts in smoothing out of the affair. She knelt at Cynthia's side and touched Tabitha's shoulder. "It sounds as though Lady Sofia's been injured and might require extra space in the landau. No doubt she'll need the attentions of a physician. Will you be able to sit up in the carriage, or would you like to rest here awhile until the carriage returns?'' Her innocent gaze hid the conviction that Tabitha would probably move heaven and earth in order to personally witness Sofia's discomfort, even if it meant having to ride on the box.

"Perhaps I could manage to sit up for the few minutes it would take to return.'' She moaned weakly again and clutched Phillip's arm while Cynthia again waved the vinaigrette beneath her nostrils. "It was just such a shock . . .''

How effective! This one would do extremely well on the boards, Andy thought.

"Lady Sofia stumbled last night, hurting her leg. It was easier to carry her back here than to return to the manor,'' Edgar interrupted. "She was unconscious for a long time.''

Due to a sleeping potion in a flask? Andy wondered.

"I was afraid I might get lost if I went for help on my own. There was no choice but to splint her leg myself and wait until morning when I knew you would arrive.'' Edgar took a deep breath and tugged at his collar. "Of course, I realize the Marchioness has been compromised by my inaction. I intend to do right by her. . . . No, Lady Sofia,'' he said, holding up a hand to stop her protests when she came hopping from behind the screen. "I accept full responsibility for this—you cannot change my mind.''

Andy swallowed a smile, taking in Sofia's silent fury. Her father was another one who would make a fine actor. The humility in his penitent pose apparently struck Tabitha as well.

Tabitha glanced between Edgar and the limping Sofia, still wearing the dress from the evening before, a makeshift splint evident from beneath the hem of her skirt. "If it was truly innocent,'' she said hesitantly, "then perhaps I could help to quash any rumors.''

Eyes downcast, Edgar shook his head. "Your offer is most generous, but we are all aware of Society's strictures and, as gentlemen, are honor-bound to follow them. Isn't that so?'' he asked the other men in the room. Each one seconded Edgar's opinion promptly, that yes, it was so.

Tabitha's nod looked almost downcast. "You are correct, of course. The scandal would have been too much even for someone such as myself to halt," she acknowledged.

Andy swallowed a snort at the conceit. Behind her, Jon choked.

Tabitha ignored the sound and bestowed a haughty look upon Sofia. "Obviously there won't be a picnic today. If you could help me to the carriage, Sir Phillip?" The Baron responded immediately to the soft command and assisted her from the cottage.

Barbara picked up one of the hampers and looked back, grinning at the remaining company before following Cynthia out. Andy took the other hamper and struggled to control her responding smile. Hands twisting, Helen fluttered about while Jon and Dominic lifted her mother. When Edgar tried to take Dom's place, the Marchioness snarled.

"My leg may be . . . broken, but it won't prevent me from strangling you." She glanced with some disbelief at her leg.

Jon stumbled. Andy covered a laugh.

Helen, still unaware of the undercurrents, patted Sofia's arm and apologized for her mother's rudeness. "I'm so sorry. It must be because of the pain." She turned back to Sofia. "We'll get you home shortly, Mama. Please don't carry on so."

Simms was waiting for the party when they returned. Any shock he might have felt at the bedraggled appearance of the Marchioness and Edgar was well concealed. He directed the footmen with the precision of a maestro, watching closely as Sofia was carried into the house. After calling for the assistance of Mrs. Simms, he sent for the doctor.

Once Tabitha, supported on either side by Cynthia and Phillip, made her way up the stairs, Simms dismissed the servants and glanced at the Marquess. "I can see it must have been quite the battle—just as you said, sir,'' he whispered out of the side of his mouth.

Andy, standing behind the two of them, chuckled. *So, the butler had been privy to the plan.* Simms turned and winked.

Edgar left to rest. Dominic went to take care of a problem one of the tenants had, after which he intended to take Helen for a drive. Barbara excused herself to go to her aunt. Except for Jonathon, the butler, and herself, the foyer was finally empty. Andy was about to make a comment on the duplicity of men when Simms's suddenly serious features forestalled her.

He glanced around and cleared his throat. ''M'lord . . . the vicar has arrived. He's in the library.''

Andy exchanged a glance with Jon. As if they hadn't had enough today, what with Dom's portrait and the plotting to compromise Sofia.

Jon massaged the back of his neck, his tension evident, and nodded at the worried butler. ''Please see to it that we aren't disturbed, Simms. Andy, come with me. You'll want to hear what Taddeus has to say.'' He took her by the arm and ushered her toward the library. ''Helen told you about the portrait?'' His lips tightened at her confirmation. ''We'll talk about it later, then.''

Taddeus Green was ensconced in a comfortable chair peacefully reading a treatise on flora and fauna, a tray with tea things at his elbow. He looked up from his book when they entered, then he greeted them warmly, his goodness shining through.

Andy smiled to herself, wondering what he would say about her father's shenanigans. Or the mutilated portrait. Her smile slipped.

The vicar stood and took her hand, seating her on the sofa. ''How wonderful to see you again, Miss Fitzgerald. The tea's still warm. Could I pour you some?''

While seething with curiosity, Andy nodded and did her best to observe the amenities. Jonathon, accustomed to the vicar's ways, went through the motions without any apparent difficulty.

She'd been wrong, Andy thought ruefully. Jon *could* do well on the boards. She managed to sit through about ten minutes of polite conversation *sans* squirming—but only because she spent at least half of that time sitting on her hands.

The vicar must have noticed. His eyes twinkling at both of them, he reached into his case and pulled out a sheaf of documents. "About that rare species I mentioned to you in my letter. There were some definite traces of its existence. These papers should assist you in proving the facts." So saying, he passed Jonathon several official-looking records.

Unable to sit still as Jon read through them, Andy jumped up to look over his shoulder. Grinning, Jonathon put the papers down and glanced back at her. *"Tsk, tsk.* No wonder that governess was let go. The manners she taught you are abominable. You might as well sit beside me." He patted the armchair at his side.

Andy didn't scold him for his teasing, or wait for him to repeat the invitation. Plopping herself down, she reviewed the first document, a notarized copy of the marriage certificate. The second document—a notarized statement from one of the witnesses to the ceremony. Eyes shining, she looked at Jon and, with a loud whoop, threw her arms around him, kissing him soundly on the cheek. "Helen will be so excited!"

"Ahem," the vicar cleared his throat.

Unable to look either at the vicar or at Jon, Andy blushed and apologized as she bent to pick up the papers she'd knocked from Jonathon's lap. "I'm so terribly sorry."

Jon laughed. "Please, don't apologize to me, Duchess. I rather enjoyed it. I wouldn't even object if you'd care to repeat it."

Andy glared at him. She grabbed the jade paperweight from his desk and would have tossed it at him—if it weren't for the vicar's presence and the fact that the carving reminded her of Burne.

Chuckling, the vicar interceded by pulling out more documents. "Richard St. James was a well-organized man, fully aware of his responsibilities. A new will was drawn up prior to the ceremony. He left the original with a solicitor there, expecting to have a more complete one done when they returned from the Continent. Since no one on the island heard of his death, nothing was ever done with this. Everything appears to be in order. There shouldn't be any problems having it recognized as a legally executed document."

As soon as Andy saw the phrase, "This will is made in contemplation of marriage to Emily White . . .," she knew the vicar was right. If it *hadn't* been there, the new will would have been invalidated by the marriage. She blinked hard several times to stop the tears threatening to spill. Jon stood and hugged her hard. Biting down on her lip as she was, she couldn't demure.

He patted her back, smiling. "I know, I know. I feel the same way." Still gripping her shoulders, he set her slightly away. "Would you like to find Helen and share the news with her?"

Andy gave him a watery smile and nodded, dashing her palm against the corners of her eyes.

"All right. And unless you happen to see them first, I'll speak to your father and my aunt. Please don't mention anything to Dominic yet, though. I'd like to find a special time to let him know."

Accepting his desire to be the one to break the news to his friend, Andy agreed. On her way to the door, she halted suddenly. Turning slowly, she darted a hesitant look between Jon and the vicar. "But what about the Baron, or should I say, Mr. St. James?"

"Leave that to me. I'll take care of that, too," Jon replied.

"Very well, then." Andy glanced at the vicar again. "If you'll excuse me?"

Taddeus gave her a warm smile. "Don't worry about me, my dear. I'll just stay and visit with Jonathon for a bit. Besides,

I need to have a few more of Mrs. Simms's tasty scones or she will never forgive me.''

Once the door closed behind Andy, Jon interrupted the vicar's account of the wildlife which could be found on the islands. ''Did you receive my message, Taddeus?''

He nodded. ''So you've made your decision then, have you? You didn't sound that positive in the letter.''

The corners of Jon's eyes crinkled. '' 'Fraid so. It appears that I'm well and truly caught, sir.''

The vicar grinned and dug into the breast pocket of his coat. ''In which case, allow me to be the first to congratulate you. She's a fine woman, but she'll give you a merry chase all the same. Won't bore you in the least, and that's important for someone like you.'' He withdrew a paper and passed it to over. ''Have you asked her yet?''

Jon shook his head. ''Can't seem to find the right moment. She's usually pounding me over some imagined indiscretion— you saw it for yourself,'' he said with another grin. ''I need to mellow her somehow, or you're right, she *will* make life difficult for me.''

The vicar stood and came to his side. ''You'll notice the names aren't filled in. I wasn't sure you hadn't changed your mind. It was all right with the Bishop. Now, if you don't mind, I'm off for home. It was a very long trip.''

''We are indebted to you for making it, sir.'' Jon shook hands with him.

''I'm just glad it had such a happy outcome, at least for your cousin. I hope that Mr. St. James won't fare badly, however.''

''They're both St. Jameses now, Taddeus. Remember, the marriage has been proven. Besides, Phillip is aware of our search. I promised to let him know of any change in his circumstances.'' Jon paused, wondering what effect the slashed portrait had on that promise. The vicar's voice recalled him and he stepped forward.

''That's very decent of you,'' Taddeus approved. He declined

Jon's escort. "I'll have Simms see me out. You've plenty to take care of now, what with both Phillip and Miss Fitzgerald. I wish you luck," he added with a final wave.

Jon closed the door and leaned his head against the frame. He didn't expect problems with Phillip. That almost surprised him. Even if he had mutilated the miniature, Phillip could probably be convinced to leave the country—especially with his desire to avoid scandal.

Andy, however, was another story. He relished the thought of convincing her, imagining how he would kiss away her excuses for not marrying him. Maybe she wouldn't be a Duchess in actuality, but she was damn well going to be his Marchioness!

After all, he loved her. He gave a slight laugh, still amazed at that fact. Love. An emotion he had never believed existed. Feeling indescribably happy in spite of all that still needed doing, Jon laughed again.

He turned back to his desk and froze at the shadow on the terrace.

Chapter Seventeen

The Baron stepped forward and shoved his hands in his pocket.

"Sir Phillip!" Jon spoke without thinking. "You heard?"

"Yes, I heard, but as you so clearly pointed out, I'm not a 'Sir' anymore, am I? It will take some getting used to." Dejected, Phillip slumped into a chair. "Should apologize. Discovered the vicar was here and I recalled the letter you'd received from him."

He glanced at Jon, distracted. "You should take better care about the French doors. They were open. Easy to eavesdrop or intrude." Phillip tugged at his cravat. "Also heard you were going to speak to me before my . . . cousin." His voice caught. "Thank you for that."

Jonathon nodded. He came around the desk and sat, hoping it wouldn't be too unpleasant an interview. So far, Phillip seemed to be taking it stoically, much like someone walking toward the scaffold for execution without expecting a reprieve. That could change. As it stood, he didn't envision Phillip being a threat to the safety of anyone, but there was still the question of the portrait.

"May I see the documents?"

Jon hesitated, trying to discern Phillip's intent. The documents were actually notarized copies. The originals were still on Jersey. He shrugged. It was unlikely Phillip would try to destroy them. Too many witnesses to their existence. He passed the copies over.

Phillip studied the marriage certificate for a few moments, his features assuming a bleakness as he did so. Putting it down with exaggerated care, he picked up Richard's will, submitting it to the same scrutiny, nodding with a grim acceptance once he completed his perusal. He looked up with a crooked, beaten grin.

"No doubt about it. These documents certainly appear to be in order. If you would be so kind as to provide me with a quill and some stationary?"

Jonathon handed him the requested items without comment and sat back.

After a few moments of scratching out directions on the paper, Phillip heaved a sigh, sanded his letter, and stood, giving it to Jon. "These are the instructions for my solicitor to start the procedure and assist the new Baron in assuming his rightful place. I believe the less fuss that's made, the more quickly the scandal will die down. In the meantime, I shall spend the next few months on an extended trip to the Continent. The portion my mother left me should help ease my way back into Society when I return."

Jon accepted the documents and put out his hand to shake Phillip's, unable to believe this man had ever destroyed anything other than a cravat. "It's very decent of you to do this."

Phillip shrugged. "No way out of it, really—especially since I intend to return to London eventually. Won't want to be shunned by the hostesses. They might take it out on my wife."

"You still intend to marry Lady Cynthia then?"

Phillip nodded. "I'll have to do it in a hurry now." He paused, studying Jon intently. "There is a slight favor I would ask of you. Of course, I would understand if you refused— I'm not really in any position to be making demands."

Jon waited expectantly.

Phillip cleared his throat. "I couldn't help but overhear the last part of your conversation with the vicar. The special license . . . I don't suppose you'd consider parting with it? It would save a tremendous amount of valuable time if I could use it." He rushed on, flushing deeply. "Cynthia and I could then marry within the next day or two and depart for our trip immediately afterward."

Jon put his hand into his breast pocket and touched the paper, hesitating. Looking at the former Baron, he felt a renewed flash of pity. Even so, he was oddly reluctant to give him the document. "What about the portrait?"

"The portrait? What portrait?"

Phillip's face was a study in confusion. . . . Wasn't it?

Jon wondered as he took in Phillip's anxious glance about the room. Was he seeking a way to escape, or was he looking for a weapon? Casually, Jon picked up the paperweight from his desk, just in case. Lightly tossing the intricately carved wolfhound between his hands, he spoke. "Dom's miniature— the one my cousin, Helen, treasured—the portrait which was grossly destroyed, probably sometime yesterday."

Phillip blanched. His gaze darted to the paperweight slapping between Jon's palms. He held up trembling hands and backed away slowly, stuttering, "I don't know what you're talking about."

Jon studied Phillip through narrowed eyes. The man was nearly blubbering, his fear tangible. Was he telling the truth? Or was he an incredibly skilled actor? Jon hesitated, unsure of what to do. Someone had attempted to murder his dearest friend. Then, Dom's image had been destroyed. He had no proof of Phillip's involvement. Certainly nothing which could be presented in a court of law. Nothing, that is, except for motive.

Jon shrugged. The only solution was to make sure Phillip left the country. That should ensure Dom's well-being. With a regretful sigh, he placed the carving of Burne out of Phillip's reach. No point in taking any chances, he thought, and reached into his pocket.

"Phillip . . ."

By now, the erstwhile Baron had backed his way to the door. He stopped fumbling with the handle. "Yes?" His voice squeaked and his eyes widened as Jon approached him.

Jon handed him the special license. "Here . . . you go ahead and take it. I can always get another one. I wish you luck with the Lady Cynthia. It may be a little difficult for you once she finds out."

"That's an understatement, if I ever heard one." His hand still shaking, Phillip accepted the license with a rueful grin. "However, I'm hoping the thought of a new wardrobe and a few baubles will help pacify her and take her mind off the loss of title. As I said, thank goodness my personal estate is still significant enough to be able to afford a few geegaws. And perhaps if I'm fortunate, someday she will be as besotted with me as I am with her."

Jon accepted a cup of tea from Tabitha, praying for salvation from her pointed questions. Just one more day, he consoled himself before donning a polite smile. "No, my aunt won't be down this afternoon. The doctor suspects she's fractured a bone in her leg."

However, he'd had to ply the laughing physician with several drams of good Scotch until the man promised to confirm the diagnosis—on the condition he'd be invited to the wedding. Still, it had been an excellent ruse on the part of Andy's father and would help his aunt save face.

"What about Sir Edgar?"

"The doctor feared a relapse from spending the night in the cool air and, as a precaution, ordered Sir Edgar to bed." Jon didn't add Edgar had snorted at the advice and was probably sitting beside a fuming Sofia even now.

Tabitha's skepticism was evident from her sniff. Patience, he reminded himself, repeating the litany silently . . . patience, just one more day.

Andy, Helen, and Barbara stepped into the drawing room, with Dom just a few steps behind. Their timely arrival was responsible for cutting off a rude comment he nearly made and Jon stood to welcome them.

Helen looked elated. Obviously, Andy had told her the good news. If only he'd had the chance to speak with Andy afterward, to tell her of what had later transpired. He needed to talk with someone about Phillip's deep game. But with the arrival of the doctor, it simply hadn't been possible.

"I'm so sorry we're tardy," Helen apologized prettily. She and her companions curtsied and seated themselves.

Tabitha shot them a quelling look before carrying out her duties as surrogate hostess. She poured out their tea and glanced about the room. She seemed almost disappointed at the thin company. Beside her sat a glowing Cynthia, her arm resting on Phillip's. Preening slightly, Tabitha nodded and signaled for attention. "I believe Cynthia has some news she would like to share with all of you."

"Oh, yes," Cynthia said breathlessly, her light flush more becoming than any rouge. "Sir Phillip has made me the *happiest* of women."

Andy nearly choked on her tea at Cynthia's choice of words. Jonathon's gaze met hers over the rim of his teacup and he winked.

Tabitha's scowl at Andy was quickly replaced with a smug smile when congratulations for the couple followed. "Yes, it is wonderful news. I'm so happy for both Cynthia and the

Baron St. James. Imagine, my little girl becoming a Baroness,''
she gushed.

Jon exchanged another laughing glance with Andy. What
Tabitha failed to mention was that the position of Baroness
was actually a few rungs down from Cynthia's current position
as daughter of a Viscount. What would Tabitha do when she
learned Cynthia wouldn't even be a Baroness? He caught Phillip's sheepish look. Apparently, the man shared the same concerns.

"It's an *excellent* match," Tabitha gloated. She looked down
her nose at Helen and Dominic, finally addressing Helen in a
saccharine voice. "Such a *shame* your mother isn't here to
share the good tidings."

"I'm so excited," Cynthia interrupted her mother. "We're
to be married by special license. Can you imagine? Phillip was
so confident that he arranged everything without my knowledge.
Isn't that romantic?'' She clapped her hands and sent her
betrothed an adoring look. "I do so love strong men who can
lead.''

Her attention returned to the others and she continued,
"We're to be married at my uncle's, after which we're on our
way to the Continent for an extended honeymoon. Phillip told
me there's no need for me to worry about my lack of wardrobe.
He's promised to purchase my *entire* trousseau in Paris or
anywhere else I might desire! *So-o-o* generous!'' Eyes wide,
she gazed dreamily at her betrothed. "Just imagine the stir
we'll cut when we return to London."

"Quite," Jon murmured politely, barely maintaining a
straight face at her prophetic words. "And you, Lady Tabitha?
Will you be returning to London immediately?''

Tabitha shook her elegantly coifed head. "I'll remain with
my brother until Cynthia and Phillip return from their tour.''

The balance of the tea was taken up with much of the same.
Jon barely managed to get any words in with Andy. Barbara's
presence on her other side didn't help, either. Their discussion

would just have to wait. He grinned, wondering how Andy would take his declaration after they had discussed Phillip, and said to her, "There are some things I need to take care of first, but I'd like to speak with you. Will you be free in about an hour's time?"

Her curiosity evident in the angle of her chin, she nodded. "Helen and Dom are going out in the curricle shortly. Papa isn't in any condition to do anything but hold Lady Sofia's hand." Andy shared a grin with her companions. "The excitement of the last few days has even exhausted you, hasn't it, Barbara?"

"Absolutely! I intend to have a quiet nap this afternoon," Barbara agreed.

Andy turned back to Jonathon. "I was going to go for a walk, but I can cut that short." She took another glance at Barbara and chewed her lip. It was impossible to ask Jon anything just now. She'd have to wait. "I'll see you in an hour's time, then." Jon's grin widened and she wondered why.

Once the company had parted, Andy spent an anxious half hour pacing the confines of the rose garden, counting out the number of steps between each wall. Then, she tried counting how many flowers each rosebush had. That didn't distract her, either. Images of torn portraits and weeping dogs interfered.

"Oh, devil take it!" she finally exclaimed aloud and marched out of the garden. Jon could just as well see her whenever she got there.

Taking the longer way—at least that way she wouldn't look *too* eager—she hesitated in the shadow of the stable as an unaccountable chill slithered down her spine. She hugged her shawl tightly and dashed onto the drive, an echoing memory of Burne's wail ringing in her ears.

Barbara was just ahead of her. Andy called out to her in relief, glad for the company, even if it would only be for a few moments. "I thought you were going to rest."

Barbara glanced beyond Andy's shoulder before smiling and

taking her arm. "I decided you had the right of it. A walk would accomplish much more than sleep, only I couldn't find you. I would've gone with Dominic and Helen, but they left before I could reach them. . . . Probably just as well. Newly affianced as they are, they need to consider how they will spend the rest of their lives with each other."

Andy chuckled as they neared the steps to the manor, and disagreed, "Somehow, I sincerely doubt they're talking about the future right now. They're probably more concerned with the present and finding a private place to exchange an embrace."

Beneath her arm, Barbara's stiffened. Andy berated her unruly tongue and flushed. "Forgive me if I shocked you."

Barbara shook her head as they mounted the steps to the front door. "You didn't. Of course. You're correct again. Sometimes, all that any of us has is the present," she added with a faint smile.

Andy cast her a sidelong glance. She'd never even suspected Barbara had a philosophical bent. What a shame that women were expected to hide all signs of intelligence.

Simms opened the door for them, but before he could close it, a commotion arose from somewhere near the stables. Barbara gripped Andy's arm when the shouts grew louder.

Simms brushed past them and dashed down the steps, running to meet the stable boy galloping up the drive. "What is it, Jem?" Andy and Barbara joined him to hear the news.

The freckle-faced boy of about twelve tugged at his forelock. "Mister Fred, the head groom, was coming up the road. He saw it all, Mr. Simms!" he exclaimed, his voice cracking. "I've got to go now."

Simms yanked at the reins, preventing Jem's escape. He held still when the horse reared, but wouldn't let go. "Saw what? Where are you going?"

"The accident . . . Lady Helen and Mister Dom . . . the curricle tipped going around a bend. I've got to get the doctor." He tugged on the reins, anxious to be off.

Andy gasped, the blood draining from her face. "Wait, Jem!" she shouted. "Are they all right?"

"Don't rightly know, miss," he shouted back over his shoulder. Simms let go and he galloped off.

Andy clutched her shawl. Simms pounded up the steps calling for help. She grabbed Barbara and pulled her aside.

Barbara was paler than the whitewashed cottage where Edgar had compromised Lady Sofia. Her mouth worked soundlessly and she gaped at Andy, shocked at the news. ". . . Dom . . . Helen . . . They're dead. I just know they are. Dom's dead. Helen's dead. Their joy is dead."

Andy grabbed her shoulders and shook her until Barbara's jaw snapped shut over the ugly words.

Jon sped past them to the stable without a backward glance and Andy gazed after him for a moment. Finally, she turned, leading the distraught Barbara into the manor.

A tense fifteen minutes passed in the drawing room where they huddled with the balance of the company. Edgar alternated between soothing a frozen Sofia and a blubbering Tabitha—a Tabitha who was too upset to notice how tightly Phillip hugged her daughter. At least Barbara had calmed down, much to Andy's relief.

When they heard Jon's commanding voice resound through the hallway, everyone, including Sofia, jumped up and ran toward the open door. Sofia finally let go of her emotions. Silent tears streaming down her face, she rushed forward with stumbling steps, not stopping until she wrapped her arms around a battered-looking Helen and Dominic.

"Thank you, God," Andy whispered, dashing back her own tears. She gripped Barbara's hand and gave her a heartfelt smile. "You see, they're all right." She watched the pair being led up the stairs to await the doctor.

"Phillip! In the library. Now!"

Jon's roar interrupted any reply Barbara was about to make. Andy shivered at his fury as his shout rang in her ears. When it reverberated against the Chinese vases, the echo resembled Burne's howl. She clamped her hands over her ears to block the sound.

Barbara's concerned voice recalled her. "Andy? What's wrong?"

When Andy looked up, the hall was empty. A sudden vision of Barbara leaving the stable yard with an anxious glance over her shoulder flew through Andy's mind. Other memories tumbled forth. Barbara gaily teasing Dom. Barbara cradling Dom's bleeding head—had her concern masked remorse? Barbara's stiff congratulations at news of the betrothal. She turned slowly toward her companion.

"You," Andy whispered in disbelief, her eyes wide, taking in Barbara's innocent appearance.

"I beg your pardon?"

"Phillip isn't the one responsible for the accidents, or the mutilated portrait. It's you." Andy shook her head, trying to assimilate the knowledge. She just knew she was right. Only, she didn't know why. She tore her hand from Barbara's grasp and backed away, opening her mouth to call for Jon. His name died before it passed her lips.

Barbara brandished a small pistol at her side before sliding it back into her pocket. Her voice pleasant, she smiled as though nothing untoward had occurred. "Why don't we go for a short ride, Andy? Everyone else seems to be otherwise occupied at the moment."

"Do I have any choice?" Andy regretted the quip immediately.

One hand still buried in the folds of her pocket, Barbara drew her closer. The outline of her fingers—and the pistol—pressed into Andy's hip. Barbara stood on her tiptoes without releasing her arm.

"Of course you have a choice," she whispered into Andy's ear with an incongruous giggle as they walked toward the door. "We all have choices," she added. Barbara frowned and patted the inside of her pocket. "Twice, I chose to make Dom's death look like an accident instead of using this pistol. A mistake I don't intend to repeat."

It was surprisingly easy for Barbara to lead Andy quietly from the manor. Everyone was too distracted by the accident to pay them any mind. As they rode away, Andy considered her chances of escape.

"I should warn you, Andy. I'm a good shot. A wonderful uncle trained me—not Tabitha's husband. He was as useless as she is."

The cold-blooded warning was deadly serious. Left with no other options, Andy realized she'd have to bide her time. Hopefully, Jon's interrogation of Phillip wouldn't last too long. She prayed he'd remember their appointment and worry at not being able to find her. She prayed he'd search for her.

Until then, all she had to do was stay alive.

Chapter Eighteen

"Damn you to hell, Phillip St. James. Stand up and fight!"

Jon grabbed the lapels of his jacket and jerked the sniveling man to his feet. When he pulled back a clenched fist, ready to throw another punch, Phillip again slid to the floor.

"I swear it wasn't me! It wasn't me." His voice trailed off. Whimpering, he brought a trembling hand to his bleeding lip, watching Jon all the while.

Relentless, Jon dragged him up again and shook him. "The reins were cut. Nearly the same trick as last time. You're lucky they didn't die when the curricle tipped." Blood, mixed with fear and rage, pounded in his ears in crashing waves. He'd nearly lost his best friends because of another's jealousy.

He shoved at Phillip's shoulder and took another menacing step closer. "Fool that I was, I believed you hadn't been responsible for the other acts." His voice quivered in anger. Anger at himself. "Or if you had, I discounted the enormity, telling myself that they'd been committed in moments of desperation. I wasn't thinking clearly."

No, he hadn't. He'd been thinking about Andy instead of

trying to find the culprit. Jon swallowed hard, trying to control himself. "But this . . . this . . ." He refused to stoop to murder, but couldn't restrain from smashing a fist into Phillip's belly.

Phillip doubled over and fell to his knees, mewling. Clutching his stomach with both hands, he looked up and pleaded, "I'm innocent. Please believe me."

Something about his tone finally cut through the red haze in Jon's mind. He hesitated, his fist still clenching and unclenching at his side. "If not you, then who?"

"I don't know." Phillip crawled and clutched Jon's trousers. "I just don't know," he repeated.

Jon reached for Phillip's padded shoulders once more. A frantic, distant barking stopped him. An icy fear swept through his veins at the chilling sound. He glanced down at Phillip, whispering, "Did you hear that?"

Phillip's head cocked to the side. "Hear what?"

"Good lord . . . Burne!" Jon glanced around the room for a weapon. Nothing else handy, he grabbed the jade carving and pulled Phillip to his feet. "You might still be of some help. Come with me and be quick about it! We don't have any time to lose."

Although startled at Jon's sudden change, Phillip obeyed. They rushed past startled grooms in the stables and, quickly saddling their horses, galloped off without explanation.

Jon's heart slammed against his chest, keeping rhythm with the pounding of the horses' hooves. Burne was still barking. Only now, they were getting closer to the baying. It was Andy. Jon could feel the danger surrounding her.

Why had he waited so long to tell her he loved her? He'd still believed it had been some sort of game. He prayed for the chance to remedy the error.

They neared a hill. On the other side was the old abbey— a place no one went anymore because of its state of disrepair. The howling stopped. Jonathon sensed that was where the danger lay.

He pulled back on his reins, gradually slowing his stallion. Phillip caught up with him and Jon held up a hand for silence. They dismounted and cautiously made their way over the crest.

Below them, Barbara and Andy appeared to be in the middle of a pleasant visit. Barbara's melodic laughter rang through the air. Phillip glanced at Jon, about to speak. Jon hushed him with another signal. They crept closer. Barbara's words became clearer.

"I've been in love with Dominic ever since my aunt introduced us two years ago. I couldn't bear the thought of sharing him with anyone. When I cut the cinch, I didn't intend to kill him. Truly I didn't. The very idea of hurting him really bothered me, but I was there to make sure he would ride slowly. I only wanted to injure him slightly. That would give me the opportunity to care for him and prove my worth. By depending on me, I was certain he would come to return my love. Only that didn't happen. He turned to that milk-and-water miss, Lady Helen, instead."

Her features twisted, reflecting the fury of a woman scorned. "I gave him two years of devotion. My only reward is a secure place on the shelf. So, you see, Andy, the fool deserves to die for rejecting me. Helen means nothing—less than nothing. If she dies at the same time, well . . ." Barbara shrugged.

She halted her tirade and gazed at Andy for a moment. "What a shame I need to kill you, though. That truly bothers me. I like you. You're bright and witty in a way most other women aren't. I've enjoyed your company. If only you hadn't guessed."

Phillip's horse whinnied.

Barbara leaped up, brandishing her pistol. "Who's there?" When no one replied, she pointed the weapon at Andy. "Whoever you are, you'd best step forward now, or Andy will meet her Maker sooner than expected."

With no other choice, Jon, followed by Phillip, surrendered.

The crazed look in Barbara's eyes was horrifying. The worst

thing was, there wasn't anything he could do about it. Jon darted a glance at Andy, relieved at her small nod. She was all right. He took another step toward Barbara, slipping his hand nearer his pocket with its hidden paperweight. Andy stood stock-still.

Barbara's head and hand wavered between Jon and Andy. "Don't think you can overpower me."

Her laughter sent another icy ripple down Jon's spine. She raised her pistol and pointed it between his eyes.

"Barbara," Phillip protested. "That isn't at all sporting."

She swung the pistol at him. "This isn't a game. Stay out of it." She swung the weapon back at Jon.

Jon's eyelids didn't flicker when, to her rear, Andy stooped and picked up a rock. He prayed Barbara wasn't a crack shot.

A sudden, fierce snarl froze the tableau.

"What in the devil was that?" Phillip whispered, finally hearing the sound which had led them to this spot.

A deep, low growl seemed to come from behind Barbara. She spun on her heel. There was nothing there.

Jon had his hand on the paperweight.

Another growl. Barbara spun again. "Where are they?" she screamed, waving her pistol in the air. Her breath came in short spurts. "I'm not crazy. I can hear them."

Another ugly snarl was the only reply to her question. This time when she spun, both Andy and Jon were ready. Andy crashed the rock against Barbara's head. The paperweight slipped from his fingers and Jonathon tackled her from the side. Phillip rushed forward as Barbara fell in a heap.

Andy collapsed into Jon's arms. He pressed her head against his shoulder so she wouldn't see Barbara's still form on the ground.

Phillip gingerly picked up the pistol. Holding it between two fingers, he stooped for the carving as well before joining them. Unable to meet Jon's eyes, he nudged a pile of dirt with his boot, and carefully extended the gun. "Here, you'd better take care of this. Barely know the rudiments 'bout the damned things—beg pardon, Miss Fitzgerald,'' he added quickly, apologizing for his language.

Still holding Andy with one arm, Jon grimly accepted the gun and pointed it away, discharging two deadly shots. "The safest way to handle something like this is to make sure the barrels are empty.''

"Yes, of course,'' Phillip stuttered before returning the jade. Andy took it. "Burne,'' she whispered and looked up at Jon.

Jon nodded and stroked the carving she held between them—a symbol of another belief destroyed. Both love and spirits could exist in this world.

"Are you all right, Miss Fitzgerald? I'm terribly sorry about all this.'' Phillip touched her shoulder awkwardly.

Still shaken, Andy lifted her head. "It wasn't your fault, Sir . . . I mean . . .''

Phillip waved his hand, his smile sheepish. "I know what you mean.'' His smile faded. "I'm sorry, too, that I wasn't much help. Told Jon I didn't like violence.''

Jon felt a cleansing laughter bubble up from deep inside and his chest shook in silent mirth. "And now, I believe you.'' He was about to apologize for the beating he'd given Phillip, when the ground reverberated.

Barbara had recovered enough to silently slip away and escape on Jon's stallion.

Andy's nails dug into his shoulders. He brushed back the hair from her face. "Don't worry. She won't get far. Not on that animal. I'm the only one who can ride him.'' He bent and kissed her forehead.

"But, Jon,'' she argued.

He pressed his fingers against her lips. *"Sshh.* By the way, I've been meaning to tell you just how very much I love you.''

Phillip forgotten, Jon grinned at Andy's disbelief and brought his lips to hers.

* * *

Several days later, everyone gathered in the foyer to bid farewell to the guests, whose departure had been delayed by the matter of shipping Barbara off to a discreet sanitarium which catered to the mad relations of the well-heeled. Jon had been right about his stallion. He'd thrown Barbara, but other than being concussed, she'd suffered no permanent damage— much to the disgust of Tabitha, Andy was sure.

At the sound of heels scraping in the hall, Andy looked back. It was the Marchioness, her arrival worthy of an Egyptian queen. Two sturdy footmen bore her carefully in a modified Bath chair, a reminder of her catastrophic injury. However, with her own shame to bear, it was unlikely Tabitha would spread any rumors about Sofia and Edgar.

Andy was pleased to see the Marchioness had forgiven Edgar. It was obvious from the soft smiles and gentle words they shared.

She glanced away and caught Phillip studying Dominic. Dom wasn't aware of it and was startled when Phillip extended a hand.

"Sorry if I made life unpleasant for you in the past . . . want to wish you well before we leave," Phillip mumbled. He flushed at not only the polite skepticism, but question evident in Dom's quirked brow and added, "Uhmm . . . the Lady Helen. I wish you well with her. She'll make a fine lady of the manor."

Andy chuckled quietly, her gaze meeting Jon's. He winked.

Dominic, however, was successfully misled by the statement. He stared hard at Phillip to see if the man were mocking him, or had simply gone as mad as Cynthia's cousin. His distracted gaze fell on Helen and he shrugged. "You've misunderstood the situation. We won't exactly be living *that* type of life."

A genuine smile crossed Phillip's features and he pumped Dom's hand again. "I don't think Lady Helen would agree with your opinion. She will probably consider any home with you to be a mansion."

Tabitha, who had been fluttering between Cynthia and the footmen in concern that nothing be left behind, finally spoke. "So sorry we need to leave in such a rush, but it's such a long drive to my brother's—I do so hate traveling! Just imagine, my darling Cynthia is getting married the day after tomorrow. I don't know how I'll survive until then. The palpitations I am suffering are almost too much to bear."

She bent forward and kissed the air above Sofia's cheek. "Such a lovely visit." Her features darkened and she whispered, "Except for *the incident,* of course." Tabitha bit her lip, as though wondering whether to say anything more. She shook off the desire and fluttered toward her daughter. "Cynthia, darling. Did you remember to take that lovely Spanish shawl Miss Fitzgerald gave you?"

The incident. Andy knew the vague words weren't a reference to the way Lady Sofia had "broken" her leg. Andy shivered at the memory of Barbara's insane duplicity and wrapped her arms around herself.

A last flurry of activity and Cynthia's party left. Jon motioned for everyone to join him in the conservatory. It was time to celebrate the betrothal of Edgar and Sofia. With all that had gone on before, it hadn't been possible any earlier.

On bended knee, Edgar placed a footstool beneath Sofia's bandaged leg. His assumed humility brought out her full laughter and she threatened to beat him with the cane she now sported. The splint had been removed, but for the sake of maintaining their story of an injury, she had to limp around for a while longer. It wouldn't do to add more grist to the gossip mill.

Jon grinned at his aunt. "Have you reconciled yourself to the inevitable then, madam, and forgiven the scoundrel who besmirched your reputation?"

The Marchioness flushed, looking years younger, and her

gaze dropped. "I have no choice but to accept the inevitable. However, forgiveness is another story," she added archly, grabbing her hand back from Edgar and shaking a finger at him. "You will be made to suffer for this, sirrah. I just haven't decided how yet." Her glowing features robbed her words of venom and she permitted Edgar to recapture her hand.

Andy's breath caught in her throat. There was that obvious happiness again. She rose and embraced the seated Sofia. "I never had the opportunity earlier, but I'd like to welcome you to the family now," she said. Sofia returned her warm hug in equal measure. Unable to believe the change in the other woman, Andy jested to cover her wonder. "I should warn you, though. You'll need to keep a sharp eye on my father. I've heard tell he cheats at chess."

Sofia blushed at the reminder of her comments during Edgar's recuperation and her voice lowered, "Yes, I've heard the same." A suspicious moisture gathered in her eyes, but it only reflected Andy's own.

Edgar passed Sofia a handkerchief. All affected, the others in the room cleared their throats until Jon stepped into the breach. "Simms, I believe it's time for some champagne."

"As a matter of fact, sir, I took the liberty of having it brought up earlier," Simms responded. He motioned to a hovering footman to bring forward several chilled bottles which had been concealed behind one of the plants.

Jon grinned. "Should've known you'd be prepared for anything."

"Quite, sir." With the tray now placed on a side table, the droll butler dismissed the footman. Mrs. Simms slipped into the room and Simms poured out two extra glasses of the heady wine.

A sense of *déjà vu* overcame Andy. Everyone, including the Simmses raised their glasses to Edgar and Sofia. The toasts began, each person trying to outdo the others in outrageousness.

When Dominic escorted a slightly giddy Helen out for fresh air, Jonathon warned them to watch out for snakes.

"The two-legged variety are the worst," Andy added. Dominic laughed. She flushed and quickly corrected herself, "I didn't mean you, Dom."

Chuckling at Andy's inadvertent insult, Jon advised the couple, "Don't be too long. We'll have a few more things to celebrate." When they left, he turned to the others. "I'll be back in a moment. Simms, you will remain here?"

His curiosity aroused, the butler raised his bushy eyebrows. "As you wish. And Mrs. Simms?"

Jon grinned. "Yes, of course. It will save you the trouble of having to repeat everything to her later." On his way out, he gave the housekeeper a fond pat to the shoulder.

Andy glanced between Sofia and her father. "About Dom's change in circumstance, do you suppose?"

Sofia sat forward, Edgar's handkerchief knotted through her fingers. "I hope so. He's fulfilled his promise not to say anything before Phillip's departure."

Edgar turned to the butler. "In which case, Simms, I hope you laid in plenty of champagne."

"There are several bottles left, sir," the butler assured him.

Helen and Dominic heeded Jon's advice and kept their walk short, returning before he did. Andy glanced at the couple, grateful they hadn't suffered more than superficial cuts and bruises from the accident. Jon's return with a packet distracted her from any further depressing thoughts.

"What have I done?" Jon asked when seven pairs of curious eyes focused on him. He laughed and spread his palms. "I'm innocent, truly." His smile softened and he nodded at Simms to refill the glasses. That done, he raised his drink. "I think it's time to toast the new Baron."

Everyone except Dom lifted a glass. Holding tightly on to Helen's hand, Dominic surveyed them. His sunny features graced with a flush, he cleared his throat. No words came out and he darted a helpless glance at Helen.

She patted his hand. "I told Dominic about his parents." Helen paused and bit her lip. "I'm sorry, Jon. I know it was your place to tell him, but I couldn't keep quiet about it any longer. You don't mind, do you?"

Jon's smile gentled. "Of course I don't."

Dom regained his voice. "My thanks for all that each of you has done." His gaze traveled the room to every individual, pausing when he reached Andy. "Especially you, Andy. And I cannot apologize enough for what you suffered at the hands of Barbara."

Tongue-tied, Andy reached to pick up her near-empty glass from the low table. It tipped, spilling the last few drops. Chagrined, she looked at Simms, who rushed forward to wipe away the traces of her accident. "At least I didn't break the glass," she said with a trace of her old awkwardness.

"All the more reason to celebrate then," Jon declared.

"If you had, it would only bring even better luck," Simms added kindly, reminding her of an old superstition. He proceeded to pop the cork on a new bottle of champagne and, swaying somewhat, refilled the glasses. "This one's on me, boys—like in the old days."

A bubble of mirth rose from Andy's chest. His nose red, Simms looked as though he were celebrating a successful bout in the ring. She joined in the toast, finally at ease with her occasional clumsiness.

Jon stood and passed the package to Dom with a hug.

Dom's eyes misted when he saw the faded journal. "My mother's?" Jon nodded. Dominic stroked the tattered cover reverently. His gaze lifted to Andy's. "Helen told me it wouldn't have been possible without your help. Thank you again." He glanced at Helen before continuing. "Indeed, we are both indebted to you." Helen bobbed her head in agreement.

Andy's throat tightened at the simple, emotion-laden words.

"Yes, the Duchess's instincts aren't bad. That is, whenever she can manage to take her mind off all that transcribing her father makes her do."

Andy tossed a cushion at Jon and the party proceeded on a lighter vein.

Andy climbed into bed, blew out the candle, and snuggled under the covers. Unfortunately, she couldn't relax. Turning on her side, she smiled as the day's events tripped through her mind. Her smile faded. After plumping the pillow, she shifted on her other side and admitted her problem.

The problem was, Jonathon hadn't sought out her company after the reception. In fact, she realized, he hadn't been alone with her since they'd returned. She shuddered and whispered, "Thank you again, Burne."

Andy lay on her back, staring up at the darkness. Was Jon avoiding her? Why? Did he regret his declaration of love? Perhaps he *hadn't* said he loved her. Perhaps she'd just imagined it.

No. His kiss had been all too real. *Her* love was real, too. Only, how had she allowed such a lighthearted libertine to worm his way into her permanent affection? Andy flipped onto her stomach, disgruntled. Love was definitely not a comfortable emotion. She flung an arm over her head.

Other than sending her a few heated looks, Jon had virtually ignored her throughout the evening, too. That hurt. She winced, calling herself every type of fool for taking such special care with her appearance before dinner and wearing one of her most daring gowns. A seductive scent, specially formulated for her on the Continent, came out of its silver case for the occasion. She'd splashed it behind her ears and in the valley between her breasts, in hope that Jon might take her for a walk.

Even now, the scent lingered, reminding her of her folly. She'd flirted outrageously over dinner, even going so far as to flutter her eyelashes at him the way she had seen Cynthia do. How ridiculous she must have looked! How she must have reminded him of the women who had tried to entrap him. Of his stepmother, whose very existence revolved around flirting and cuckolding his father until he'd succumbed to an apoplectic fit and choked to death.

But then again, perhaps he *didn't* look at her so negatively. The one time Jon had spoken to her at dinner, he'd said it had taken him a long time to really believe that most women weren't like his stepmother. The force of his statement took her by surprise and she lost herself in the heat of his hypnotic gaze . . . only he didn't say anything more.

By the time Jonathon had dragged her father off for a few private words after dinner, Andy had given up on regaining his attention. She excused herself, claiming she needed to rest.

Now as she lay between rumpled sheets, Andy steeled herself against an urge to cry and began determinedly to count sheep. It wasn't until the rosy fingers of dawn crept through the curtains that the age-old remedy for insomnia worked.

Chapter Nineteen

What was taking her father so long? He should have been there by now, his visit with the vicar in the village over. Andy shielded her eyes against the glaring sun and looked around the valley surrounding the gamekeeper's cottage.

According to the note Simms had passed her, she was to meet him at the gazebo. She hadn't felt like going there for a number of reasons, not the least of which was the memories it invoked, and had changed the meeting place to here. Perhaps Simms hadn't given him the message? Andy shook her head. More likely he had been detained by the vicar. At the same time, she wondered what her father had to say that couldn't be said at the manor.

Andy sighed, still unable to believe her father and the Marchioness were getting married the next day. She glanced at the stream. Its cool water bubbled invitingly over the rocks and she succumbed to the temptation. Removing her shoes and stockings, she hiked up her skirt and hopped onto an old fallen tree which straddled both bank and stream. With one cautious foot in front of the other, she made it to the end of the log without incident.

Perching down on the very edge, she drew her gown to her knees and dropped her feet into the water. Its cold made her squeal, then laugh—she hadn't done this in years. It felt wonderful. She lifted her bare head to the sun's healing rays, not caring that it would give her a rash of freckles, and splashed her feet playfully the way she had as a child.

She stopped the splashing to ripple her fingers through the water thinking that, like the trail left by her movement, the wedding would bring initial changes. What then? Would life settle back into a routine, just like the now still water? How would she fit in?

Sofia and Edgar planned to move to his estate after a brief honeymoon trek through the Lake District. Both wanted Andy to continue making her home with them, unless she desired otherwise. Odd, how they made it sound as if she had some choice. Although she had her mother's portion, she wouldn't feel comfortable setting up her own establishment. Not yet anyway. Perhaps later.

One thing was sure. Next week, Andy was going to visit one of her cousins. Perhaps her nephews and nieces would keep her busy with their antics. She desperately needed something to distract her from what she was leaving behind.

Jonathon.

An effervescent vision of the Marquess floated through her mind—an image so strong she could almost see it reflected on the water. She imagined his bold features, with his lips curved into one of his wickedly innocent, captivating grins—which always irritated the stuffing out of her!

Frustrated, Andy paddled her feet in the water, as if dispelling the mirage would clear her thoughts. No point in dreaming about that scoundrel. So what if he *had* said he loved her? He'd followed the declaration with indifference. Well, perhaps not completely so. He had tried to get her alone once or twice, but without success. It only meant he hadn't really tried.

The hard gallop of a horse recalled her. Her father. Relieved, she stood and waved, barely managing to keep her balance when her perch swayed. With the sun directly in front of her, it took a moment to ascertain the features of the arrival . . . and it wasn't her father.

"Hello there, Duchess," Jon greeted her after tethering his stallion to a nearby tree.

"I'm expecting my father."

"He's been delayed." He gave her a long, serious look. It vanished when he noted her bare feet. His features broke into a grin and he removed his own boots and stockings. "An excellent idea," he declared, striding onto the fallen tree.

The log rocked and Andy cringed. "Jonathon, don't!" Her body swaying, she spread her arms for balance, nearly slipping into the water. "Jon . . . please go back."

"Not to worry, my dear. I'm an old hand at this. Besides, not only will this ensure I have your undivided attention, but it will also mean you won't be able to avoid my company— the way you have been lately. Most unkind of you to tease me with your beauty the way you did last night, then escape."

The log steadied. Andy sat, refusing to pay his flattery any mind, and glared at him. *"I've* been avoiding *you?* Isn't the shoe on the other foot?"

"Missed me, did you?" Jon laughed. With total disregard for their safety, he moved closer. "You don't mind if I join you, do you?" The log rocked again while he seated himself.

"Would it make any difference if I did?" Her body adjusting to the slight swaying, Andy hugged her knees to her chest and stared straight ahead.

"Probably not," he answered companionably and dropped his feet into the stream. "Ahh," he sighed. "This feels heavenly. It's been ages since I've done this."

Andy shot him a sidelong glance. Slowly paddling the water,

he really did look contented, even though his breeches were getting wet. Eyes closed, he'd leaned back on his palms. She decided she might as well enjoy herself, too, and stuck her feet in the water again. The splashing water helped dispel her melancholy. As small sprays flew, Andy realized Jon was right. It did feel good.

"Does your aunt swim?"

"Pardon me?" Jon asked, startled by the question.

Smiling, Andy gazed at a broken branch floating down the water. "When I was younger, we often went to the coast for holidays. Papa always made a point of finding a deserted bay where we could swim."

"Another one of your unladylike accomplishments? Goodness, you seem to have a veritable font of them."

Not put out, Andy merely grinned and bent to scoop up a handful of water. Without warning, she repaid his insolence by showering him. The log swayed.

"Whoa, easy there, Duchess." His glinting eyes hinted of retribution.

Laughing, Andy ignored the warning. Jon, though, fell oddly silent. She glanced at him. He was staring straight ahead, his feet stilled.

"Actually, we all swim—my aunt as well as Helen, too," he said, finally answering her earlier question. "We used to sneak away from my uncle on summer afternoons to do just that."

Inwardly, Andy cringed. She'd learned enough from working on the genealogy to realize that life with the old Marquess had been unpleasant. An abusive individual by all accounts, Malcolm had been concerned only with his own consequence and comfort.

How difficult it must have been for Jon to enter such a household after first his father, and then stepmother, died. Thank heavens he'd had the Lady Sofia to hold most negative influences at bay. Sympathetic to his situation, she reached out and silently touched his arm.

Jon covered her hand, wrapping his fingers through hers, and edged closer. Andy gulped nervously when the log rocked. With one hand against the rough bark, she clung to Jon with the other. Overhead, a gyrfalcon screamed.

Jon looked up at the majestic bird. "Looking for prey, no doubt." He gave a short laugh. "Sometimes, that's how I felt in London—like prey."

Still silent, Andy glanced at his clenched jaw.

His cynical gaze met hers and he shrugged. "A simplistic comparison, perhaps, but it's true. Oh, I'll admit I enjoyed the attention my position and wealth brought me. . . . I was *very* green when I first went to Town," he snorted. "But I was free, grasping for all life had to offer. After a while, though, it became tiresome. Finally, I joined Wellington's ranks—as much for distraction as to infuriate my uncle who was dead-set against his heir risking life and limb."

A self-deprecating laugh escaped his lips. "I made the mistake of returning a hero and the fawning worsened. Then, some woman or her mama would try entrapping me. Because of my uncle, I couldn't come here to escape."

She'd never seen him so introspective and tightened her grip on his hand. He'd listened to her. The least she could do was to return the favor. Andy recalled Helen mentioning much the same tale when they had first arrived. It certainly explained his "devil-may-care" attitude. No doubt it helped him remain elusive . . . and single.

Andy bit her lip, suddenly worried. Had she made him feel trapped? Was that why he'd been avoiding her? Her fingers curled into her scar but Jon reclaimed her attention.

"I took to alternating between arrogance and charm. No one dared mock me, unsure of how I'd react." Jon glanced at Andy. His eyes deceptively innocent, the corner of his mouth slanted wickedly.

Wary, Andy tried to pull her hand away. He tugged it back. "No one mocked me, that is, until you, Duchess. You never hesitated to puncture my sense of consequence." His gaze now hooded, Jon leaned forward, bringing his face ever closer to hers.

Andy could barely swallow. The heat flooding through her had nothing to do with the sun beating down upon them. She couldn't even *see* the sun anymore, focused as she was on Jon—the man she loved. The man she'd be leaving soon. Her lips parted to welcome his kiss.

Their makeshift bench rocked violently. Unbalanced, Andy gripped Jon's shoulders. Her eyes widened. "Jon . . ."

His comical look of disappointment was the last thing Andy saw before they plunged from their precarious perch, and into the stream.

Andy sputtered to the top, laughing, feeling cleansed even as weeds clung to her. Beside her, Jon was already treading water. He shook his head, spraying Andy with droplets of water. She splashed back, the sound of her hand smacking against the water frightening nearby sparrows.

"What have you to say about my ability to swim and my sense of adventure now?" she teased.

"I'm not sure." His eyes glinted with reflected sunlight as he pondered her question. "Actually, I think I'd rather have you clinging on to me for dear life. However, Duchess, I must object to your method of cooling my ardor.

Andy pursed her lips even though she didn't mind taking the blame for their position this time. "It worked, didn't it? Personally, I think it was a rather innovative idea, one I shall keep in mind the next time someone becomes too forward."

Jon growled and dove under the surface.

Andy floated happily in the water, waving her arms about lazily. It had been so long since she'd swum. Her only regret was that she was wearing one of her better gowns. Not only would it be ruined, but it also got in the way of her pleasure.

Unexpectedly, she choked in water. Jon had grabbed her by the ankles, submerging her, all the while ensuring her safety by clinging to her waist as they both kicked their way to the top. Still coughing, Andy combed wet strands of hair from her eyes. Dead twigs poked her fingers and she glared at Jon in accusation. "You, sirrah, are nothing but a cad and a scoundrel."

Jon nodded. "Undoubtedly. As a matter of fact, I'm sure I've heard that somewhere before." His face came toward hers once more. "Now where was I before I was so rudely interrupted? Ah, yes. I was about to kiss the extremely desirable woman who was sitting beside me."

Andy took in his wolfish grin and momentarily consigned her conscience to perdition. Her fingers slipped to grip his wet shoulders. Touching him, the corded muscles beneath his lawn shirt only fed a growing wave of desire and her grip tightened. She kicked her feet under water and boldly surged toward his lips. Just this once, she thought.

They sank, still clinging to each other. When their feet touched the shifting silt on the stream floor, Jon pushed them to the surface. By the time they broke through the water, they were both gasping for air.

Jon noted the current had carried them quite a ways from their original spot. "We'd best return to shore. Even streams such as this aren't the safest place to swim."

Andy nodded and began swimming to the shore. "I'll race you," she called out over her shoulder.

"I love races," Jon warned and swam abreast of her. "Winner gets a kiss."

Andy chuckled, losing her rhythm, and Jon pulled ahead.

It didn't come as any surprise to find him waiting for her on a high embankment and she gratefully accepted his assistance in climbing from the stream. Wet and bedraggled, Andy grasped her undone knot of hair between both hands and wrung it out. Her glance fell on the skirt of her gown and she sighed at the mud there. "Another gown ruined." In addition to all the hems she'd destroyed during her Season, she thought.

"Actually, I rather like the way it looks," Jon mused.

"You would!" Andy blushed and tugged at her bodice, trying to pull the clinging material away from the curves it outlined.

Jon's hand stilled her. "Don't worry about it, Duchess. Besides, I need to claim my winnings before you change your mind. I wouldn't want you to renege on our little bet."

Her feet were on solid ground now. She had to bring her racing heart to earth, too, so Andy stepped back with a laugh, trying to nullify the intensity of his gaze. "I didn't agree to any wager, Jonathon."

"It doesn't matter, Duchess." He put his arms around her in a loose embrace and rested his forehead against hers. "Besides, with such a wager, there really aren't any losers." He brushed first her lowered eyelids with his lips, then stooped to crush her mouth.

Effectively silenced, Andy clutched his shoulders and tasted him. He tasted of fresh air and sunshine. He tasted of dead vegetation from the stream. He tasted of himself and she knew she'd spend her lonely nights remembering these last private moments with Jon. Instead of weeping at the thought, she shivered, as though a sliver of ice had chipped away at her very soul.

Misunderstanding her trembling, Jonathon pulled away. "Come, Duchess. We'd best get out of these wet things, or you'll catch your death." He took her hand and led her toward the trail.

Still breathless from his embrace, Andy followed him in a daze. Muddled, she struggled to match his confident pace. Her gaze traveled the length of him as he strode in front of her. Longing pierced through her and she stumbled.

Jon looked back in question. Andy gulped and glanced away, startled to note they had arrived at the gamekeeper's cottage.

When he smiled and pulled her toward the steps, Andy dug in her heels. This was going too far. It was time to escape or she would lose what few shreds of dignity she had remaining by declaring her love.

"Jon, I think we'd best return home."

"I'm glad you think of it as your home, too, Duchess," he replied, ignoring the essence of her comment. He tugged her toward the door.

She yanked back.

He grinned and opened the door. "I see you're in the mood to play games again." Not bothering to close the door, he reached for her, his fingers trembling, and pressed a hurried kiss to her forehead. "After I've shown you a few of my favorite games, we'll talk about you making your home permanently with us."

Her mind warring with her heart, she stepped into his open arms. Whatever he'd said about making her home with his family didn't make sense. This—being within his arms—was home. The words she'd meant to horde spilled out. "I love you, Jon."

Instead of laughing as she'd feared, he groaned and kissed the pulse throbbing at the base of her throat. A hand slipped to the buttons there, gripping the fragile material of her gown. Unfortunately, he gripped too tightly and the cloth around the buttons ripped.

"Why do we always have such a problem with these accursed things?" he sighed, staring at the buttons which had come loose in his palm.

Andy gulped, trying to still her frantic breathing, embarrassed at her wanton behavior and whispered words of love. Unsure of his motives, unsure of herself, she swallowed again and tried to pull away.

Jon pulled her back. "I'm afraid I cannot let you go just yet, Duchess."

"You must," she insisted before taking in the change of his grin. That dangerous innocence again. "Jonathon . . ."

"I'm sorry, but that won't be possible. It seems we're expecting company any moment." His smile growing even more angelic, he waved a hand.

Slowly, dreading who she might see, Andy turned and blushed furiously. They'd been discovered.

Unfortunately, they'd been discovered by her father and the Marchioness. When Andy saw them nearing, she considered the possibility of darting to the safety of the screen Sofia had once been hidden behind. However, Jon now stood in her path.

Sofia's lips pursed and her grip tightened on the basket she held. A pair of large fringed ears appeared above its edge and she absently ruffled the fur of the tiny Papillon pup. Her brow arched as she examined the condition of Andy's gown. "It appears we arrived just in time, Edgar. That is, I *hope* we arrived in time. Did we?" she asked, nailing Andy to the spot with a piercing gaze.

Focusing on the little pink tongue licking Sofia's hand, Andy nodded silently at the pointed question. Behind her, Jonathon chuckled. Andy directed an elbow into his ribs. How could he laugh when they should be thinking how to escape from this coil?

Seemingly ignorant of their situation, Jon drawled, "Actually, Aunt Sofia, you arrived a little too early for my liking."

Andy stomped a heel on his foot, appalled by his audacity. Didn't he realize what this meant? "Jonathon, you dolt," she hissed over her shoulder. "Stow it!"

Sofia heard and choked. Pressing a fist against her mouth, she exchanged a severe look with Edgar.

Andy groaned. They were well and truly lost now. She withered under Sofia's gaze. Fortunately, this time the Marchioness chose to berate her nephew.

"Yes, Jonathon. That will do. There will be plenty of time for that after the wedding. By the way, Andy, this is a gift from Jon. He asked us to bring it should it arrive while he was out." She shoved the basket at her. "I understand his name is Burne."

Dazed, Andy accepted the pup and froze. *Wedding!* "There isn't going to be any wedding!" she finally screeched. The small dog barked in chorus.

"I'm afraid that's where you're wrong, my dear," her father interrupted gruffly. "The two of you have no choice."

Jon leaned into Andy's back. She felt his body shake with suppressed emotion.

"Your father's right, you know. I'll just have to do the honorable thing."

The suppressed emotion was laughter!

Andy took one look at his now-martyred expression and punched him on the shoulder. His pained yelp relieved some of her stress. "There's nothing honorable about you!" she sputtered. Burne took exception to the jiggling and nipped Andy's hand. Soothing the dog with soft strokes, she turned to her father, trying to reason with him. "But, Papa . . . Nothing happened."

"I'm grateful to hear that, child, but that doesn't change a thing and you know it." Both his words and his stance were implacable.

Andy shot Jon a scathing glare, unwilling to take the blame this time. "This is all your fault!" He cocked his brow as if in reminder of her own hungry kisses. As if she needed any reminders. . . .

"That will do, Andrea!" the Marchioness reprimanded. She removed her shawl and draped it around Andy. "Not that it helps much," she snorted, stepping back to study the effect.

"Lady Sofia." Andy reached out to touch her arm.

"I do not like to repeat myself, young lady," Sofia declared. "We'd best leave the gentlemen here to work out the details," she said more kindly and led Andy out the door.

Andy dragged her feet. It was like going to a funeral—her

own. This wasn't how she expected the relationship with Jon to end. She had wanted to treasure sweet memories of their parting, not shackle a reluctant Marquess. She glanced down at the basket in her hand, wondering what to do with the dog. Burne . . . what a wonderful name for the tiny creature. He nudged her fingers with his damp nose. Andy stilled as pieces of his conversation with her father penetrated her thoughts.

"I'll arrange for a special license, Sir Edgar, and the matter can be taken care of before the end of next week. That way, you won't need to delay your own honeymoon by much."

Edgar frowned. "Now just one moment. I thought you said nothing happened."

"Of course nothing happened," Jon replied.

Andy turned, adding her vociferous agreement. "Honestly, Papa, nothing did happen. It's true." The Marchioness tugged on her arm and she fell silent.

"You see?" Jon nodded at Andy.

Andy's gaze darted between the two men. As much as she loved Jon, she wouldn't force him into an unwanted union. Why wasn't he trying any harder to escape the tightening web spun by their relatives? Puzzled, she swung her head back to her father.

"Since nothing happened, I'll have no havey-cavey, hole-in-the-wall ceremony for my only child," Edgar insisted.

Andy glanced at the Marchioness. In spite of the fact that they themselves were to be married on the morrow by special license, Sofia didn't appear to be in the least offended. In fact, she looked rather amused.

"What's sauce for the goose . . . ?" Jon inquired.

"Is *not* sauce for the gander," Edgar disagreed. "I'll not have the niece of a bishop and an earl married with anything less than what's due to her consequence. Is that clear?" Not waiting for Jon to reply, he continued with his plan. "Your wedding can follow on the heels of Lady Helen's and Dom's. The banns will be read properly."

"Oh no, Sir Edgar," Jonathon argued. "It is inconceivable that I shall wait that long to claim my bride. It only takes three weeks for the banns. After that, your daughter is mine."

Andy swallowed in the face of his possessive gaze. It was something she'd never dreamed was possible. "Jon . . . you really don't have to do this."

"Yes, he does!" Edgar and Sofia declared simultaneously, both of them struggling to choke back laughter. Burne barked, as though adding his agreement. The older couple succumbed to chuckling.

Andy swung her head back to them. Basking in the heat of Jonathan's gaze, which was quickly melting away her reservations, she had almost forgotten about their audience.

"By the way, Duchess . . ." Jon began with a self-deprecating grin. "I don't know if I had the chance to mention this earlier . . . I was rather preoccupied and might have forgotten. There's something you should know."

The innocent look was back in his eyes. It was all Andy could do to prompt, "And just what might that be?"

Jon studied her for a moment. "I seem to have forgotten . . ." his voice trailed off. "It isn't about Burne. My aunt already told you he's my gift to you. It's simply that I love you, Duchess. I'm positive I told you that before. The same still holds true, by the by."

Everything faded away as Andy stared into his eyes, mesmerized. She watched his lips move, but couldn't concentrate on the words. She flushed when he stopped and looked at her expectantly. "I beg your pardon?" Under the shawl, her hand pressed against her pounding heart.

"Will you marry me and be my Marchioness?"

"Oh, yes!" she finally managed with a weak smile. She wanted nothing more than to throw her arms around him, only Lady Sofia's grip held her back. Andy shot a guilty look at her father and the Marchioness, both of whom looked immensely pleased.

Edgar rubbed his hands together. "Well, I'm glad that's settled. Off you go now, my dear. I understand Burne's bed is already in your room." He bussed her on the cheek before grimacing at her still-damp gown. "You look positively dreadful. Sofia will see you home safely, won't you, love?" he asked, kissing the Marchioness as well.

Sofia nodded with a tender smile, gently stroking his cheek in return.

"But Andy and I have some unfinished business to take care of," Jonathan interceded.

Lady Sofia stared him down. "It will just have to wait for another few weeks." Her expression softened and she reached up to ruffle his shaggy hair, forgetting he was no longer a small boy. "And congratulations. I'm very pleased with your choice of a bride."

As the Marchioness led the way, Andy paused and looked over her shoulder at Jon. He blew her a kiss.

"Until later," Duchess," he called out, his eyes promising so much.

Andy smiled dreamily. Her footstep stilled in midair at her father's chuckle, followed by something which sounded as if a back was being clapped.

"That was well done, m'boy. How ever did you get Andy so wet? It was almost as good as my trick with Sofie's leg."

Andy turned. Jon was grinning and pumping Edgar's hand. "My thanks for your help, sir. This couldn't have been done without you."

"Oh, I was pleased to do it. After all, one good turn deserves another and all that," Edgar demurred.

Andy groaned and stared at Lady Sofia's suspiciously heightened color. The woman evaded her gaze. Andy placed a hand on her hip and glared at both her father and Jonathon. They noticed and abruptly halted their conversation, shuffling their feet, exchanging anxious looks. She folded her arms through Burne's basket and tapped her foot.

Jonathon winced. "Andy . . ." He began hesitantly. "I can explain, really . . ."

Andy shook her head, cutting off his entreaty. "I'm warning you right now, my lord . . ."

Jon's forehead furrowed. He stepped forward and reached out his hand. "Blast my cursed sense of humor. Andy, please listen to me."

"No, you listen to me, sirrah." Andy struggled to bite back her laughter. "I just want to warn you . . . I'll have a lifetime to get even with you for this." She couldn't contain her smile any longer and turned away, fairly floating toward the tethered mounts placidly chewing away on the grass under the trees. She shook her head—Jon and his plotting. Only he had gotten carried away this time and had forgotten his lines.

She darted one more glance at him over her shoulder and met his suggestive leer. Her laughter was carried away on the breeze, joined by the frolicking barks of Burne.

Beyond them, atop the hill, the shadow of another dog raised its head as if in welcome, then disappeared.

ROMANCE FROM JANELLE TAYLOR

ROMANCE FROM FERN MICHAELS

DEAR EMILY   (0-8217-4952-8, $5.99)

WISH LIST   (0-8217-5228-6, $6.99)

AND IN HARDCOVER:

VEGAS RICH   (1-57566-057-1, $25.00)

YOU WON'T WANT TO READ
JUST ONE—KATHERINE STONE

ROOMMATES   (0-8217-5206-5, $6.99/$7.99)
No one could have prepared Carrie for the monumental changes she would face when she met her new circle of friends at Stanford University. Once their lives intertwined and became woven into the tapestry of the times, they would never be the same.

TWINS   (0-8217-5207-3, $6.99/$7.99)
Brook and Melanie Chandler were so different, it was hard to believe they were sisters. One was a dark, serious, ambitious New York attorney; the other, a golden, glamourous, sophisticated supermodel. But they were more than sisters—they were twins and more alike than even they knew . . .

THE CARLTON CLUB   (0-8217-5204-9, $6.99/$7.99)
It was the place to see and be seen, the only place to be. And for those who frequented the playground of the very rich, it was a way of life. Mark, Kathleen, Leslie and Janet—they worked together, played together, and loved together, all behind exclusive gates of the *Carlton Club*.